DIVINE
JUDGMENT

- The Divine Chronicles Book 3 -

I0653874

JOANNA GRACE

ABW-WJP, LLC
P.O. Box 337
Lindale, TX 75771

This book is a work of fiction. Therefore, all names, places, characters, and situations are a product of the author's imagination and used fictitiously. Any resemblance to actual persons, living or dead, places, or events is entirely coincidental. The author acknowledges the trademark status and trademark owners of various products referenced in this work of fiction, which have been used without permission. The publication/use of these trademarks is not authorized, associated with, or sponsored by the trademark owners.

Copyright © 2014 by JoAnna Grace
Second Edition

All rights reserved. No part of this book may be used or reproduced in any manner whatsoever. For information, address ABW-WJP, LLC, P.O. Box 337, Lindale, TX 75771. Email: arrowbkw@gmail.com

2022 Cover Design by Moorbooks Design
Book design by Champagne Formats
Printed in the United States of America

Library of Congress Control Number Data
Grace, JoAnna.
Divine Judgment / JoAnna Grace.
1. Fantasy romance—Greek mythology—Fiction. 2. Romance—Fantasy—Fiction.
3. Sagas—Romance—Fiction.
Fiction. | BISAC: FICTION / Romance / Fantasy. | FICTION / Romance / General. | FICTION / Sagas.
PCN # 2016911678. 2014
ISBN 978-1-940460-10-9

www.authorjoannagrace.com

JoAnna Grace

CONTEMPORARY ROMANCES

The Roles We Play

Riverview Romances

Why The River Runs

A River Between Us

PARANORMAL TITLES

Divine Chronicle Series:

Divine Awakening

Divine Destiny

Divine Judgment

Divine Encounter

Divine Pursuit

Divine Deception

Divine Justice

Blake Pride Series:

Pride Before the Fall

Break Her Fall

The Harder They Fall

Divided We Fall

Rise After the Fall

For more information on JoAnna's books, signings, events, and more, Sign up for the NEWSLETTER at http://eepurl.com/B_DM5!

A Note From Jo

Thank you, dear readers, for once again picking up a JoAnna Grace novel. I hope you enjoy it. It brings me great joy to hear from you. Please connect with me on social media:

Facebook: facebook.com/joannagraceauthor
Instagram: instagram.com/authorjoannagrace

Want updates delivered to your inbox?
Make sure you're in the know.
Sign up for my newsletter today! Visit http://eepurl.com/B_DM5

Do you want to help an author?

Leave a review!

Your opinion matters. Every review can help.

Share a link to this book on social media!

Like, follow, tag Jo, and share this book with your friends.

Support Indie Authors!

Did you know that an Indie Author fronts all the
cost of production?

That's right. We appreciate every person who purchases our
books because that's how we continue to produce more.
Independent authors, cover designers, editors, and formatters
work hard to bring readers quality products and stories they can
fall in love with.

Like. Share. Follow. Subscribe. Tag. Review.

It all helps the Indie community!

Share the Love.

DEDICATION & ACKNOWLEDGEMENTS

Thank you to everyone who has waited patiently—and not so patiently—for this book. You, the readers, are amazing and your dedication to Ryse and Avery is inspiring. This is all for you, my friends!

Thanks to my hubby and my midgets for walking this journey with me—especially during those times when it was more like me dragging you along. I love you so dearly. Thanks for understanding my need for a space to call my own—both in the world, and in our home. We've torn down walls this year in every way.

A very special thanks to Cheryl and Mom who always listen when I call in a tizzy about characters, plot holes, and brain-drain. You've talked me off the cliff, inspired new twists, and emotionally invested in my books as much as I have. I couldn't have asked for better people to lean on.

Thanks Jelaine for once again plucking the cover idea from my head and making it a reality. Thanks to Anna, Angi, Pam, Cheril, Olivia, Connie, and John for your assistance along the way. We've had some interesting conversations, right? Cheers to many more. Thanks to my Thursday morning coffee buddy, Melissa, for pulling me out of my writer's cave for some social interaction. Thanks nurse Tiffani for your insight and your big heart. Love you girls! To my OWG Sisters: Thanks for supporting me and telling others about your crazy author friend. Shimmer on, ladies. Shimmer on.

Last but not least, I am thankful to God, who has given me a purpose and the tools to see this thing through. Thank you for consistently placing people in my life who teach me, sharpen me, encourage me, and don't think I'm crazy for hearing voices. 'Preciate it!

PROLOGUE

RYSE'S HAND SHOOK AS HE HELD THE TORCH. HIS BODY TREMBLED, rejecting the obligation that he must fulfill. Tired eyes stared at the pyre stacked high with wood and flowers.

Set her body on fire…

Zeus's words echoed in his head, bouncing around in the space that was empty but for those commands. It was a painful numbness, to be so full of sorrow and dread, yet hollow at the same time.

Atop that pyre lay Avery's lifeless body wrapped in white silks and lace. Even in death she was so beautiful it made his very bones hurt to look at her. He shuddered. Reddish-brown hair spread out in a halo around her face. What he would give to bury his hands in it once more and feel the warmth of her body in his arms.

Set her body on fire…

He nearly crumbled to his knees at the thought. Over two centuries he'd walked this Earth and had never felt the love and desires and pleasures of it until Avery came into his life. Such a short time he'd had with her and it wasn't enough. Ryse couldn't say goodbye. He couldn't set the pyre ablaze, even though Zeus commanded it. How could he damage her body? How could he destroy the shell that held her loving spirit? It seemed so final, so permanent. His feet were stuck to the floor and his hands shook. His knuckles turned white under the strain.

"Master," whispered a deep bass voice that hinted of the African plains. That voice had called him from the deep many times in the last couple of days. "I would assist you, should you need me."

Ryse turned to Hammon. His bloodshot black eyes nearly blended with his midnight skin. Ryse shook his head once. This was his task, his burden, and his test. It was a challenge of his faith in the gods, not Hammon's. Ryse looked to his mother. Dynasty held onto his brother Hayden; both of them knew his suffering. It was only the day before that his mother had set his father's pyre aglow, cremating what little was left of Troy's body after his gruesome murder. Somehow, his mother had found the strength. He could too.

Set her body on fire. Let her spirit be released from the flesh.

Ryse grit his teeth and touched the burning torch to the wood and watched the flames catch. As the logs went up one by one, Ryse stepped away and joined the few trusted people allowed in the temple. His family stood beside him, ringed by his Elites. Hammon, Philippe, Cutter, Yankee, Brenden, and the newly added Dante knelt in prayer as Ryse did. Never in all his years had he prayed so fervently. He looked up only once to see the silks catch fire and turned his head away. He couldn't bear the sight of her body burning to ashes.

He prayed Zeus had kept his word. He prayed his faith was secure in a god who had molded his life and guided his steps for over two centuries. He prayed that Rhea, mother of Zeus, Poseidon, and Hades, who had created Avery for him, once again showed him favor and returned his beloved from the world of the dead.

Set her body on fire. Let the flesh go and have faith in the gods. She will rise from the flames, a goddess among immortals.

The temple shook. Thunder echoed off the stone walls. Ryse was on his feet in an instant, examining the pyre that still blazed. Avery's body lay untouched by the flames.

An explosion filled the temple with a cloud of smoke. A great wind whipped around them, sending flames and sparks dancing in a tornado. Columns of fire circled the room even as the Elites poised to fight the unknown threat.

Fire consumed all the oxygen, making it hard to breathe. Ryse was ready to send everyone away. No sooner than he had the thought, the tornado was sucked back into the pyre—into Avery's mouth. Horrific screams echoed in the temple as she convulsed. He was beside her in an instant. The burning wood was gone and her body writhed on a slab of white marble.

Ryse's blood pulsed hard through his body. What had they done to her? The gods had promised to bring her back to him, but not like this. *Please* not like this.

Her eyes popped open and Ryse picked up her head in his hands. "Avery. My love."

She looked around in wild confusion until her eyes met his. Their usual emerald color swirled with blue and white, a sign that she was closely linked to the afterlife. A frightening thought.

"Ryse." She held him close. "I can't stay long. Rhea. It's Rhea."

"No. They promised you would return." He caressed her hair over and over again. They wouldn't take her. He would break every bond he'd ever made if Zeus and Ares betrayed him.

"I will. Trust me, Ryse. Trust in Rhea's promise. Have faith, baby. I'll be in your arms again soon." Avery pulled his head down and kissed him with the passion of a woman given a second chance at life.

Ryse soaked up her love, let it fill his entire being.

"Take care of my body. I'll be with you again."

Ryse held on tighter as her body went limp in his arms. The life in her eyes faded. The colors seeped out and left only white. Rhea had called her back. "Avery, don't leave me," he begged as he shook her shoulders. "I need you. I love you."

The edges of her lips tilted up as her eyes tried to close. "I love you too, so much even the gods will not keep us apart. Protect me until I return." Her voiced faded, her eyes closed, and Ryse' whole universe had shifted.

Alive. Avery was alive. He could see her chest moving with each strong breath. Under his palm, he could make out the beating of her heart. Yes, she was alive and he would do as he promised.

"Hammon!" he screamed. In all the chaos, he hadn't noticed his Elites coming to his side.

"Here, Master. I'm here." A long-fingered black hand touched Ryse's shoulder tentatively. "We are all here, sire. We have seen." His men surrounded him with their strength. From the expressions on their faces, they looked to be as shocked and frightened as he was, but none of them shied away.

"Where is my mother?" Ryse searched and found Dyna on her knees by the altar. She rose and came to him. "We will make her comfortable. No one is to see her, no one is to know she's alive. If word gets out she's in this vulnerable state—"

"She'll be a target." Brenden, Avery's guardian and friend, said. "We have to hide her."

Ryse nodded. Of course. But where?

"I can't sense her." Hammon touched Avery's forehead. His eyes squinted in concentration. "Can anyone else? Can you feel her aura at all?"

Ryse searched inside himself for the bond that linked them. It was there, strong as ever. But the rest of the men shook their heads, as did his mother.

"The gods shield her." Dante spoke up. Of all the people in the room, he would know. His gift was to absorb and block the talents of other Olympians. It made him a very unpopular man among his peers, but a vital ally to Ryse. His assessment was crucial. This meant Avery could be hidden in plain sight and no one would know.

"We will put her in my suite," Dyna said. "No one is allowed entrance and, if people are seen coming and going, all will think it is to attend to me." Dyna leaned over Avery and kissed her on the cheek. Her tear-filled eyes met Ryse's. "Hanna and I will tend to her, my son."

Ryse nodded, and pulled his mother into his arms. Even though he had always limited contact with others, Dyna was the exception to every rule. And now, with his father gone, she was as much his charge as Avery.

"It's a good idea." Hayden, who had been silent thus far, came to join their embrace. His face was pale of his usual color and his eyes puffy. "The protection spells on her rooms are unbreakable. Father made it so."

Hayden's voice quivered at the mention of Troy. Their father had been murdered only two days ago. The family had not the time to grieve properly. They had burned Troy's body as their traditions dictated, but with everything that had happened after his death, they hadn't stopped long enough to mourn appropriately. Avery's situation pulled all their attentions.

"So be it." Ryse nodded in decision. "Let's make sure the path is clear to Mother's rooms and I'll carry her. Hammon, cover us. Dante, use your gifts to shield me so that no one in the vicinity can track my movements."

Hammon's eyes went white as he channeled his powers. "The path is clear, sire. None are around the temple."

As Ryse lifted Avery's body into his arms, Dante touched his shoulder. He hesitated making contact, but Ryse had commanded it. It was an odd sensation, having the young warrior block his powers and his aura. Dante's eyes were the same sand color as his hair and, when he used his gifts, the black of his pupils disappeared.

"I won't be able to keep this up long," he panted, beads of sweat breaking out along his forehead. "Trying to contain your aura is strenu—"

Dante never finished his sentence. Instead, he fell to the ground.

"Ah, shit." Yankee rolled his eyes after checking the boy's pulse. "We've got a fainter."

For some reason, this tickled Dyna. The queen slapped her hand over her mouth when she giggled. But she had already attracted the attention of the men around her. As hard as she tried to gain her composure, she couldn't contain the huff that passed under her fingers.

"My sincere apologies. It's really not the time." She cracked a smile and pink crept up her face. "But you have to admit, it is comical. Poor child didn't have a chance at containing your aura. What were you thinking?" Dyna leaned down and passed her hand over Dante's face, using her blessed touch to awaken him. The soldier's eyes fluttered open and looked up in question. Dyna gave him a warm smile. "Easy, child. I think you bit off more than you could chew."

"What happened?" Dante staggered to his feet.

"You passed the fuck out. That's what happened." Yankee

chuckled and slapped the blushing soldier on the shoulder. "Come on, lightweight."

Ryse recalculated his plan. The group headed out of the temple and entered the palace through one of the hidden tunnels. Hammon went ahead of them and cleared the way, sending out his senses to pinpoint any Olympians working in the lower levels. He derailed a butler and maid who were trying to freshen up the hallway that led to the queen's private rooms. Ryse didn't let down his guard until they were safely behind the closed door and protection spells.

Hanna, Dyna's Shadow Lady, was waiting in the suite. She was the only person other than the Elites who could know of Avery's condition. Dyna had already placed protective walls around her mind so that no one with telepathy could find out their secret. Hanna would be an important part of this charade.

Hanna pulled back the fresh linens and Ryse slid Avery's body between the sheets. They positioned her just right and tucked the blankets around her form. Ryse felt her pulse. It was slower than normal.

"She lives, my son." Dyna touched his arm.

"I know." Knowing, even seeing, didn't give him much hope. Only Avery's promise gave him faith of her return.

CHAPTER ONE

The Heavens- City of Olympia

"CRAP, CRAP, CRAP. DAMN IT TO HELL." AVERY SLAPPED AT her skin, shook herself off like a dog sheds water. "Fire? Really. You have to transport me with *fire*?" She glared up at Rhea, who stood waiting patiently. Avery coughed and hacked, trying to get the heat out of her throat. It took her a moment to realize she wasn't on fire and she wasn't having trouble breathing.

"Fire is a part of who you are, beloved. It is not my fault that you have not embraced it."

"It flippin' hurts!"

"Your irreverence is disturbing." Rhea folded her hands in front of her and frowned.

Avery's brows rose. She paced toward the goddess and crossed her arms over her chest. "Irreverence? You set me on fire. *Twice*. You created me and stuck me on Earth, gave my father a vision that caused him to take me into the human world, and now, after I've finally found Ryse and fallen in love with him, *and* figured out who I really am, I'm dead. Now I'm pulled every which way but right, in and out of my own dang body. Did I miss anything? Oh, yeah. You set me on fire."

"Twice," Rhea finished for her, her lips twitching. "I do enjoy your spirit. Worry not; I shall return you to your mate in due time." She gathered Avery into her arms and offered comfort.

Avery shivered once more. The memory of the flames still freaked her out. It was only after her tantrum that she comprehended where she was and took a glance around. "So this is Heaven, huh?"

There was…nothing. Rhea and Avery were surrounded by an endless sea of nothing. She figured Heaven would be like what she saw in the movies: white lights, lots of gold and silver, shiny crap. Instead, she stood in a void. There was no white light, but no darkness either. If she squinted, she could make out color, but not really.

"Would you prefer the afterlife to look like this?" Rhea waved her hand and a golden street appeared under her feet, leading to a city clad in gold and jewels. There were vivid colors, great temples floating on clouds…and every cliché the human race had ever depicted as eternity.

"This isn't it either, is it?" Avery sighed.

"Maybe you would prefer this?" The scene changed and Avery's heart nearly broke in half.

It was her childhood home in Texas. The farmhouse with a wraparound porch sat pristine in the middle of hay pastures. Smoke even rose from the chimney. A faint scent of Mama's fresh baked bread wafted past her nose.

Before she could stop herself, tears rolled down her cheeks and she turned to Rhea. "I had no idea the gods of my husband would be so cruel." Her anger lashed out like a whip at the goddess.

"It is accurate, is it not? This is the place you felt most at home, the most at peace."

With a defiant swipe, Avery cleared her cheeks of moisture. "Yeah. But you know darn well that place is gone and so are the people in it. So why don't you quit with the picture games?"

"As you wish." Rhea's arm cut through the air and Avery's childhood home was gone. In a blink, they stood high on a grassy hill so perfectly green that each blade looked hand painted. Their feet rested on the cool white marble of a grand temple.

Avery peered up and up and higher still to the ceiling, elegantly decorated with frescos of the gods. "I've seen this place."

"It is the city of Olympia in the realm of the gods. When we left the Earth, we recreated our cities and temples together here."

"Cities?" Avery questioned.

"Athens, Delphi, Olympia, exactly as they would have been on Earth."

Rows of stone buildings with intricate carvings of the gods they hosted dotted the valley below. The temple of Zeus was the most prominent. A dozen circular pillars lined the exterior; white limestone stacked as high and mighty as the god it paid homage to.

"Will my parents be here? In one of these cities?" Hope lit in her heart at the thought she might be reunited with her family again.

"Your mother was human and I'm afraid, upon death, her soul went to a place that I have no access to. Your father, however, anxiously waits to greet you." Rhea held out her arm and pointed to a figure emerging out of the valley below.

"Daddy!" Avery took off running, her feet moving as fast as possible toward the open arms of her father. She jumped and he caught her with a strong grip. He was just as she remembered. Tall, brown hair, heavy build, with the warmest hugs in the world.

"Avery, my precious girl, how I've missed you." He kissed her cheek over and over again as they both wept. "I'm so proud of you, baby." Loving words fell from his lips repeatedly, as if he were making up for a decade of not sharing his love with her every day. "I love you so much."

"Daddy, I'm sorry. I'm so sorry about everything. About Jerry and Mama, and everything."

He held her face in his hands. Green eyes, exactly like hers, were filled with tears and emotion so deep it stirred her soul. "Don't be sorry about your mother, baby. I knew when we were mated that her humanity would be a part of the deal. She was worth every sacrifice. She gave me you." He kissed her forehead again. "No father has ever been as proud of his daughter as I am of you."

Rhea approached, a kind smile on her face. "I owe your parents a great deal, Avery. I wish I could bring them together again, but that is far beyond my control. I can only offer you the knowledge that your mother is in a similar place and her soul is at peace."

"Thank you, goddess." Her father bowed to Rhea. "Thank you for bringing me my child and for keeping her from a true death."

"I have things I must attend to. Your time here is short, Avery. Enjoy this gift. For when I return, you will face your fire and your killer."

Avery swallowed hard. *Ugh.* The thought of facing Salina again made her nauseated. Instead of dwelling on that thought, she took her father's hand and they meandered down the paths of the Heavens. Question after question, topic after topic, father and daughter caught up on as much as possible. When she spoke of Ryse and how much she loved him, her father grinned. But there was a sadness in his eyes.

"You are in for a very hard life with him, Avery. He will not be an easy man to love."

"No, Daddy. He's a very easy man to love. What's hard is makin' him see that."

"If anyone can do it, if anyone can love him enough, it's you." Her father sighed and she knew their time was nearly up. "You've become so much greater a woman than I ever imagined. For so long, I feared what would happen to you without your mother and me there to guide you." His face softened, his green eyes shone. "But you're so strong, so determined. Maybe a little quick on the trigger when it comes to attacking people." He chuckled. "You should be more careful."

"Trust me, I will. Dang. Dyin' hurts," she joked, but rubbed at her chest, still able to recall how the knife had punctured her chest over and over again.

Her father put his hands on her shoulders and looked her in the eyes. "As much as I love you, my sweet girl, I don't want to see you again for many, many centuries. Not until you and your mate rest in the Heavens together."

"I promise, Daddy. I'll be more careful. But I also made promises to Ryse, and I won't stand by and let him fight his demons alone."

"That's my girl. I love you, more than you can fathom." He pulled her in for a hug and Avery tried to memorize everything about him. She wouldn't get a chance like this again and she didn't take it for granted.

The Heavens- Holy City of Delphi

Lysandra entered the main temple of Delphi. The ancient city had once been on Earth, but now it was a place of solitude for the gods only. The tray she carried held oils and herbs for the Pythia, the triad of Oracles who oversaw the temple. She delivered the supplies and knelt down to receive her next order. Three naked women sat chanting in a shallow pool of water that smelled of sweet oils. No males were allowed into the sanctuary and no one except temple priestesses were given entrance to this room. Their lack of clothing aided in their focus. There was no reason to hide their bodies. The nudity didn't bother Lysandra; she was used to it. When she came into the sanctuary, she too had to be unclad. It didn't take her long to realize clothing was a waste of time in the temple. No one saw her but the Pythia. When she did venture beyond the temple, her robes and drapes weighed her down and were abrasive against her skin.

"Lysandra," called one of her mistresses. "I see you."

She gasped as the Oracle trained her white, glowing eyes on her face. "Me? Why would you have a vision of me?"

"Come." The Oracle held out a hand so pale it was nearly translucent.

Priestesses in training were not supposed to step foot in the pool. Lysandra's heart pounded as she touched the Oracle's hand and stepped into the warm water. As she lowered her body, a vision came over her. She was accustomed to visions, had them all the time. This experience was different.

She saw a woman with long, reddish-brown hair. The mass of curls spread out on a pillow, her hands folded over her chest. Was the woman dead? No. Not dead, but not living either. Time began to slip backwards and she saw the men who placed the woman in the bed with such care. The scenes rewound all the way back to the moment this woman was murdered. She saw it all. Her death, her lover, her true identity. Lysandra screamed as the vision ended in painful clarity.

Avery, mate of Thracian Master and Olympian Prince Ryse Castille, was in the spirit realm while her body lay in the Haven on Earth.

"Did you see it?" It wasn't an Oracle who asked the question, but the mother-goddess, Rhea. The Oracles crawled to her robes and touched them in reverence. Lysandra knelt down, her face nearly in the pool.

"They need you, Lysandra. I am sending you to the Haven in the earthly plain."

"Mistress?" Lysandra was appalled. "You don't mean among the *humans*?"

Rhea stroked the heads of the Oracles who fawned over her. The urge to join them was strong, but the possibility of having to go to Earth was like foot soldiers marching across her chest into battle. Their feet pounded a heavy rhythm over her heart and stomping their air from her lungs. Lysandra rubbed a hand over her sternum trying to relieve the pressure.

"Yes. 'Tis your destiny. You will learn much and be of great service to the gods. Go meditate and receive the knowledge that I bring. Your time will come soon."

"Is this—" She breathed deeply, closed her eyes against the pain of the cold truth. "Is this because I'm...*damaged*?"

The Pythia swiveled their heads to her. They stared with unblinking, lifeless eyes that knew too much. Everyone in the temple sensed it. She'd never fit in, never been fully one of them. That was why she'd never ascended to the Pythia, why she remained a temple priestess.

"Damaged?" Rhea questioned. "You are not damaged, Lysandra. You are simply too full of color to live in this white realm. It's time for you to discover who you were meant to be."

Lysandra made her way to her sleeping chambers and sat on her mattress. She was leaving the Heavens and going to the Earth... among other Olympians...and if her vision was accurate, she would be meeting the warrior with sandy blonde hair and unique eyes of the same color, the one who went unconscious when he touched Master Ryse. This magnificent warrior had her heart racing the most.

The Heavens - City of Olympia

Avery's heart broke as she walked away from her father, once again following Rhea. At the same time, she was full of love and peace. Finally, she was able to say goodbye to her father in a way she could be happy with. Rhea had given her priceless closure.

"Avery." The goddess pulled at her arm to bring Avery beside her. "Meet Helios, the god of fire."

Avery's body went cold. Helios was a walking fireball. We're talking straight out of a comic book – a man on fire. Even his smile seemed to glow orange and red.

"Ah, my new student." His words crackled like burning logs, more of a sound than an actual enunciation of syllables.

"I shall leave you to your lessons." Rhea inclined her head to Helios and he bowed deeply in return. Then Rhea was gone, and the god of fire's attention was solely on Avery. "Are you ready to learn your craft?"

"Yeah, 'bout that." Avery bit her bottom lip. "Not so much."

"Call upon your fire," he commanded, accustomed to being obeyed.

"What? No." Avery shook her head. "That flamin' crap is scary and bad things happen. It's not like it did me much good against Salina. I mean, no offense. It clearly works for you."

"You have not mastered the art." Helios held up his hand when Avery opened her mouth to argue. "Silence. You will learn. You will not argue. What emotions were you feeling the first time your gift manifested?"

Dear gods, she was really going to have to do this.

"Rage." Avery bowed her head, thoughts of Frank's bleeding body haunting her mind. "Sorrow."

"That is where we shall begin." Helios waved his hand and the world twisted. Olympia was gone and Avery stood in her childhood home again, just in time to watch Jerry stab Frank. Bile rose in her throat and her body shook. As she had been that horrific night, she was tied to a chair in her living room. Jerry, who had once been considered a close friend, slammed a knife into the chest of his partner, and Avery's treasured friend, Frank. Jerry's laughter made her retch. In her head, she knew this was only a memory. She had survived this night and moved on with her life. Her heart, on the other hand, felt the pain anew. She didn't want to watch her friend get tortured again. She didn't want to experience the loss and helplessness again.

"No. Don't make me relive this. Please," she begged, sobbing as Frank's blood coated her bare feet once again.

"Control your fire, Avery." Helios pointed a flaming finger at her body.

Fire? She held up her hands and, sure enough, flames danced over her skin exactly like Helios's did. Her entire body was consumed. The nightmare became real and kerosene flooded her veins.

"Nooo!"

CHAPTER TWO

Earth- The Haven

RYSE OBSERVED HIS COUSIN, EVANDER, TOUCH NIKKI'S FOREHEAD AND close his eyes in concentration. He was one of the most powerful Paeans in the Olympian world and he had come down from Chicago as soon as he could.

"She's barely functioning."

"What?" It was Brenden. The poor boy was worried sick about Nikki. Since the moment she said Salina's name during her confession, her mind had been in a coma. Now her body was beginning to show the effects. Her skin was yellowing and every breath was more labored than the last, even with the assistance of the ventilator. There were bluish bruises under her eyes and her cheeks sank in. A central line attached to her upper arm kept her fed. Neither Olympian magic nor modern medicine helped. Nikki was barely alive.

Evander stood and spared Brenden a glance before he spoke to Ryse. "Salina planted a virus in her mind. It's much more than a telepathic tripwire like I originally thought. Her brain is slowly telling her body to cease functioning. I have to admit, and forgive me for saying it," he said, "but it's rather impressive. She had help. I've known Salina her entire life. This is far beyond her skills."

Ryse scrubbed his hand over his face. "Can you fix it? Can you un-program or—"

"No." Evander shook his head, his tone resolute. He kept glancing to where Bren stood at Nikki's bedside. He knew; they all did. "Only the gods can undo this, Ryse." His blue eyes, a rarity in their family, were sad. His brows dipped low in frustration. "If they don't intervene soon, she'll die. Her body is shutting down. Her heartbeat is already weak and her lungs barely pull enough air to keep her alive. I can make her comfortable by cutting off her pain receptors in the brain. That's about it, cousin."

Bren stormed out of the room, slamming the door closed behind him.

"Sorry," Ryse said to Evander. "He and Nikki were just beginning their relationship, but his feelings are deep."

"I understand." Evander sighed. "I wish I had better news for him. For you both."

Ryse allowed Evander access to Avery's body after swearing a blood-bonded oath of secrecy.

"Avery?" asked Ryse.

"She's fine, physically. But her aura is gone from me. Her brain activity is rapid but scrambled. The gods have hidden her well. Whatever she's doing up there, they don't want anyone to figure it out. I wouldn't have believed her existence if I hadn't seen it."

The men talked more about the events leading up to Avery's coma and Nikki's deterioration. Evander grieved with Dyna for her loss. Evander's mother was Troy's sister. The siblings had been close until she willingly left this world for the Heavens.

"When the smoke clears from all this," Evander said as he clasped arms with Ryse before his departure, "I am in need of your tracker's services."

"Hammon?" Ryse's eyebrows rose.

"It seems there is someone new in my region. They evade my tracker and I believe there is more than one."

Ryse crossed his arms over his chest. "Trouble?"

Evander gave him a sly grin that reminded him of his father. Their family's blood was strong and Evander had the same dark features as

Ryse, Hayden, and Troy. "Curiosity." His smile widened more. "You know me; I'm a sucker for an enigma."

The men shared a laugh. "Now you have piqued my curiosity, cousin. Perhaps I will join Hammon on this wild goose chase of yours."

"I hope you will be otherwise detained by your Grace, Ryse."

"Me too, Evander. Me too." Ryse hesitated before he shocked his cousin by embracing him with a firm slap on the back. It was something Avery would do and he thought to try it out. "It is good to see you, cousin. Don't be a stranger."

Evander's breath left him in a rush. He couldn't meet Ryse's stare, but he blinked rapidly. "I, yes, I won't."

As Evander's car drove out of the Haven's realm and into the human world, Ryse stared off into the sky. All he thought about was the color blue, the movement of the white clouds, and the feel of the breeze as it picked up his hair. He took a deep breath. What would it be like to be Evander? To have a simple Olympian life to return to? His cousin had a clinic in the human world that served the civilian Olympians living in that realm. From what he had said, Evander's life seemed easy. He went to work, helped people, came home, and entertained a woman every now and then. He drove cars humans drooled over, lived in a mansion, and didn't hold back from enjoying the luxuries of life.

So very different from what Ryse faced when he returned to the palace. There was luxury, sure. But not the carefree life Evander enjoyed.

"What's on your mind, brother?" Hayden strolled over to him. The last few days had been hard on his younger brother. Hayden wasn't supposed to exist at all. The gods only gave Deities one son, one heir. The rest of their children were usually female. There was only one Prince—except for Hayden. For some reason, his foolish brother had it in his head that it should have been he who drank the poison instead of their father. And Ryse knew Hayden would give anything to switch places with Troy.

"I was thinking about being normal."

Hayden gave a sardonic laugh. "What the hell for?"

"Nothing. It's nothing. How is Mother?" Ryse followed Hayden as he headed into the gardens for a walk.

"She watches over Avery, prays constantly. She made Hanna take Father's clothing out of the closet. No one else is supposed to know, but she keeps one of his shirts under her pillow." The men shared a knowing look. Their parents had been mated for centuries. Although Dyna knew her husband was in the realm of the gods, it didn't make living in this place without him easier.

"I will glory in the moment I separate Salina's head from her shoulders," Ryse said, his anger a livewire in his veins.

"The Avondales travel this way." Hayden's words brought Ryse to a halt. "They will be here by this evening."

"What do they know?" Ryse asked, his words hard and cold.

Hayden shook his head, pushed his black hair off his face. "Only that Father passed. They come to comfort our family." He huffed and looked out across the grounds. "Now we have to tell them how he died."

Ice settled in Ryse's muscles. That was one conversation he did not want to have. No matter his hatred for Salina, he had a deep respect for Charles Avondale, her father.

"How are you, Hayden? We've had little time to talk." He studied his brother closely.

"You know me; I can drink my way through anything. It's all rainbows and unicorns and shit."

Ryse took a deep breath and sat silent until his aura washed over Hayden to let him know he was serious.

Hayden clenched his jaw and shrugged with jerky movements. Anger radiated from his aura. "The gods punish me, I think."

Ryse crossed his arms and frowned. His silence forced Hayden to continue.

"They taunt me. Every night, every time I close my eyes, I dream of a woman I might never have. She seems so real. She gives me peace." Hayden's bottom lip quivered, his voice cracked. "Until I wake up. Then I'm back in this hell of death and confusion. I'm left wondering if the gods get a kick out of it. What's the point of it all? Father's death, Salina's betrayal, Nikki's foolishness, Avery's absence. Why? I'm so sick of their games." Hayden struck the stone wall he leaned against, causing his knuckles to bleed. He shook his head and scoffed.

Ryse sighed. Damn, he wished he had some answers. "Avery told me to have faith. And honestly, right about now, that's all I can do. I have to have faith in her, if nothing else. There is a purpose for all this, brother. We must find it. Together." Ryse held out his hand and Hayden gripped his forearm in return.

"Together."

Brenden sat on the edge of the bed next to Avery. She reminded him so much of his sister, Meg. At least Avery would live. It crushed him to think about losing both Meg and Nikki. He didn't think his heart could handle it.

"She's dying, Avery," Brenden confessed in a hushed voice. "I actually fall in love, and she's dying. Did she tell you I kissed her?" He huffed, wiped his nose, and cleared his throat. "Finally took that chance. It was perfect. Thanks to Salina, I'll never get to do it again. I guess it's a moot point, though, huh? Even if she weren't dying from this virus, the gods would punish her anyway for what she did. It's not her fault. You think they know that?"

"Of course they do, darling."

Lady Dynasty entered her suite on the tail end of his comment. She took one look at Brenden and her lovely face softened. It was a mental adjustment to see her in black mourning robes. Her dresses were usually bright and cheerful as she was. Today, she mirrored her clothing, depressed and heavy.

Brenden wiped his wet, red eyes and turned his face away. "My apologies, my queen. I wanted to—"

Dyna held up a delicate hand. "Do not apologize, warrior. I often speak to her as if she could respond."

They both looked down at Avery's sleeping form. Bren's cheeks grew warm as he addressed Dyna again. "I guess you don't like the fact that I'm upset over the woman who killed your husband."

"I know the person who killed my husband, and the woman you

worry over is not the murderer." Dyna walked over to the window and peered out. "To be honest, before I knew what had truly happened, I was angry with Nikki. Now I understand her motives, her actions, the hand that forced her. I understand why it had to be Troy." She turned her lavender eyes on him. "Nikki knew she could not harm someone Avery loved most. Ryse. Hayden. Me. And even Troy. But Nikki knew that for Salina to get the punishment she deserved, she had to do something drastic."

"Hayden hates her," Brenden said.

Dyna nodded, her waves of knee-length blonde hair rippling with the movement. "Hayden is grieving. His words are birthed from that grief. Do not hold it against him."

Yankee interrupted to announce that the Avondales were less than two hours away. Dante accompanied him and would escort Dyna to meet her guests. The three warriors waited in the sitting room while Dynasty and Hanna freshened up.

Yankee and Brenden had a love-hate relationship based on their mutual respect for Ryse and love for Avery. This evening, he hoped Yankee would keep his trap shut. His nerves were shot after hearing Evander's diagnosis of Nikki and he couldn't handle asinine comments.

However, Yankee took up a post by the door and sat down with a book. Brenden was tempted to make a smartass comment about him being able to read at all, but he didn't want to engage.

Yankee watched out of the corner of his eye. But when he spoke, it was to Dante. "Can't believe you fainted." Yankee shook his nearly bald head and chuckled. "Fucking pansy."

Dante crossed his arms over his broad chest. "You try leashing the power of a Master Thracian and see where it gets you, tough guy. He would put you on your ass too." He rubbed the back of his head. "Couldn't one of you have caught me? I've been dizzy all day."

The three warriors chuckled. But the joke didn't last long.

After a moment, Yankee spoke up again. "Look, little brother. I might be the last person on Earth you want to see right now, and I don't give a shit—"

"Yankee, not now—"

"—because I get it."

Brenden hushed.

Yankee pursed his lips. His eyes darted between the other two men in the room. "Yeah, we all know. You love Nikki, but you need to be with Avery. I get it. Not everyone could do what you're doing, sticking to your duty and all. But you need to get something through that furry head of yours; you too, Ken Doll." He referred to Brenden's shape-shifting blood and Dante's clean-cut blonde hair. Yankee rarely addressed people by their given names. Gods forbid he show that kind of respect. "For men like us, love isn't in the cards. We're soldiers, my brothers. Our future is written in blood. Do yourselves a favor and get the L-word out of your heads. The only woman we need to worry about is lying in the next room."

Brenden sighed. It was disheartening, but maybe Yankee was right. Thracian soldiers assigned to high-profile Olympians rarely mated or held steady relationships. It was simply the way of their world. He'd been foolish to think that anything could ever work out with Nikki. Maybe if he hadn't been so distracted, he would have been able to save both Nikki and Avery. He had fought and earned the title of Guardian. Fat lot of good he was to either of them in the end.

CHAPTER THREE

PURE ACID CHURNED IN RYSE'S STOMACH AS THE DEITIES FROM EUROPE exited their vehicle. Charles, Filene, and Ashton were far more modern than his family. Even though they had their palace in the Olympian realm, they often chose to linger in the human world. Especially Ashton. He looked like he had been interrupted during a photo shoot at the beach. His striped white shirt was open at the top, rolled up at the arms, and hung over khaki pants. Most women would throw themselves at his feet, and many had.

A faint hum began in Ryse's temple. *Dear gods, get this over with.*

Charles, with his custom tailored suit and designer glasses, was not known to be a vain man. He simply desired the finer things in life. Charles and Troy had been like brothers during their younger years. The two men could not have looked more opposite. Charles was blond with blue eyes, which he'd passed down to his children. Even his wife had the same features.

Filene was as beautiful as his mother but that was where the similarities ended. Filene was not as tall, nor did she have exotic eyes like Dynasty. She kept her light-colored hair short and flipped out around her head. Unlike the floor-length gowns his mother wore, Filene walked confidently in a short dress suit and high heels.

"Dynasty." Filene held out her hands to greet her oldest friend. Upon their contact, tears rolled down her cheeks.

Perhaps no one but Ryse noticed the way Dynasty stiffened in her arms.

"My dear friend. I'm in shock. I'm simply in shock. My heart is broken for you. To lose your mate and so tragically. I'm sorry, Dyna, so very sorry. How are you even breathing right now? I cannot imagine the depth of your suffering."

Filene's sympathy was real, but Ryse wondered if it would last when the smoke cleared.

Dynasty smiled at the other woman. "My sons keep my heart beating. It is the will of the gods that I am here. I pray daily for their strength and they lend it to me."

"You look well. Truly, you have their grace." Filene hugged her once more.

Ryse and Hayden greeted Charles and Filene warmly. Kind words were exchanged, condolences were given, and when Charles choked up, his honest pain was expressed. Ashton offered his sympathies, but he lacked the emotion his parents conveyed. Then again, even as a child, Ashton had been composed, the proper gentleman.

Ryse greeted all the Thracian soldiers who accompanied the Deities. These were his men, even above their duties to their charges. One of them was Xavier, Dante's father. He would be anxious to see his son. Unfortunately, it would not be a happy reunion.

"Where is Salina?" Filene asked. "I would have expected her to greet us."

"She is not in the palace right now. I'm sure you will see her later." Hayden's words were not a lie. Salina was in the prison, not the palace.

"Let's go sit and talk, shall we?" Dyna said as she and Filene walked arm and arm to the library. The room was more intimate and the conversation that followed would be hard enough, especially if the Avondales thought others could hear.

"Will you tell us what happened to Troy?" Charles asked. "There is much speculation and I wish to get to the bottom if it." He took a seat across from Ryse while Filene and Dyna sat next to one another, clasping hands.

Ryse waved off Hanna, who served warm drinks to everyone. If he added heat to his already churning gut, it might erupt. And what the hell was that humming in his head?

Before the European Deities arrived, Ryse, Hayden, and Dyna had discussed what would be revealed and what would be kept secret. There were some things the Avondales didn't need to know—*yet*.

Dyna let her sons tell the story of her husband's death. Hayden began. "Father held a brunch in honor of Ryse's mating. That morning, Mother had a vision of his death. She didn't know when or how, only that it was inevitable."

Filene gasped. "How terrible." She covered her mouth with her hand and began to cry. She knew all too well the burden of a Divine Grace's visions. Tears rolled down Dyna's face as she accepted the affections from her friend.

"Forgive me, Ryse." Charles shook his head. "In all the confusion, I forgot that you've been mated recently. What a blessing. Where is your Grace?"

"Hayden should continue." Ryse pinched his lips and looked away. He had to play the part of grieving widower, after all. Charles's head tilted a fraction, his brow furrowed.

"Before Ryse and his bride could drink from the sacred chalice, Avery, Ryse's mate, noticed her Shadow Lady acting strange. Being the smart girl she is—was—she put the pieces together."

"Her Shadow Lady killed Troy?" Ashton blurted. "A *maid* killed a king? You can't be serious."

"It's a bit more complicated," Ryse mumbled and cast Ashton a pointed glance.

Hayden explained about the champagne, the poison, how Troy had been eaten from the inside out. The graphic nature of the murder caused Charles cringe and Filene to cover her mouth with the back of her hand as if she were going to be ill.

"Why?" Filene cried out. "Why would she do such a thing? And where is Avery? Where is your mate, Ryse?"

No one spoke. The words were razors and no matter how you handled them, they would cut into the souls of everyone in the room.

"Dynasty," Filene pleaded, leaning in close. "What are you not saying? Please, let us bear your burden. We love you. You shouldn't have to go through this alone."

Dynasty cried in earnest as she lifted a hand to touch Filene's cheek. "I wish I could keep this from you, my dearest friend. By the gods, I wish things were not as they are." Dynasty stood and came to stand behind Ryse, leaving Filene on the other side of the room with her family.

Ryse leaned over on his knees and finished the hardest part of the story. "Nikki was under a great telepathic compulsion. The moment she confessed the name of the person who programmed her mind, she went into a coma. She is on death's door as we speak."

Ryse let the Avondales fill in the blanks. They knew their daughter's skills. They knew her Olympian gifts.

"Ryse." Charles said his name through clenched teeth. "Where is my daughter, *exactly?*"

Ryse held his narrowed-eyes stare, but said nothing. Charles knew.

"What? I don't understand? What does Salina have to do with this?" Filene looked to Dyna for the answers. Ryse's mother put a shaking hand on her throat.

"Oh dear gods and goddesses." Charles rose from his chair and began to pace the room. He ran his hand over his hair.

"Charles?" Filene glanced from Ryse to Dyna to her husband. "Darling?"

"She did it, Filene," he spit out. Charles braced his arms on the back of her chair and hung his head. "Salina used her telepathy to make that girl murder Troy."

That was when the chaos began. Filene left her chair in a fit of anger. She threw her arms in the air as she denied every possibility of her daughter's involvement. Ashton tried to defend Salina; he argued that she wasn't nearly powerful enough to plant a virus in someone's mind. Charles turned the color of English peas and murmured about being sick.

Hayden, Dyna, and Ryse stayed seated and kept their heads about them. This family had to come to the truth in their own way. There was no easy way to learn that your daughter, your sister, was a murderer.

"No," Filene screamed. "I don't believe you." She stood in front of Ryse, who rose to meet the challenge. He towered over her, but she didn't shrink back immediately. "It's lies. What proof do you have? All of this is preposterous. My daughter wouldn't kill a fly, much less murdered a man who she viewed as family. And why? She has no motive."

"We can provide you with witnesses and all the proof you need, Filene. But do you really want to hear it?" Ryse watched the indecision on her face.

Finally, she steeled her spine and slapped Ryse across the face. "Yes. I want proof. I want to talk to these witnesses. I don't believe any of this."

Charles gained his footing and took his crying spouse into his arms. His eyes stayed on Ryse. His wife struck the Thracian Master and, according their laws, she could be put to death. "Filene, why would they lie about this? There is no logic in blaming this on Salina unless she is guilty. Why would they hurt us in such a way unless it were true?"

Filene pushed him away. "That is our daughter. How can you believe this so easily?"

"Because I trust Dynasty, I trust Ryse and Hayden. And I know that a darkness has grown in our daughter for the last few decades. I didn't want to see it, and now Troy is dead because I chose to bury my head in the sand. My friend, my leader. He's gone." Charles coughed and sat down, his head hanging nearly between his knees. His aura was overpowering, rolling over everyone in the room in waves of hot anguish and pulses of sickening turmoil. Even Ryse recoiled under the tsunami.

Over the next couple of hours, the Castilles explained Salina's actions to the Avondales. Although Salina's primary motivation was to get to Ryse, it didn't fly with any of them. Certain details were left out. Ryse's instincts told him that they didn't need to know about Salina's connection with the teleporter. There was plenty to her story without those details. When Hayden told of how Salina stabbed Avery, they all paused.

"She—" Ashton swallowed hard and turned his head to Ryse. "Salina murdered your mate? Your Grace?" As a prince who hadn't yet found his Grace, Ashton could appreciate the heartbreak Ryse felt.

Every Deity Prince longed for a Grace. "I'm sorry, Ryse. Salina has always been somewhat fixated on you, but this is far beyond what anyone could have expected. A Grace is a gift to the race, not just the man. That's a horrible tragedy. You have my deepest sympathies."

Ryse nodded to him and kept his eyes averted like he was trying not to cry. He rubbed at his temples not only to play the part, but also to try and relieve the buzzing in his head.

"I want to see her." Filene was ready to collapse. "I have to see my child. I want to know why she did this."

"No, Mother," Ashton said. Ryse flipped his stare to the young Prince and narrowed his eyes. Maybe it was his imagination, but the buzzing in his head seemed to be worse around the other Prince. Ashton regained his composure. "I should see her first. She might talk to me if you're not there. You know she's always confided in me." He looked to Ryse. "I don't want to upset my mother any more than necessary. If Salina is mentally unstable…"

Ryse took the hint. "Fine. General Falcon will take you to her cell." Ryse stood to leave. "I want to meet with Xavier to discuss security measures. If you find out anything…"

"You'll be the first to know," Ashton assured him.

Ryse was far more concerned with the way Ashton's aura never wavered, never showed any emotion, as if it had been frozen.

— ·— ⚬ ·—

Dante would not let his nerves get the best of him, even if he did have the urge to cringe and cower under his father's scrutiny. It was a gut reaction, one he'd lived with his entire life. Decades of his father talking down to him about his lacking performance had chipped away at his confidence. With a deep breath, he remembered that he was no longer a child. He was an Elite.

Dante's father, General Xavier, was one of the few Olympians to show his age. Silver laced his brown hair and wrinkles spread from the edges of his eyes. Not that the man looked old by human standards, but most Olympians didn't develop gray hair until their fifth century of life. Xavier was heading into his sixth century. Until Dante's birth, the general and his wife were not blessed with sons, but a dozen daughters. After Dante's birth, they had more daughters still, hoping for one more son.

Dante knew they kept trying because Xavier was not pleased with the son he was saddled with. Dante's powers were more defensive than offensive. He was not hard and blunt, like his father, but compassionate and tactful like his mother. He was a fine soldier, so the general said, but he was not a leader and would never achieve the rank of his father and grandfather and great-grandfather.

A disappointment Dante lived with every day.

When he first came to the Thracian Training Center, he was quickly categorized as a second-tier warrior. He could not control fire or wind, he could not run faster than the eye could see. His strength was that of an average Thracian soldier. Physical tracking did not come easy to him and he couldn't read the auras of others like most trackers could. The Earth did not bend to his will, the metals of the Earth did not come at his command.

He was nothing special; nothing amazing or stunning.

When his fellow students did understand his gift, the semi-seclusion began. The men would be happy to talk to him, study with him, and have lunch together. But no one wanted to spar with him. No one wanted to share a dormitory with him.

Not that he blamed them. If his power was an offensive one, something useful like manipulating water or telekinesis, he would be protective of it too.

However, Dante was the eraser of gifts. One touch, and he could disable powers. Coming or going, he neutralized the threat. To shake his hand was to be a mere mortal temporarily. In that moment, Dante could get an intimate feel of their powers.

Even the mighty General Xavier didn't like to embrace his son, as proven by his greeting when the Avondales arrived at the palace. Xavier had acknowledged him with a quick visual assessment, then dismissed him with a head nod. "Soldier."

"General." Dante bowed his head slightly. There were no handshakes, no hugs, no happy reunions with the father he hadn't seen in the last couple of years, nothing. Dante might as well have been a faceless soldier in the crowd to his father.

What made him lift his chin higher and not feel the sting of rejection was the fact that he stood beside Master Ryse. The Master of all Thracians world-wide invited him to this meeting. Dante was an Elite apprentice, taken under the wing of the five most deadly men in the Olympian world. All because one woman didn't glance over him the way his father had.

Avery.

She *saw* him. For that, Dante had devoted his life to the princess, earned the gratitude of the royal family, and now could accept the cold shoulder of his father without guilt stabbing his heart.

Victory and pride swelled in his chest as he sat in a meeting with the Master and the general. Xavier had heard all the accusations against Salina and requested a private audience with Ryse.

"He does not have to be here simply because he is of my blood," Xavier to Ryse, waving off Dante as inconsequential.

Of my blood was much different than *my son*.

"No, he has to be here because he was privy to Salina's actions from the beginning." Ryse delivered the words without looking at Xavier. He sat down and waited for Xavier to follow. Hammon was also in attendance and nodded to Dante take a seat on the opposite side of the Master.

Xavier did not miss the position of his seating. His jaw tensed and his eyes narrowed a fraction. "I was not aware of him achieving any accolades to earn him a place beside you, Master Ryse." Xavier's body language betrayed nothing of his agitation. No one in the room knew the general like his own son. Dante saw the way his fingers drummed on his thigh and his lips pinched together, creating thin lines around his mouth.

"Your *son*," Ryse accentuated the familiar term, "has proven to be a valuable asset. I believe his talents have been overlooked far too often. However, that is not why we are here."

"Of course. I would like to know exactly what happened. You may feel free to give me the details that were too harsh for the family. I need to be abreast of the situation, for their sake."

Dante paid close attention as Ryse vaguely explained the circumstances of Salina's capture. But he would not make a move to punish her until he heard from the gods, who had been silent far too long.

"Nothing like this has ever happened in the history of our people and I find the absence of Ares' instruction a telling sign that I am not to make a hasty, rash decision. Until the gods express to me their wishes, I want you to be aware of all the security measures we will take. It is not meant to be insulting, but simply to protect those under my care."

"I understand, Master. Whatever you need, I will provide and aid you in your—"

"Your assistance will not be necessary. My Elites will handle all interrogations and General Falcon will have a team doing searches of all visitors and their belongings." Ryse's immediate shutdown caused Xavier to blanch, but the man said nothing. "I'm surprised that General Gaston did not come with you. Why did he remain in Europe?" He referred to Xavier's only superior officer.

"With Charles and Ashton both gone, he thought it pertinent to continue having a powerful presence in our country."

"Understandable."

Their business was finished only minutes later. There wasn't too much that passed between the two men. Ryse and Hammon left in order to allow Dante to speak to his father.

He stayed seated, but Xavier stood and paced the room. "How far are you from finishing your training?"

"A couple weeks, although recent events have caused me to place schooling on hold."

"Humph." Xavier shook his head. "I bet. I can't believe you're in the middle of this mess. Didn't I tell you to keep your head down and lie low?"

"It was not a conscious choice, Father. I had to step in. It's my duty to protect the Deities, isn't it?"

"It matters not. You will say only what is necessary and we will get you out of this place as soon as possible."

"I cannot leave." Dante didn't push his father often—or ever. But circumstances had changed. *He* had changed.

"You can and you will. Your training is nearly complete; you have no purpose here now."

Dante pushed back his chair and leaned over the table on his knuckles. "I do have a purpose here. I will not leave."

"Do not forget your place, soldier," Xavier yelled, reminding Dante of his true position in his father's life. "You will obey orders. I know they have at least taught you that."

Xavier stormed out of the room before Dante could let him know exactly what he had learned.

As an Elite, even only an apprentice, Dante answered only to other Elites and Master Ryse. Avery, of course, when she woke up, would be his mistress and he would gladly follow her lead.

Now wasn't the time to inform Xavier of such things. But the time would come and, when it did, Dante feared it would be an ugly scene.

CHAPTER FOUR

ASHTON WAS MORE THAN ANGRY WITH HIS PATHETIC SISTER. HONESTLY, killing dogs? Bloody freaking dogs? What the fuck was she thinking? Why bother? Then to use a Shadow Lady as an assassin…yeah, brilliant. Nothing could go wrong with that plan. Idiot. She'd made so many mistakes. Screwing the scientist as blackmail. Trying to get Avery to commit suicide. And getting the teleporter killed? Bloody. Fucking. Hell. If the gods weren't already going to have her head, there would be shit to pay with the demons. As it stood now, his little sister was a pig waiting to be slaughtered. Ryse Almighty was going to have to chop her blonde head right off her shoulders.

Admittedly, the bastard Prince looked rough. Despite her mistakes, Salina had killed Avery and it made Ryse weaker. He was prey now and the rogues could thank her for that.

Ashton walked down into the pit of jail and was shown to Salina's cell. His parents were still too upset to come see her; at least, that was what he'd convinced them to think. But he'd seen this one coming. Salina's ambitions had always blinded her common sense. When the cell door opened, it took his eyes a moment to adjust to the dim light.

"Ashton." Salina flung herself into his arms and he nearly fell over. Thracian guards came to pry her off, but he waved them down.

Damn, she stank. He wanted to gag.

"You've got to get me out of here. You can fix this. I know you can."

He laughed and Salina recoiled. "Salina, my darling, do you have any clue what a bloody mess you've made? You've killed the Grand fucking Deity, a Divine Grace, and apparently, a good dozen Thracian soldiers. I can't help you out of this." He raised his hands with a shrug and chuckled.

The only clean thing was the cot. He couldn't sit down, so he stood still, careful not to get dirty. This cesspool was far beneath any-one of royal blood, but she'd earned it.

"Ashton," she pleaded, trying to sound innocent and seductive, kneeling in front of him. "I didn't kill anyone important. It's not my fault those Thracians felt the need to sacrifice themselves to save their princess. I had nothing to do with that stupid maid killing Troy. I adored Troy; you know that."

Ashton bent down to look her in the eyes and whispered, "And Avery? Did you have nothing to do with the knife that plunged itself into her heart over and over again? Innocent of all charges, huh?"

A glare of unadulterated hatred crossed her beautiful features, making her appear positively maniacal. "No, that bitch got what she deserved and I'm glad she's wandering the afterlife. Ryse has belonged to me since the night I took him into my bed and I will not share."

"You've killed his mate, Salina. The gods will determine your *in-nocence* of the other charges, but you've murdered his Divine Grace in a room full of witnesses. He's a wreck over her." Ashton leaned down until he was but a breath away from her. His eyes bored into hers. "Know this, sister. He will not hesitate to run his blade straight through your neck when the time comes." His finger trailed across her throat slowly.

Fear bloomed in her eyes. She shook her head wildly. "No. No, he wouldn't kill me. Not my Ryse. He's been inside me, Ashton; a part of me."

He examined his cuticles, bored with her theatrics and delusions. "Half the Olympian population has been inside you, Salina. It's not nearly as glamorous as it once was. Trust me."

"What will you do while you're here if not champion for my life?"

"I'm watching, Salina. Every move those Castilles make, every rotation of the guards, every Thracian in training will have eyes on them. I must carry on the mission. But you? You're far past my aid."

Salina stood and ran her hands over her long, tangled mess of blonde hair. "Daddy. Daddy will get me out of here. Daddy will not let me die." Her desperate conviction nearly made him pity her. Nearly.

"He's heard everything. He's talked to witnesses, he's spoken in depth with the scientist you—what was the word—*raped*?" Ashton shook his head, took a deep breath. "I doubt he will even try. You've botched this one up royally."

"I can't be killed. I won't be killed." She lifted her chin. "I'll tell the gods everything. I'll—"

Ashton had his hand around her neck in a blink. He pulled back her hair so hard it made her gasp. "If you think for one second that *they* will help you after you've cost them a teleporter, you're far more insane than I thought." He twisted her hair and she winced. Her eyes watered. "Listen and listen good, you whore. If you think the wrath of the gods is cruel, wait until your soul gets to Hades."

Her eyes rounded.

"Haven't considered that, have you, Salina? For killing a Grand Deity *and* a Divine Grace, you will be sent straight to the fiery depths of Hades for all eternity. And that, my sister, is where the demons are. You can either go down as a martyr for their cause or you can go down as a sniveling, spineless rat. Which do you think the demons will welcome?" He tossed her back on the cot and dusted off his hands more than necessary. "Think about how you want to play this, Salina. If I were you, I'd go with anger to the gods and pray the demons think it's good enough rebellion." Ashton looked back as Salina righted herself on the bed. "Demons have no mercy, and a tender morsel like you would be a prized gift."

Tears dripped down her cheeks, cutting through the grime on her face. She nodded her head in understanding. If Salina had a brain, she would play her cards right and maybe her eternity wouldn't be pure torture.

"Get cleaned up, Salina. Our parents want to see you and I'll be damned if they are going to see you like this." He flicked his hand at her as he walked out of the cell.

Two hours later, Ashton stood out of the way. He'd delivered his warnings to Salina privately. Now his parents had to face their murderous daughter. As much as he hated to admit it, this was one thing he would keep his mother from if he could. Per his request, Salina had been moved and cleaned up. Filene didn't need to see her daughter looking like a pig in squalor.

Now they sat at a table, the three of them. Salina on one side, his parents on the other. Guards were outside the door, his parents' personal Thracians stood inside the room upon Ryse's insistence.

Tears ran down Filene's face and, despite her anger, reached over to take Salina's hand.

"Why?" she whispered. "How could you do this?"

Salina cast a quick glance in Ashton's direction before she answered. "I wanted her gone."

Filene drew back her hand, covered her mouth, and closed her eyes.

"Ryse was supposed to be with me," Salina continued. Her voice never betrayed her. It was firm and unwavering. "I thought that when we, when we were together, it meant the gods had given him to me. A true Deity doesn't break his celibacy, except for his mate. You've both said it time and time again. Ryse slept with me. I thought it meant he would be mine."

"Did you use your telepathy then?" Charles' question held the heat of his disgust. "To get him to bed?"

"Only a little. I promise."

Salina lies so easily, Ashton thought. He knew better. She'd used every ounce of her Olympian magic to get Ryse to sleep with her. When he realized what transpired, he left her immediately, blaming himself for something forced on him in his weakest hour.

Charles stood, wiped a hand over his face, and around to rub his stiff neck. "Do you have any idea what you've done, Salina? Can you conceive of the consequences of your actions? The gods will punish you for this and there is nothing anyone can do to stop them."

"You could—"

"No." Charles cut her off with the slashing movement of his hand. His head shook back and forth. "No, child. I will not, *cannot* defend you in this."

Salina tilted her head to the side, looking at their father. Her jaw went slack and her eyes squinted. "I'm your daughter. I'm a Princess. Aphrodite gave me—"

"You're a murderer," Charles screamed over her. He leaned over the table and slammed his fist down. "You. Are. A. Murderer. He was my oldest friend. Troy was like a brother to me and you had him killed. I can't even fathom the magnitude of it."

Filene tried to calm him down, but there was no getting through to him. Ashton had never witnessed his father so enraged. Perhaps he wasn't a spineless tool of the gods after all.

"I didn't want that girl to poison Troy," Salina confessed. "I wanted her to kill Avery. How was I supposed to know they were so closely bonded? She had only been assigned a couple days. I've had my Shadow Lady for over a century and we can barely stand each other. I never meant to hurt Troy or Dynasty. You must believe me."

"She was his mate, Salina," Ashton said as he rolled his eyes. "What did you think, that he would come running to your bed after you killed her?"

Salina pinned him with a hard glare. "He's mine. He's always been mine. I'm a princess; she was a farm girl. She didn't deserve him."

"The gods chose her. The gods—"

"Damn the gods," Salina shouted and everyone halted. With those three words, she'd stopped them all in their tracks. "When was the last time the gods showed their faces around here? No one has faith in them any longer. They have abandoned us and the people worship *us*. We have become gods to the people." She crossed her arms over her chest. That outburst was too close for comfort. Ashton needed to get his parents away from Salina before she said something that would condemn them both.

Thankfully, Charles righted himself. "You bring shame to this family, to our country, our religion. Yes, you were a Princess, and you had an obligation to the people beneath you. Because of your greed, your petty jealousy, and your promiscuous ways, you have separated your-self from this family."

"Charles?" Filene looked up at her husband. "What are you saying?"

Salina's eyes widened a fraction.

Ashton straightened from his post against the wall. His father couldn't seriously be—

"You are no longer a princess." Charles could have been made of stone. He was unyielding. "You are no longer a part of the Avondale clan, and you are no daughter of mine."

Salina looked first to Ashton and, for a split second, he thought she was going to spill everything. Her mouth hung open and her eyes were the size of dinner plates. She turned her attention to Filene. "Mother?"

"Come, Filene, Ashton." Charles helped his wife stand and mo-tioned for his son. "Our business here is done. Her life rests in the hands of the gods now."

Right before they left, his mother broke. She ran to Salina and pulled her into her arms and began to sob hysterically. "You will al-ways be my child," his mother declared, then looked to her husband. "She will always be my daughter. I'm her mother. I can't, I simply can't *quit*." Filene wiped her face. "I will pray to the gods every day for her soul. They must forgive her if she repents."

"First," Charles said with a growl, "she must feel remorse. I doubt she feels anything but her own selfish desires."

He left without another word. Ashton pried his mother off Salina and took her to the temple, where she began to pray fervently. *Such a waste.* Salina had a point. His mother was devoted to gods who barely showed their existence anymore. The time was coming when they would no longer be needed. That was when he would step in to take their place.

CHAPTER FIVE

DANTE STOOD AT ATTENTION, HIS HANDS CLASPED BEHIND HIS BACK, his eyes straight ahead. In front of him, Xavier paced as usual. The man was incapable of standing still, a nervous habit thankfully not passed down.

Finally convinced that he needed to hear Dante's full accounts of the last few days, Xavier cornered him in the billiards room the next morning, the same room Lady Dynasty had pulled him aside in not long ago. Her message had been clear; be sure of your choices and get ready to deal with the consequences, good or bad.

Dante had made up his mind, and his loyalties, he knew, were in the right place. Too bad that place was not where his father wanted them to be.

"Avery picked you from the crowd, you say?" Xavier rubbed the salt and pepper hair on his chin.

"Yes, sir," Dante answered with crisp words. He hesitated to reveal too much to his father.

Xavier had been with the Avondales for the majority of his long life. As soon as Ashton was born, he asked to be assigned to the child. From that day forward, the Prince hadn't made a move without Xavier's knowledge.

Given the fact that Ashton's sister was a murderer, Dante was apprehensive about revealing things about the Castilles. Some events were common knowledge and there was no use lying about them.

"And you said you know *for a fact* Salina planted suicidal thoughts into the woman?" Xavier narrowed his eyes at his son.

"Yes, Father. I know what I sensed."

"Could you have been mistaken?"

"No."

"Are you sure you are capable of sheltering another person with touch? You're not making this up?"

"Of course not." This was bordering on insulting and Dante's blood pressure rose with every doubting question. Did his father think he was a complete imbecile?

Xavier shook his head, unbelieving of his son's tale. "Your powers are young, still developing. Are you absolutely positive—"

"*Yes*, Father," Dante insisted, tired of the onslaught of questions. The Master Thracian and a room full of seasoned soldiers believed him. Hell, the Grand Deity believed his testimony. Why was it so damned difficult for his own father to have a little faith in him?

"Do not take a tone with me, soldier." Xavier faced him, puffed out his chest. "I have the authority to ask such questions and you will answer them without attitude. Remember, I am a general and you are not."

Dante relaxed his stance and crossed his arms over his chest. Xavier's nostrils flared at his sudden change of stance and the utter lack of respect he showed. If a pissing match was to take place, Dante was ready. He had spent all night praying for Ares to give him the strength and words to properly deal with Xavier. If his father wanted to ignore their biological relationship, he could too.

He remembered the way Ryse had put a hand on his shoulder and looked him in the eyes. *"You are one of my Elites, apprentice or otherwise. Avery chose you by direction of the gods and now you stand out, independent from other Thracians. Remember that, my brother. You are no ordinary soldier any longer."*

With those words firmly embedded in his mind and heart, Dante leveled his gaze at his father. "You are correct. I have not earned the title of general. However, I have earned the title of Elite and am now directly under the authority of Master Ryse. I don't fall into the military hierarchy, but rather stand independently. How did Ryse put it, oh yes—*above it.*"

The haughtiness faded from Xavier's face. "I beg your pardon?"

"You heard me. As an Elite, I can answer you how I please or choose to ignore you altogether. Although I would prefer to be civil about this."

Xavier's eyes widened, his nostrils flared, and he took an involuntary step back. Ripples of rage and power poured from his aura, the heat and energy of their waves rattling the pictures on the walls.

Dante's message had not been well received. Being inducted into the Elites was all some Thracians strived for their entire careers. Elites were revered and respected, the cream of the Thracian crop. Although he would never admit it, Xavier had once idolized them and strived to join their ranks, to have the ultimate power and title of a Thracian Elite. Only being Master could be a greater honor.

"You're lying," Xavier said, practically foaming at the mouth with bitterness. "Like you're lying about Salina. Why the hell should I believe a word you say? You've been nothing but one disappointment after another."

Dante motioned his arm towards the door. "We can go find Ryse together, if you wish. I'm sure he will happily set the record straight, as will any of the Elites."

"That is the problem with the *Elites*. Ryse takes these random soldiers and gives them freedom to run amuck, obeying no one, answering to no one. Those men have no honor, no sense of loyalty. They are renegades, not warriors. Nothing more than killers for hire. Some of them are not even of Thracian blood at all. You should examine your priorities."

"We answer to Master Ryse and we answer to the Grand Deity."

"Convenient, since the Grand Deity is dead," Xavier sneered as he kept his pacing. But his ego had deflated a fraction.

Dante kept his eyes focused just above the man's head. "Yes, tragically, thanks to the sister of the man you serve. Perhaps it is not me who needs to examine priorities?"

Xavier backhanded Dante. The swing was so fast, so hard, that it stunned them both. Xavier had reacted too quickly to control his strength.

"I will not allow you to speak ill of Prince Ashton. He has been more of a son to me than you have."

Dante slowly turned his head back to his father, touching the stinging place on his cheek, and his fingers came away red and slick with blood. That didn't stop him from asserting himself. It was past time for this confrontation. Xavier had voiced what Dante knew all along. Ashton was the powerful son he'd always wanted.

"And I will not let you speak ill of Master Ryse or his Elites. They are far closer to being family than you ever were."

"If your mother heard you say that…" Xavier shook his head. "What a disappointment you've become, Dante."

"Only to you. My Master and my mistress think differently. So does my mother, not that you've ever cared to ask her." That fact gave him the courage to face down his father. Avery valued him, loved him. Ryse accepted him into the Elites with no questions, no hesitation. His beloved mother sent him letters nearly every month, speaking of her love and pride. That was all he needed. Xavier's expectations were never going to be met and Dante'd accepted that long ago.

Xavier huffed; his expression was an ugly mask of blatant disgust. "And you think Ryse will keep you around now that his Grace is dead? Don't you comprehend, you daft child; you were merely her play thing. Your talents will be of no use to the Master Thracian." He laughed and raised a brow, thinking he'd found a wound to salt.

His victory was short-lived. Dante nodded, pursed his lips, and walked up until he was eye-to-eye with his father.

"I've already proven you wrong, and you're too *daft* to see it. If you will excuse me, *General*, I have an Elite meeting to attend. I'm sure you will get the notes later." Dante walked out of the room and left his father to stew with his rage. The satisfaction in his gut was well worth the wait. After all these years, he had not only lived up to being the best soldier he could, he had surpassed even Xavier's expectations.

Brenden met Dante in the hall on the way to their meeting. Bren's eyes zeroed in on the line of broken flesh and blood.

"Where the *hell* did you get that?"

Dante touched his cheek, but shrugged it off. He did not want to make more of this than there was. "Minor disagreement with General Xavier."

"General? Not your *father*?" Bren asked, examining Dante.

Yankee approached them and grabbed Dante's chin, turning it to see the gash. The man had no concept of personal space.

Dante ignored him and answered Bren's query. "Yes. It seems familial ties don't take precedence to military rank."

Yankee's smug grin grew. "Did you pull the Elite card? Bet that pissed him off. Fucker. He drew blood."

The three of them continued down the hall to the conference room Hammon had specified. Dante shrugged again, uncomfortable with the conversation. "He was not pleased."

Philippe joined the parade and rattled off in Italian, pointing to Dante's face. *Great, another mother hen.*

"English, man. Speak in English." Yankee rolled his eyes.

"Your *faccia*?" Philippe spoke to Dante and ignored Yankee, like most of the men did.

"General Xavier," Dante said.

Philippe went off on a tirade in Italian. Dante knew just enough to catch something about killing Xavier, or hacking off his balls, something to that effect. He hadn't known Philippe long and his Italian was rusty, so he could pick out basic words.

"English, jackass," Yankee spit out. "We no speak-ah de Italian-ah." He punctuated the words with pretend sign language that looked more like gang signs. One of these days, Yankee was going to piss off the wrong person and said person was going to give him the ass beating of a lifetime. Dante hoped like hell he was there to watch.

Philippe shook his head, his curly black hair bouncing around his ears. "Eh, idiots." He opened the door where Cutter and Hammon waited.

"Oh, *that* you can say in English?" Yankee muttered and closed the door behind them.

Bren and Dante exchanged a glance. Philippe could speak English fluently most of the time. He simply spoke Italian around Yankee to irritate him.

They gathered around the table and took their seats. Hammon stood at the head and examined them all. He was so tall and thin he could be mistaken for fragile. Dante knew better. Underneath his baggy black leather jacket was lean muscle. Hammon was a hell of a fighter and the best tracker in this realm. His skin was black as night and blended with the black clothing he favored.

Hammon's dark eyes scanned the men and damned if they didn't land on him. Dante froze in his seat, hoping if he avoided eye contact nothing would be said.

"Let me guess; I should see the other guy?" Hammon teased with a slight smile.

"Minor disagreement with my fa—General Xavier, sir." Dante's jaws clenched, his cheeks blazed. Respect for Hammon ran deep; he was not a man to disappoint. Dante had been raised with legends of his greatness.

Hammon took in a deep breath and clasped his hands in front of him. Expectant. Patient. He didn't have to speak; he didn't have to voice a question. His expression alone prompted Dante to spill. Hammon had that effect on people.

"The general seems to think the Elites are running amuck, answering to no one and having no loyalty nor honor. I set him straight and he was offended."

Men began to complain until Hammon held up his hand. He continued to stare at Dante, somehow knowing there was more. There was no use trying to get anything past him.

After a moment, Dante finally sighed. "He also thinks that Master Ryse will kick me out now that I'm not Avery's play thing."

"You were Avery's play thing?" Yankee's brows rose on his forehead. "Nice job, Ken Doll."

"Shut it," Dante warned.

Hammon crossed his arms over his chest, reached up to touch his chin. "I assume you put him in his place?"

Dante nodded and pointed to his cheek. "I'd say he heard me."

"Did you strike him in return?"

"Only his ego, sir. That hurt him bad enough, I assure you."

Cutter, Yankee, Philippe, and Hammon exchanged looks. He could only imagine what that was about.

"All right." Hammon flipped open a leather portfolio and began the meeting. They had a lot to discuss, but somehow, he knew all the men were bothered by the fact Xavier hit him.

Surely they all thought him the weakest link for not fighting back physically. Maybe he should have. Maybe he should have hit his father with the same burst of anger. No. He couldn't think like that. Hitting his father would have brought him down to the same level of disgrace. Instead, Dante had been the bigger man and walked away from Xavier's childish tantrum. Besides, his father was a seasoned warrior. A physical altercation would mean little to him. Being outranked by his disappointing son hurt him far worse.

The Elites would see it that way. He hoped.

Finally, he thought, relieved when the meeting concluded an hour later. His face hurt, not that he would whine about it. He stood to leave, but Hammon asked him to sit at the head of the table. None of the others had risen from their chairs.

"Sir?"

Hammon touched a button on the intercom system and paged General Xavier.

Dear gods of Olympian. "Sir, I have to ask that you let me fight this battle on my own. He is my father and I will deal with him."

"No," Hammon answered abruptly, cutting off any arguments.

"You are Elite," Cutter explained, his Chinese accent punctuating each staccato word. "As Elite, you are brother. There are no battles you fight alone."

"That's right." Brenden rose to his feet. "Xavier strikes you, he might as well have hit us all."

"He drew blood, Ken Doll. We can't stand for someone to mess up that pretty face of yours." Yankee came to stand by Brenden and patted Dante on the cheek...the injured one.

Philippe motioned again for him to sit at the head of the table by slapping the back of the chair twice. "We cannot allow our loyalty to be questioned. He must be taught we are a united front; otherwise, he will see us as weak and others will follow."

"You know," Yankee whispered to Philippe. "If you can speak English like that all the time, it would be polite."

Philippe turned away from Yankee and rattled off curses in Italian, causing everyone to chuckle.

Hammon, Cutter, Philippe, Yankee, and Brenden formed a wall behind him. Even as dread rose in his gut, he was honored to have such men at his back.

Xavier entered the room and his footsteps faltered when he saw the six men facing him.

"Elites." His jaw clenched and his chin tilted upwards.

"General," the Elites acknowledged as one.

Hammon, their leader in Ryse's absence, took point. "General, it has been brought to my attention that you have a problem with our squad."

"That was a private conversation."

No denial, Dante noted.

"You made it public when you left your mark on the face of our brother," Hammon said.

"My son had no right to share details of our conversation."

Dante rose. "Oh, *now* I'm your son? Earlier, I was merely some soldier under your boot."

Xavier was about to argue when Hammon held up a hand to silence him, a move that caused the general to blanch. "Dante is one of us. He is no longer simply another solider. He is no longer merely your blood relative. He is a member of our ranks and we take any attacks as a group. You insult him, you insult us all. You strike him, you strike us all. His blood is our blood. This," he pointed to Dante's gash, "is unacceptable not only from one soldier to another, but from a father to a son. You shame yourself, general. Do not let it happen again, or we will have no choice but to show you how deep our loyalty to one another runs. Punishment shall be swift and blood will spill. You are dismissed."

Xavier practically had smoke coming out of his ears. He thought about arguing; Dante could see it in the way he opened his mouth, then shut it quickly. Instead, he bowed his head slightly and exited the room, shooting Dante a pointed glare before retreating.

Dante released the breath he'd been holding and sat down, resting his elbows on the table. "This is going to make the holidays awkward."

Yankee threw back his head in laughter. The others joined him and, finally, Dante cracked a smile as his brothers slapped him on the back and shoulders.

He'd never been more humbled. If he weren't already devoted to the Elites and to Master Ryse, that display of solidarity and brotherhood would have sealed the deal.

CHAPTER
SIX

R YSE BARRELED DOWN THE HALL, ASHTON FOLLOWING IN HIS WAKE. HE
had things to do and Ashton's petty issues were inconsequential
at the moment. Again, his head hummed in Ashton's presence.
What caused that?

"I don't appreciate your thugs trying to intimidate my general."

"I'd be careful of your vocabulary, Prince Ashton. My Elites are
rather touchy today, and possessive." He kept walking so Ashton
couldn't see the smile on his face. The way his men had handled Xavier
was no less than he expected and he was damned proud.

"This is no joke, Ryse. Those men have no right to speak to a general in such a manner."

Ryse turned, nearly causing Ashton to run into him. His Thracian
blood made him at least six inches taller than the other prince. "They
have every right. They protect their own. I'm sure you understand that
after my father's murder, we have closed ranks and will tolerate no
threats, no matter how small."

Before either of them spoke again, they were knocked back
against the wall with a blast of power coming from an aura so violent
it could only be from one of the gods. Ryse ran to the epicenter of the
blast, uncaring of what Ashton did.

Everyone in the palace made their way outdoors, where a crowd gathered. No one could defy the electric force pulling them to one place.

In the middle of the crowd stood Hermes. His aura was a beacon, signaling all the Olympians in the Haven to his location. The people knelt at his feet, awaiting him to speak. Hermes met Ryse's stare. His eyes glowed with the white light of the gods, his robes fell in sheets of white and purple to his winged feet. An outstretched hand beckoned Ryse forward, then he reached out to call Charles.

Sons of Zeus, he spoke in their heads. The gods did not need to use mortal words. *Thou art summoned by the gods of Olympia. I shall take you unto the council. Gather the guilty, prepare your households, for all kings of this mortal realm shall gather. There is another who must accompany you. The second son shall answer to Zeus.*

Ryse looked around to see Hayden, wide-eyed and searching for his brother. Ryse shook his head slightly. It was not wise to show fear in front of the gods, especially one as cunning and deceptive as Hermes.

"My Lord, our king has been murdered. Shall I go in his stead?"

Hermes' eyes narrowed on Ryse. *Yes. You are the heir. You shall go. I will return before sunset tomorrow. Make your preparations.* Hermes' body glowed until the light burned so brightly, everyone had to turn away. Gale force winds swirled from where he stood and knocked people off their feet.

When the wind ceased and light faded, Hermes was gone.

After a moment of stunned silence, the crowd erupted. Some prayed aloud, some worshipped, some screamed in fear. A god had come to them for the first time in centuries. History was made.

Ryse reacted immediately. There was much to be done. A gathering of all the kings was unheard of. If Hermes appeared to them, he would also visit the other Deities. With Troy dead, Ryse and Hayden being summoned to the Heavens, it left General Falcon with the responsibility of the Haven. Unease settled in his gut when he realized how vulnerable the Havens around the world would seem without their kings. Ryse had to conference with the generals, prepare them for what might come.

Elites and Thracians went into action. There was protocol set into place and now it would be implemented. All over the world, Havens with Deities and without were locked tight. Olympians living in the human world were contacted with the chance to journey to the nearest Haven. Once the Deities were gone, the Havens would be on hard lockdown. Thracians would patrol their borders and those soldiers working on the outside would be on high alert.

While everyone was distracted, Ryse snuck in to see Avery. The sight of her made his heart ache. Soon he had to leave and she would be vulnerable. Time in the Heavens passed differently than it did on Earth. What might seem like only a day or so to him would be weeks or even months to her.

"Wake," he whispered, willing her to follow his command. "Please, my love, open your eyes." He clenched his eyes shut, his jaw so tight it could break. Tears threatened to spill. "I need to know you will be safe while I'm gone. You can't defend yourself like this. Wake up." Ryse pressed his lips to her forehead.

Avery never moved. Heart heavy and burdened, he rose to leave.

His mother stood silently behind him. Tears streaked down her cheeks. She rubbed her hands together in jerky movements. "This is a miraculous occasion, you journeying to the Heavens."

Gods love her, she was trying to be strong. Ryse went to her and pulled her into the cradle of his arms. She clung to him like he was a lifeline.

"What is it, Mother?"

"I will be alone with you and Hayden gone and Avery in this state. What will I do in your absence? I've never been alone."

Ryse gently took her by the shoulders and made her look into his eyes. "You will not be alone, Mother. Hanna is with you. Yankee will be here, along with Brenden and Dante. Hammon, Cutter, and Philippe will be aiding General Falcon, but they too will be checking on Avery. Today, everyone in this Haven witnessed a god revealing himself. The people will seek out your guidance. They need to know your faith is strong and they will follow you. Remember our people, Mother, and you will never be alone."

Dyna took a deep breath and straightened her back. She wiped her eyes clean. "Yes, I must remember my station. Our people will surely be overwhelmed. Perhaps after you leave, I can travel through the village and minister to them. Many are camped by the portal. They will require provisions." She touched a hand to her chest. "Having a god in our realm; what a miracle. These are interesting times."

"That's the Divine Grace I know." Ryse embraced his mother once more.

Over her shoulder, he cast a glance to Hanna. She tipped her head in silent acknowledgement. Even if it cost her life, she would protect his mother.

Not too many people knew of Hanna's gift. If they did, they would be terrified. The power she wielded had a price, though. The greater words of power she called on, the weaker she became. Telling a person to have a nice day made her feet tingle and her hands go numb for hours. Manipulating a person's actions would knock her to the ground, her legs crippled for a day or two afterward. Ryse had only seen her pass out once and he prayed he never had to see it again. She had willed Andreas, her mate and fallen Elite, to live, and it had nearly killed her too.

That night, Ryse sat at the dinner table with Dyna, Hayden, and the Avondales. Charles, Filene, and Ashton were quiet. They all were. A great chasm had formed between their families and neither party wanted to admit it. Filene had never looked worse. Her usual physical perfection was a far cry from the red-eyed, pale-faced, twitchy woman at the table. Then again, his mother was also the picture of distress. Pastel gowns had been replaced by black while she was in mourning. Troy loved her hair loose and that was how she'd kept it for decades in order to please him. Tonight, it hung down her back, tied with a strip of ribbon.

"How are the grape crops this year?" Dynasty asked. The members of the Castille family, left abroad, kept up a winery and supplied the Avondales with fine wines.

Filene's head rose and tilted sideways a fraction as if she couldn't believe Dyna was asking about grapes at a time like this.

"They are wonderful. Thank you," Charles answered when it was clear his wife would not. "Hayden, my boy, how go your studies and history documentation?"

"Very well. I have much to write these days. Unprecedented events have happened." Hayden realized what he said and looked back down at his plate.

"I'm sure you do." Charles' shoulders slumped. "I'm sure you do."

Ryse took a drink of his wine when Filene met his eyes.

"Are you going to kill my daughter?"

Hayden fumbled with his silverware and the only sound in the room was cutlery hitting the floor. Charles cleared his throat, but didn't move to change the subject. All eyes turned to Ryse.

Slowly, with more control than he realized he had, he set down his cup and leaned back in his chair. He spoke low and calmly. "I will do as the gods instruct me, as I have done for two and a half centuries."

"Will you not even attempt to spare her life?" Filene cried out. The woman was on fire inside and it burned in her words and her wild eyes.

Fury built in his gut and he could feel his eyes glowing with the light of the gods. Only the unshed tears in his mother's eyes kept him from exploding in rage. "I will obey the gods. Perhaps they will show her the same mercy she has shown to others."

"She's but a misguided child," Filene argued, but Ryse didn't listen.

Unable to take any more of this topic, Ryse pushed back his chair and stood. "Forgive me if I can't stomach your concern for her. My father and my Divine Grace are *dead*. Dozens of my Thracian brothers are dead. If I have the chance to beg mercy for anyone, it will be for them."

"Ryse." Charles stood and held out his hands to stop his remarks. He was known as a peacemaker and, while Ryse respected his attempts, it was useless. "Please, son. We are all hurting for the loss of Troy and your Avery. We simply don't want to add more death to the situation. Please, sit down and let's finish our meal. In the coming days, we will all need our strength. No more on this subject. I promise." He cast a stern glance to his wife, who looked as if she might argue. Instead, Filene turned her eyes to her plate and moved food about with her fork.

Dynasty's eyes pleaded with him, so Ryse nodded to Charles and took his seat.

Not another word was spoken during the meal on any subject.

Dynasty pulled a blanket tighter around her shoulders. Flames danced in the hearth and she recalled how Troy's body had burned like the wood. So had Avery's, yet miraculously, her body was reborn and in the next room. At least in her mind, Dyna knew her beloved's death had not been in vain.

If only she could convince her heart. For over two centuries, that man had been by her side and loved her so mightily she never once doubted they would be together forever, even in death.

Sleep eluded her during the nights after his murder. Every time she closed her eyes, all she saw was the grotesque way he had died. She could still hear his screams and see the fear in his eyes when he looked up at her. When she did sleep, her nightmares were full of blood and death and anger.

Who would have thought she could hate someone the way she hated Salina? A child she had known since birth, the girl was akin to family. Now? Now, Dynasty wanted to see her dead.

"Grave things haunt your eyes, mistress." Hanna adjusted the blanket that fell when Dyna used a tissue to wipe her eyes.

"Forgive me, Hanna. I know this is painfully familiar for you as well."

"I've had years to deal with my grief, mistress. You've only had days."

"Will you sit with me? Tell me how you ever overcame your sadness. All I want is to curl up in our bed and never come out again until the gods call me home. If not for my sons, for Avery, I think I would."

Hanna, always conscious about the words she spoke, sat down and thought for a moment. Her gifts could not affect the events of the past, only the future. Still, she meditated on each word, played with the long, black braid of her hair as she spoke. "When my beloved died, I thought my heart would break into a million pieces and never beat again. It was the little reminders that hurt me so deeply. To go into our home and see evidence of his life. A cup here, a shirt thrown across the bed, his shoes in the corner by the front door. The smell of his clothing, the lack of his warmth in my bed, eating alone, not hearing his terrible singing as he bathed, the absence of his weapons." She sighed and her breath hitched. "Those were the things that stung my soul. I knew he died honorably, but no matter the means, he was still lost to me. Perhaps it makes me a terrible citizen of this Haven, but I wanted to tell his fellow soldiers to curse their honor. I wanted my husband back."

"How did you carry on?" Dynasty wiped fresh tears from her eyes, understanding all too well what Hanna meant. Cleaning out Troy's clothing was like taking a hammer to china, smashing her to uneven shards.

"There are days when I'm not sure I have. There's not a day that passes that I don't think of him. I must believe the gods have a purpose for me, though."

"Usually, when I'm in distress, I call upon Filene. Now, in my darkest hour, I have lost both husband and dearest friend. Perhaps your purpose is to comfort me? Would that be a disappointment to you?"

"No, mistress." Hanna smiled with deep affection. "I miss Andreas with every fiber of my being, but if my testimony might help you, his death will have saved two lives. Ryse's and yours."

"I'm so blessed to have you with me." Dyna reached for her hand. "Andreas was an honorable man, Hanna. I know he is serving in the halls of the gods, where only the most distinguished of Thracians have a place."

Hanna, her eyes misting over, nodded quickly and bit her lip to stop the trembling.

The two widows sat in companionable silence as the fire crackled. Both of their mates had died horrific deaths from the same poison. Surely the gods would not let this evil claim another woman's husband.

CHAPTER SEVEN

B RENDEN WENT DOWN TO THE MAKESHIFT HOSPITAL ROOM WHERE NIKKI was held. Wires and tubes stuck every which way from her body. In the last few days, she had lost a substantial amount of weight and her cheeks were hollow. Dark circles formed bruises under her eyes. Flaming red hair that had once shone with radiance seemed dull and flat. Every moment, she slipped further away and he could do nothing to stop it.

Just like he'd been unable to stop Avery from dying or his sister Meg so many decades ago.

Wasn't it only a couple days ago that he'd fought Ryse in the arena and Nikki nursed his wounds? It seemed like so much longer since their first kiss. His heart clenched as he thought about how Nikki had taken care of him that night. Ryse had given him the ultimate test of his strength and he had the bruises to prove it. Nikki's hazel eyes had been full of adoration and compassion, drinking him in. She'd checked his bandages a thousand times and he'd teased her about using it as an excuse to touch him.

"If I wanted to touch you," she'd challenged, her lips quirking up, "I wouldn't bother with excuses. I'd simply reach out and place my hand here." She pressed her palm against his chest, then slid the other one to his neck. For all her bravado, she was shaking; not that he was going to mention it.

His body tightened at her nearness. The sweet scent of her shampoo, something floral and soft, filled his lungs. He took a deep breath, memorizing every layer of her scent, his animal abilities recognizing so much more depth than the average Olympian could.

"Nikki, my beautiful Nikki." He bent his forehead to hers, closed his eyes, and wrapped his arms around her tiny waist. She was so small compared to him, like she could float away with a strong wind. Yet she had a will of iron, firmly planted in her beliefs and duties as a Shadow Lady.

"Brenden?" she whispered, forcing him to open his eyes with the catch of her voice.

"Yeah, Red?"

"I'm afraid."

Those two words made every Thracian instinct shift into protection mode. "About what?"

"I've been trained so hard to be the best Shadow Lady possible. It's a great source of pride for me. My family finally came around and they're proud of me. Especially given that I am in Avery's service."

"You should be proud, Nikki. You're amazing at your job." He ran his hand over her thick, red hair. So soft.

"My teachers never prepared me for this." She reached up and touched the scruff of his jaw. "I was never taught about relationships or love or how to balance my duty with a personal life. I don't think I'm supposed to fall in love, much less with the Head Guardian of my mistress. I adore Avery." She looked up at him with wide, fear-filled eyes. "What if I mess this up? I'm terrified of failing her. But I'm terrified of how I feel for you too."

Brenden closed the distance between their lips and gently coaxed her into a kiss. "Whatever happens, Nikki, I'm with you. Look at Avery and Ryse. Look at how strongly they love each other. A love like that endures. So will ours."

Her shy smile was forever engraved on his mind. He'd do anything for that smile.

Now, in the darkest hour of her life, Bren vowed to stand by her side. When she woke up—and he had to believe she would or else he would go insane—she was going to have to deal with the reality of what had happened. He couldn't stand to think about the guilt she would carry.

He would be there to help her, to share the load and bear the burden.

"Don't leave me, Nikki," he whispered in her ear. "I'm not giving up on you. The gods will have mercy; I know it. If Dynasty can forgive you, then surely the gods will too." He looked at the lines on the screen that showed her pulse. The beats were sporadic, much too far apart. "Hermes is taking you to the Heavens, baby. Hold on one more day. One more day for me, Nikki. That's all I ask." Brenden bent down and pressed his lips to hers. "I might not be able to go with you, but I'll never stop fighting for you."

Hayden downed another shot of alcohol with a proof so high that humans couldn't stomach it. The substance would put him to sleep. Thank the bloody gods.

Comfortable in his bed, he waited impatiently until the alcohol relaxed his body. He had someone to meet. With Hermes summoning him and Ryse to the Heavens and the thought of all that entailed, it was a miracle he could relax at all. Hello, self-medication.

The haze began to form and his pulse increased. The sweet scent of lavender and roses filled his head. He stepped onto the stone path he knew so well and made his way to the arbor. He could barely contain himself. In the middle of the garden sat a fountain—the same fountain that sat in the gardens behind the Haven. The dream was a replica of the reality.

Something changed. Frantically, he tried to find his night angel as the picturesque garden morphed into a ratty apartment. Lush, green grass changed into green shag carpet that had been old thirty years ago. Dingy walls in desperate need of paint replaced flowers. The fountain melted into a beaten down, raggedy sofa bed. In the middle of that bed, curled up in a thread-bare blanket and shivering, lay his angel.

Her black hair fell against the pillow, her face so serene it was heartbreaking. What was she doing in this place? Was this where she lived? Dear gods. Hayden looked around again. The shelves were bare. The walls were peeling. Rat poison sat in a corner. One radiator heater, not nearly enough to warm the space, worked overtime. The place was a drafty dump.

"Oh no. No. This isn't right. You're not supposed to see this." She sat up in the bed, the thin blanket cradled to her chest.

"What's wrong?" Hayden went to her and sat on the edge of the bed, or cot, more accurately. It groaned and creaked with his weight. "Where are we?"

Black eyes glistened with unshed tears. Her bottom lip trembled. "This is my place. This is where I live. I can't believe you're seeing it. Why didn't we go to the gardens?"

Hayden shook his head. "I don't know. I started there, but then I came here."

Tears crested her lower lids and fell down her cheek. She ran her hands through her hair. Usually, in his dreams, the black mass appeared perfectly groomed and hanging down her shoulders. Tonight, it was braided and strands escaped around her face. Instead of long, flowing, white gowns, she wore a baggy jersey and cotton shorts.

"I hate this place. It's cold and dirty even though we clean and clean and clean. I never wanted you to find me here."

"Hey, whoa." Hayden pulled her into his lap and closed his eyes at the perfect feel of her body against him. She smelled of winds over the ocean, fresh and warm. "I don't care about all that. I want you safe. Are you safe, at least?" He kissed her hair while she took time to answer.

"I think so. I don't know." She turned her face to his and her eyes went over every feature like she was trying to memorize everything about him. "You're so handsome."

"And you're the most beautiful creature the gods ever created." Hayden sighed as he touched her silky hair. Her facial features were delicate and soft, lovelier than anything he ever imagined could exist. Her eyes were dark brown, almost onyx, rich and warm. Latte-colored skin felt smooth under his touch.

Could he be in love with this woman because she was a creation of his every fantasy? He had to believe she was more than an apparition formed in his mind.

"I don't know how much time we have, but I need you to listen, my angel. I might be gone for a while."

"What? Why?"

"I'm going to the—" The word frozen on his tongue, his mouth gaping open, but soundless.

Damn the gods. Once again, he couldn't reveal the information that might help them find each other.

"Where?" she asked.

"I can't say. But I don't know how long I'll be there. It could be weeks, months even."

"You won't sleep?" Her head tilted like she couldn't understand.

"It doesn't work like that."

His angel's eyes misted again and those tears ripped his heart in two. For months, they'd spent nearly every night together. Sometimes for only minutes, sometimes hours. But they couldn't speak the words that would lead them to each other. They didn't exchange names, they couldn't say the cities they lived in. Nothing vital.

It was a cruel joke of the gods; he was convinced of it.

"You don't know when you will be back?" When Hayden shook his head, she nodded with understanding. "Will you kiss me then? Please? Give me something, anything to hold on to."

Hayden's breath left in a rush. "Gods, yes, I can do that." He brought his lips down on hers and the wonderful taste of her mouth sent him straight through the clouds. Not hesitating, his angel opened her lips and let his tongue slip inside. She let out a soft moan and moved to sit across his lap, her legs circling his waist. Instantly, he grew hard beneath her. What he would give to be inside her, to claim her as his mate and have her beside him in his waking hours.

Hayden lost all inhibitions in this dream. Up until this point, their interactions had been guarded, their touches quick and gentle. Once he went to the Heavens, there was no telling how much time would pass on Earth. It wouldn't be long for him, but it might be for her. Minutes in Heaven could equate to days on Earth.

He let her take anything she wanted and loved every moment of it.

She kissed him with abandon, plundering his mouth and running her hands over his neck, his chest, through his hair. Her hips moved against his erection, teasing him to a painful state. She kissed him like—he paused—like she was saying goodbye.

Hayden pulled her face back and saw her sweet lips glistening, felt her panting breath on his neck. "You do understand that I'm coming back, right? I won't leave you forever. I can't."

"How do you know? What if this is the last time we have together?" The desperation in her voice about did him in.

Hayden took her head between his hands. "I. Will. Find. You."

"Not if I find you first." She smiled at him and his world fractured into beautiful lights like a kaleidoscope. By Zeus, no smile should bring a man to his knees like this. She had to be his.

He *had* to find her in real life.

"No, oh *no*," Her hands went to her head. "I'm leaving." Frightened eyes met his. "I love you. Come back to me. I'll wait." She shouted her promises as the unknown force took her from him.

Hayden woke up and shot up in his bed. His breath was labored and he could still feel the taste of her on his tongue, his body still aroused and pulsing with unfulfilled need.

"Shit. Just...damn it." He flopped back down and rubbed his hand over his face.

As soon as he returned from the Heavens, no matter what the gods decreed, he was going to form a mass search for his night angel. Now that he knew what a hovel she lived in, his resolve was firmer than ever. She was real, and with the gods as his witness, he would find her and bring her home.

CHAPTER EIGHT

RYSE AND CHARLES WERE THE FIRST TO MAKE THEIR WAY TO THE PORTAL. Tension hung heavy between them. Never one with flowery words, Ryse remained silent.

"I don't know what I've done wrong with my children," Charles confessed.

Ryse studied the other man's face. His brows pinched together and dipped low. Lines bracketed his lips and Ryse detected a tremor in his hands.

"I look back on Salina's young life and can't seem to find that place where she began to change into something *unholy*." Charles looked up at Ryse. He was not a small man, but Ryse towered over most. "Am I so blind that I'm missed the cosmic shift in my daughter?"

Sympathy flooded Ryse's heart. He didn't have children and he couldn't imagine the disappointment and guilt Charles must feel. "Salina was a delightful child, Charles. I remember her youth well. It wasn't until the last few decades that she began to turn into something…unholy, as you put it." Ryse then addressed the white elephant that had always hovered between him and Charles. "I take part of the blame of her descent into this madness. I shouldn't have gone to bed with her. It was a poor decision then, and it has cost me everything now."

Charles sighed. "None of us are perfect in our actions, Ryse. And I think Salina was sliding downhill long before she seduced you. I know she used her powers on you, son. After losing your companion and friend, she swooped in like a vulture. Do not carry this guilt with you. My dau—" he bowed his head, shook it once before continuing, "Salina is a powerful telepath. I don't think you could have refused her, even if you had wanted."

"If I am not to bear the guilt of Salina's actions, then you can't either. Her choices were her own and so shall be her consequences."

Charles's lips formed a tight line across his face, but he nodded once. "I want you to know, Ryse, that I truly respect you and your family." He took in a deep breath and straightened his shoulders. "No matter what the gods decree, I will not let it diminish that respect."

As Ryse shook his outstretched hand, he knew they had come to an understanding.

Only moments later, Hayden joined them as they stepped into the clearing. Every person in the Haven had gathered. Only Hanna and Avery were missing. Thousands of faces focused on the epicenter of light that formed where he stood with his brother and Charles.

A great flash of lightning shot to the Earth as Zeus opened a portal and Hermes glided onto the grass. His unearthly eyes glowed as he searched the three men.

One king is missing.

Ryse shook his head. "My lord, all that are in this realm have assembled."

Hermes unblinking stare landed on Hammon. *You are a king, are you not?*

Hammon stepped forward from the crowd and knelt to one knee. "I passed on my crown willingly, my lord. My heir is now the ruler of our people."

You shall attend this gathering, ancient one. Zeus demands it.

Rising to his full height, Hammon approached and stood next to Ryse. All the men were tense. Deities hadn't been summoned since Troy had been appointed Grand Deity. Even then, the gods had come to Earth, not the other way around.

Where are your criminals?

Ryse held up a hand to signal the Thracians who held Salina under guard. Two men held her by the arms, her body in chains and shackles. She walked with her head high, her nose in the air. Those Thracians who willingly defended Salina were next. None of them could meet Ryse's eyes. Behind them came four men carrying Nikki's near lifeless body. Brenden had the front corner of the cot. His eyes were haunted and blank.

The crowd parted and made a path to Hermes. As they reached the circle where the god stood, the huge portal flashed and crackled with electricity. The swirling white and gold oval was the gateway into the Heavens for the living. The only other way to enter was to die.

Seven soldiers exited the portal. They were giants to most of the people in the clearing. Only Hammon and Ryse could compare. None of the seven showed any emotions. They didn't heed the people standing around, gasping at their grand appearance. These were the guardians of the Heavens, Zeus's personal soldiers. Each man had a bare chest except for the crisscrossing leather straps that held the massive swords strapped to their backs. Thick leather belts held up their white, flowing pants.

One soldier stood to the side of the portal, a gate keeper. The rest calmly took over the duties of the Thracian soldiers. Their eyes saw everything, but focused on nothing, as if they were machines, not men. Ryse knew some of their faces, though. These were fallen Thracians who had found honor in the sight of Ares. Their duty extended into the afterlife. Every Thracian prayed this would be his fate upon his death.

Two of them bowed their heads to Ryse and placed a fist over their hearts. "Teacher."

He returned the gesture. Pride swelled in his chest to see his predecessors and some of his students holding this honored position. Every Thracian from the training center had joined the crowd. Ryse hoped this new crop of young soldiers held the same reverence for the seven soldiers of Zeus.

He stood still as they moved to take control of the prisoners. Brenden's nostrils flared when the soldier came to take his handle of Nikki's bed. Ryse figured this would be hard on him. Brenden didn't know if he would ever see her again. None of them did. The heartbroken man bowed to his Master, then turned and left. He didn't stay to see the ascension. Ryse knew he returned to Avery's side, but to everyone else, he simply looked distraught, grieving over a lost lover.

It is time. Hermes waved his arm towards the portal. Together, Ryse, Hayden, Hammon, and Charles stepped foot into the electric barrier. Everything in Ryse's world turned brilliant, blinding white. Air left his chest and the building pressure in his body caused him to scream. No sound came from his throat. The bone-crushing pain intensified before his eyes rolled back in his head and his world went black.

— —· ⚬ ·— —

Ashton held his mother's trembling hand as all the men stepped through the portal and made their way to the realm of the gods. He had to admit, it was unsettling to see his rock-steady parents nervous. Usually, his father held a reserved respect for the gods, and his mother mentioned them like most would mention the weather. They were not devout as they had once been. Did they regret that now that Charles was off to face the gods? Were they actually afraid for their lives or their status? Filene hurried to the temple to pray and he let her go. That answered his question. Hell, he'd thought his mother had forgotten how to pray.

Useless fear, he thought with a huff. Salina had murdered the Grand Deity and a Divine Grace in cold blood and none of the gods swooped in to punish her or stop the events. Even now, they were too preoccupied to come to Earth. They sat on their thrones and called the Olympians like dogs. Hermes might as well have whistled and handed out bone-shaped treats. They didn't care about earthlings anymore.

The gods had abandoned the Olympians and only the rogues were smart enough to figure it out. The rest of these pathetic bastards had a rude awakening in their future. The only beings paying attention to Earth now were the demons. Ashton had seen the writing on the wall months ago and these events only confirmed what he already knew. The gods were out, the demons were in. If any of these Olympians wanted to survive, they had better start playing for the winning team.

Ashton glanced over at the blond man who kept glancing at him. "Is that your son, Xavier?"

The warrior behind him stepped up to his side. "Yes, sire."

"You're angry with him?"

"Disgusted, sire." These words were said through clenched teeth. "If I may speak freely, I think there is more to this story. Dante is not nearly as useful as they make him out to be. I should know."

"What are you saying?" Ashton tilted his head and examined the boy. Dante held out his arm to escort Lady Dynasty back to the palace. The queen smiled up at him. "He's not a bad-looking chap. Maybe they are getting more use out of him than we think. You think your son is capable of such?" Ashton looked into Xavier's sand-colored eyes.

"After his actions the last few days, I put nothing past him or those *others*. They think they are so superior." Xavier's lip curled up in a snarl.

"That's the problem with all the Olympians in this Haven, isn't it, Xavier? Perhaps the gods are punishing the Castilles and the Elites. We should further their cause."

Xavier's lip kicked up to an infinitesimal smile. Ashton recognized the cunning expression. "What did you have in mind?"

"We're stuck here until Father returns. Might as well take notes. Who leads the Elites now that Ryse and Hammon are gone?"

"Philippe. The Italian."

"Keep him occupied. Who else?"

"The Asian man is next in line. Yankee is an arrogant sonofabitch, keeps to himself. Brenden, the animal boy; he's so caught up in his pathetic heartbreak that he's weak and blind. Then there's Dante." He let out a huff. "Those three are nothing to worry over. Brutes, not too much brains. I'll keep Philippe and Cutter distracted."

"Good. I'll deal with Dante. He's their weakest link."

Ashton and Xavier exchanged a nod.

Dante was a prime target. With Hammon gone, the Elites were now down another man. If he could get Dante away from the others and burrow into his mind, Ashton might find the one thing he needed to put an end to the Castilles.

THE HEAVENS

CHAPTER NINE

RYSE AWOKE TO THE SOUNDS OF LAUGHTER AND A THICK IRISH BROGUE. The sound was familiar, but it was impossible that he recognized it.

"Rise and shine, princess. You been sleepin' long enough. Too much more beauty rest and you'll be as good lookin' as me."

Ryse's eyes flashed open to see a face that still appeared in his worst nightmares. Not because of the man, but because of the way he died. A smiling brute with red hair, pale freckled skin, and hazel eyes greeted him.

"*Andreas*." Ryse tried to hop up, but was disoriented. The room spun and stars danced in his vision. His stomach had taken a roller coaster ride and wasn't back yet.

"Aye. I've only seen you stumble once before and it was from drink."

Ryse cleared his head as he examined the seven-foot mammoth in front of him. It was Andreas' face, but his body was twice the size. "I must be drunk. 'Cause it seems there's more ugly to you now than when I last saw you."

Andreas's laughter echoed and he pulled Ryse into a manly hug. This was his way; Andreas was one of the most physical people he'd ever known. He hugged, he touched, and he constantly made contact with others. "It's good to see you, my friend."

Ryse had to be dreaming. Did he die after all? Had the gods tricked him? He had to be in the Heavens because he had watched Andreas die in the same fashion as his father. The battle had been decades ago and Andreas had been the first Elite warrior Ryse commissioned.

"What?" Andreas queried when Ryse kept staring.

"I saw you die," Ryse whispered, his voice thick with emotion.

Andreas' happy face grew solemn. "Aye, you did. And because you taught me so well, the gods showed me favor. I'm a soldier of Zeus and I have you to thank, Master."

Air left his lungs and he thought he might really screw up and cry. This was his long lost best friend standing in front of him, living, a soldier of Zeus who thanked him and called him "Master."

"Easy now, lad. Don't want to be lookin' like a couple o' Nancys." Andreas slapped him on the shoulder and winked. He knew. Of course he knew. This was Andreas. "Besides, I'm not the only one up here anxious to meet you."

Ryse took a second to look around and gather his faculties. He was in a stately room clearly designed to let people recover from the portal. There were benches and maidens handing out goblets of water. Hayden sat with his head between his legs as a young woman held a damp cloth to his neck. Charles was still passed out on one of the benches. Hammon attempted to stand and wobbled. Another maiden caught his arm and steadied him.

"What the hell happened in that portal?" Ryse asked.

"Yer soul was separated from yer skin, lad. Nasty bit o' work. That's the only way to get in. I've heard it's not as bad goin' back."

"By the gods, I hope not. Wait, then. Where is my body?"

"In the portal. Safe."

"How do you know?" Ryse questioned. He stopped walking, hesitant to leave his skin unattended.

Andreas gave him a smug grin. "Have time to stop and smell the roses, did ya? In case you haven't noticed, Master Ryse, you fared much better than the others. None linger in the portal. Don't you worry." He motioned for Ryse to follow him.

By then, Hammon had taken notice of who was in the room.

"Andreas!"

"Hammon!"

The two men embraced and exchanged heartfelt words of joy. Ryse often forgot that Andreas hadn't only been his loss, but Hammon's as well. The two had been friends long ago. It did his heart good to see them reunited.

"You've had a hellova time with that one, Hammon." Andreas nodded over to Ryse. "I can't believe you haven't run him through with yer sword yet."

"I've been tempted, old friend." Hammon's shining smile stretched ear to ear.

"Now I remember what it was like having both of you mothering me. By the gods, you two separate." Ryse clapped them both on the backs as they shared a rare moment of familiarity.

It took a few more minutes for Charles and Hayden to join them, but finally, all the men were back in their right minds and on their feet. Andreas opened the tall, ornate doors and they beheld a landscape Ryse couldn't have imagined, even in his wildest dreams.

Rolling hills with the greenest grass the eye could fathom. Temples of stone that were once erected on Earth now stood out in white contrast. People milled about, made their way into the temples, and carried tomes he could only guess the age of. His jaw hung open when he looked into the skies and saw the planets, the entire solar system so close he could spin the rings of Saturn or touch the rust-colored soil of Mars. All of creation and the mysteries of the universe were in those skies.

"Welcome to Olympia, lads," Andreas said as a broad smile stretched across his face. His arms encompassed their surroundings. "Welcome...to the Heavens."

"Holy Zeus," Charles whispered in awe.

"No words. There are no words. How am I supposed to document this place when I have not the vocabulary?" Hayden spoke in a daze, taking in every detail. Surely he would find a way to write his experiences down to share with future generations.

They all followed as Andreas made his way down the hill on a white, stone-paved path. Ryse turned back to see the building they'd come from. It was a small temple with round columns, just enough to hold the portal. More soldiers stood guard at the doors.

"First, you must all be purified." Andreas directed them to another white-stoned building. "Enter and allow the priestesses to cleanse you. The gods want to get this matter sorted. They don't like havin' all of you here and yer homes unattended. The great council convenes as soon as all the Deities are done."

"Have the others arrived?" Hammon asked. His inquiry was for one Deity in particular.

"Yer son has arrived, Master Hammon. He anxiously waits in the temple of Zeus," Andreas replied with a kind smile. He slapped Ryse on the arm and then gripped his forearm. "You and I will catch up later. I have missed you, old friend."

"And I you." Ryse's voice was thick with emotion.

Andreas bowed to them all, his hand fisted over his heart, and turned to leave.

"I will see you again, right?" Ryse asked.

"Aye, I got a pint with yer name on it!"

"They have pints here?"

Andreas spread his arms to encompass their surroundings once again. "It is Heaven, after all." His carefree grin stretched ear to ear. Seeing Andreas so happy, so full of purpose and—*life*—gave him the greatest sense of relief and hope he'd ever experienced. If Andreas had found such overwhelming peace in the afterlife, surely his father would have the same peace. Ryse didn't know what he expected of the afterlife, but thus far, it was everything he could imagine and more.

"Brother?" Hayden called from the entrance of the cleansing temple.

"Coming." Ryse allowed a smile for Andreas.

The cleansing was both a physical and mental exercise. Having maidens in white robes wash down his body as he stood in a shallow pool caused him great humiliation, even if he did have a towel draped around his waist. The women's faces were covered, but they saw enough. Going from public nudity to meditation didn't work so well for him. He was wound tight again.

"Only when you clear your mind and heart can you enter the holy temple," a woman whispered. "Close your eyes, warrior." He could have sworn there was a hint of laughter in her tone.

Ryse closed his eyes and tried to get rid of the noise that had taken up permanent residence in his head over the last few days. He tried to concentrate on the one thing that always soothed his soul. Avery.

With eyes closed, he remembered the way her hair felt as the soft curls sifted through his fingers. As he took a deep breath, he caught her scent: soap and berries sprinkled with sugar. By the gods, she had smelled so sweet the night she had taken him into her body. His mouth watered to taste her again, to kiss her lips and taste the richness that was dynamically Avery. He'd give anything to hold her once more and hear her laughter or her southern voice of honey as it caressed his ears.

"And you shall, Ryse Castille, Master Thracian and Deity Prince."

He opened his eyes to see the owner of the voice that ended his trance. The woman stood tall and, even when Ryse rose to his full height, she was still taller. Her jet black hair was loose and fell in a silky wave to the floor along with navy-colored robes. Her eyes, the most intense glacier blue he'd ever beheld, stayed steady on him. In his heart, he knew this woman.

"Rhea." Her name was whispered in awe.

"I am."

Ryse stood quickly. "Avery? Where is she?"

The woman never blinked, but she did curve her lips into a ghost of a smile. "She is well, Master Thracian. Walk with me." She linked her hand in the crook of his elbow. They left the temple and crossed a field full of lavender blooms, the purple sea spreading out for miles. "She was not supposed to die."

"Then...why?"

"Free will. When I created the Olympians in the dawn of time, I fashioned a civilization of intelligent creatures who knew their place." Her hard tone surprised him, but he remained silent as she spoke. "My people worshipped me, they adored me because I created them for that purpose. Over time, I saw where I had made a mistake. The people didn't worship me out of thanksgiving or appreciation. They were simply created to. Their affections were stale and tasteless on the tongue.

Their prayers were but a series of meaningless, memorized words. Which would you rather have, Master Thracian, an army of soldiers who follow because they were programmed or an army of those who choose to do so?"

Ryse nodded his head. He fully understood. Loyalty out of choice and faith ran much deeper in the soul than loyalty out of habit or tradition or fear.

"Upon realizing my mistake, I bestowed upon my sons the obligation to watch over my creation. I spent millennia scrutinizing the decision to endow free will to the people. I determined that if we, the gods, gave them something worth following, they would choose us on their own."

"That's where the Deities came into play?"

"Yes," she said and smiled. She flicked her wrist and the purple blooms of lavender turned into yellow tulips. Rhea made a soft noise of displeasure and flicked her wrist again. The field changed to an endless vista of blue roses, just like the ones he'd given Avery when they first met.

"The gods were to guide you. Zeus, in particular. He wanted the responsibility and I gave it to him. Over time, he has forgotten his duties and he has let the people fall into disarray. The bloodlines are diluted. Olympians breed with humans and those of different lines. The original gifts of the gods have died out or mutated. Take your Elite, Brenden, for example. He should not exist. He is a genetic anomaly, a monster in the truest sense of the word."

"He is a good man," Ryse snapped defensively.

Rhea held up her hand. "I speak only of his blood, not his heart. I see the value in the man. He is loyal and will be of service to Avery. My point is that my creation has shifted the balance of power and I cannot have that. They forget who gave them life and who can take it away. A people without religion, without purpose, and without a moral guide are doomed. Look at the myriad of human civilizations that imploded because they became lost to greed and power. I cannot have the Olympians doing the same. I would rather destroy them all than watch them kill one another slowly by giving in to selfish desires. That is why I created Avery. She is of pure blood, no matter who birthed her.

You are twice-blessed by the gods, a son of a Deity; no purer blood exists. The two of you are the beginning of a new lineage, one that must guide our people back to the gods. Do you understand?"

"Yes, I do." Ryse's jaws clenched.

Rhea touched his cheek and brought his face up so she could see his eyes. "Salina is only the beginning. There are others out there who are far more destructive. You must take up your sword and wage war against those who threaten your world." Her face hardened and, for the first time since their walk began, he saw the creator of the universe in her eyes. This goddess was power personified. "I was not exaggerating when I said I would rather extinguish the Olympians than watch them fall to ruin. And I have the capacity to do thusly."

Ryse swallowed the lump in his throat. The goddess was quite literally putting the fate of the Olympian world in his hands. If he didn't take care of the problem, she would.

"Go. You have a trial to attend and I have a Grace to raise from the dead."

CHAPTER
TEN

RYSE ENTERED THE TEMPLE. THE COMBINED AURAS OF ALL THE GODS and Deities in the room left him breathless. How long had it been since such a monumental gathering? All the earthly Deities in one place, the gods and goddesses perched high on their thrones and the lower gods filling the standing room.

The white marble temple was cold and hard, but with the many bodies filling the space, one would never know. Soaring three stories into the air, suspended under the dome ceiling, was a massive sphere resembling the Earth. Continents and oceans, brown and blue shapes swirled with the white of clouds. The sphere rotated precisely as the real Earth would.

Light spilled in from the tall windows around the sphere and flooded the circular room below. On one side were the thrones of Zeus, Poseidon, and Hades. The three sat higher than the others that stair-stepped down from there. For once, he was thankful for his mother's teachings on the gods. He knew each of them. Ares, Athena, Artemis, Apollo, Hera, and Hestia sat on the next row. Hermes, Hephaestus, Persephone, and Aphrodite were nearest to the floor.

"Come now, son of Zeus and Ares," Hera called out to him, her elegant hand stretched forward. "We've been waiting."

The room hushed and many faces turned to him. As he made his way through the throng, he wished like hell he could be invisible for once.

In the center of the temple was an open area surrounded by a continuous marble bench. There sat the other Deities. Charles represented Europe. Hammon and his son Eekon represented Africa. Dimitrious of Russia, Gabel of Australia, and Amais of South America. The only continent that didn't have a Deity was virtually uninhabitable. Hayden sat near Hammon and visibly sighed when Ryse made eye contact. He'd saved his brother a place.

Ryse greeted each Deity, some he had not seen in many decades. Each man offered his condolences on the loss of his father. But each man also said Troy was lucky to have found the afterlife, after experiencing it for themselves.

The conversations in the room started again and created a low hum. Ryse was thankful no longer to be the center of attention. Yet he was soon the center of a goddess's attention.

"Master Thracian. You are made of flesh and blood after all." Athena made her way over to him, her body barely covered in the leather strips that held up her weapons. Her eyes traveled down his body and back up again, pleased with what they saw. "I was beginning to believe you were only a myth."

Ryse bowed his head to her. "My goddess."

Making one complete circle around his body, Athena came to stand directly in front of him, so close he could smell the leather she wore. "I contributed my blood to your Grace, did you know that?" She raised a single brow. Her face was hard and square, more masculine.

Ryse was a pro at his poker face; even in front of the goddess of war, he would not show his intimidation. "Thank you, Athena."

The goddess leaned in and her cold eyes met his. "It will come in handy later."

Athena winked and turned away, dismissing Ryse to take his place with the other Deities.

"What's *that* supposed to mean?" Hayden whispered from beside him.

"We shall see, brother. We shall see."

Ryse's attention went to Zeus. The god, clad in gold and so

beautiful to look upon, stood and held out his arms. Every person watched him. The room went deathly silent, as if even the walls awaited his next command.

"Sons and daughters, gods, goddesses, and earthly deities; what joy it gives me to have you gathered in my temple. If only it were for celebration and not for this solemn event." Zeus lowered his hands and motioned for those who could to be seated. All the gods on the tiers below him sat on their thrones.

"Never in the history of our race has there been such a meeting of power. Perhaps that is why this council is necessary now. We will hear the testimony of those associated with the murder of my son, Troy. Who better to recall the death, than he?"

Zeus waved one hand towards a door. The marble slab swept open and Ryse's heart stopped.

"Father," he and Hayden exclaimed in unison. Ryse reached for his brother instinctively, but Hayden had already gripped his sleeve.

Troy, or at least the spirit of him, floated into the chamber.

"You may embrace your father," Zeus said. "For your parting was sudden and painful. You shall be gifted this chance to once more be together."

Troy looked to the men and a huge smile crossed his face. Spirit became flesh with each step he took toward them until Ryse felt his father's arms around him, solid and strong. Troy pulled both his sons against him and wept.

"My boys. My beloved sons. How I love you. Forgive me for not telling you every day how proud I am of you."

Hayden cried on his father's shoulder, but Ryse simply closed his eyes and wished Mother was here to see her husband once again.

Charles stood back and waited until the men had separated. Then he dropped to his knees in front of Troy. "Forgive me, my oldest and dearest friend, for the circumstances that led you here."

Troy took Charles by the shoulders and helped him to his feet. "You are a good man, Charles. I do not hold you accountable for Salina's actions. Do not trouble your heart, my friend."

Charles' lip quivered as he bowed his head to Troy and took his seat again.

"I forget how emotional the humanoids can be," Athena said to Ares. He tilted his head and looked at the men like bugs under a microscope.

Troy grimaced and urged Hayden and Ryse to sit down again. "Shall we continue?"

Zeus brought out the Thracian traitors and Salina. Soldiers threw her down onto the marble floor. It took her a couple of tries to sit up with her hands tied behind her back and her ankles bound together. She finally sat on her knees before the chorus of gods. Her blonde hair fell down her back in matted sheets. Ryse felt pity on her until she looked over her shoulder at him and snarled like a feral animal. He growled back, memories of her hands plunging a knife in Avery's chest staining his mind.

"Cast your eyes away from him," Zeus bellowed at her. "He is the least of your worries...for now."

Ryse saw Charles in his periphery. The Deity sat straight and poised, never once looking at Salina, but focusing on the gods.

The last person brought into the chamber was Nikki. She was still unconscious and appeared to be closer to death than when Ryse saw her last, as if her spirit was clinging to life with an iron grip. The soldiers gently lowered her to the floor, using much more finesse than they had with Salina.

"Apollo," Zeus commanded.

With a nod of acknowledgement, Apollo left his throne and knelt beside Nikki's weakened body. He touched a finger to her forehead. Healing words, spoken in ancient Greek, entered her body as a river of light. As if evacuating the disease, light chased a black mist from her mouth, ears, and eyes. The particles of shadow drifted in a tornado above her head. The thicker the cloud of evil became, the more Nikki's body came to life. Her cheeks filled in, the bruises from her eyes disappeared. Color returned to her face and her breaths deepened.

As if the mist might infect him, Apollo slowly backed away from Nikki and the swirling black cloud.

All around the temple, people began to whisper. But their voices were muted by the rumbling growl of Hades.

When the god of the underworld rose from his throne, Ryse

realized he was made of the same black mist. The implications were unnerving. Particles formed legs and arms and a torso. Ryse could even make out ghostly, skeletal facial features. Hades was not like Zeus or Poseidon. He did not consist of a human-like body.

The cloudy figure floated down over Nikki and absorbed the blackness that sprang from her mouth. A hand formed as Hades touched Nikki's cheek. "Poor child," he rumbled like thunder, his voice more of an echo of great power. "Your body was not created to survive such black magic."

Hades whipped his head around to Salina and red eyes formed against the darkness. "Such magic should not be on Earth. You have been a busy girl."

Pure, unadulterated fear sent chills over Ryse.

Salina shivered, but tilted her chin up in defiance. She said nothing. Then again, why bother denying anything to a god? Hades knew. They all did. The evidence of her deeds had come from inside Nikki.

Salina had been consorting with demons.

Hades floated back to his throne and the mist formed a body as he sat. His red eyes never left Salina.

A female scream broke through the moment of silence. Nikki sat up with a jolt and gripped her head with her hands. Apollo touched her once more, ending her terror. She slowly lowered her hands and looked about her.

Her hazel eyes went wide when Hestia, goddess of the hearth, extended a hand to help her up. Nikki gawked at the goddess and accepted her aid. She had trouble gaining her balance, but the goddess was patient and held Nikki's arms until she could support her own weight.

"Am I dead?" Nikki whispered.

"No. You are in the temple of Zeus to account for your actions."

For a second, Nikki looked confused. She glanced around and finally saw Ryse and Hayden. Her first reaction was one of relief. Then, she eyed Troy and recognition dawned on her face.

"Oh no. Oh dearest gods, no. What have I done?" She gripped her head again and lost her footing. Nikki slumped down to the floor and would have fallen over had Troy not gone to her.

"Easy, Nikki. Breathe." Troy held her shoulders.

"Forgive me. Oh, Troy, please forgive me. I'm so sorry." Nikki sobbed uncontrollably, gripping Troy as though her life depended on it.

Ryse couldn't stand the hysterics any longer. Nikki was emotionally damaged and if her testimony was to be of any use, she had to calm down. The reality of what she had done was too much for her gentle soul to bear.

"Can someone not calm her mind? Is there any way to help her?"

Zeus held out a hand and Nikki's crying faded. She was still aware of her surroundings, but she wasn't in a frenzy of emotion. "Stand, Shadow Lady. Speak your truth and recollections."

Nikki nodded and told the gods exactly what led her to giving Troy a champagne flute of poison and then going into a coma. They murmured amongst themselves when she implicated Salina in the crimes. Poor timid Nikki stood shaking after her testimony was heard.

"Why Troy?" one of the gods asked. "Why not someone else?"

"It had to be one of them," Nikki explained. "That was the compulsion. I couldn't give it to Avery. It went against the fabric of my being. Not Master Ryse; he is my mistress's mate. Avery loved Prince Hayden so much, and Lady Dynasty too. I knew she loved King Troy, but I also knew—" Nikki fretted, her eyes darting over to Salina. "If the Grand Deity was murdered, someone would finally pay attention to the problems Salina was causing."

"Someone, as in the gods?" Zeus clarified. Nikki nodded, her eyes full of tears, her arms wrapped tightly around herself.

Salina gave an indignant huff. The sneer on her face said she enjoyed delicate Nikki making her point.

Ryse and Hayden exchanged a look. They finally understood. Even Nikki, so devoted to her path and the will of the gods, could see that there was a disconnect between the Olympians and their creators.

"My, my, my." Rhea walked through the crowd and into the center of the temple where Nikki stood, commanding the attention of the room. The gods and goddesses bowed from their thrones; those in the audience went to their knees.

"This child went to such great lengths to get your attention." Rhea's tone was hard and cold.

Thankfully, Ryse's dealings with her did not include that tone. It was enough to freeze the room.

"Mother, blessed one," Zeus greeted her with a kiss on the cheek, then on her hand.

"Is this what it takes for you to turn your attention back to our creations?" The mother-goddess scolded her children and many of them had a hard time meeting her eyes. "Do you not see the desperation in this child?" Rhea touched Nikki's long, red hair affectionately.

Zeus bowed his head to Rhea. "Forgive us, Mother. We were shocked by these events." His eyes speared Salina. "We never would have thought our appointed children would ever turn on one another."

"Think again," Salina sneered.

Ryse wanted to slap his hand over Salina's mouth. Did she *really* smart off to the mother-goddess? Was she trying to damn her soul to eternity in the underworld?

"Silence, you infectious pustule of our society," Rhea snapped at Salina. "You bring death and treachery to our people and have the audacity to speak in my presence? Hold your tongue or I shall remove it."

Athena rose from her throne and conjured a long sword. The tip of the blade ended up at Salina's throat. "One more word, I dare you."

Rhea turned her attention back to Nikki. "I understand your motivations, child. I commend you for not betraying your mistress. For that reason, I shall not strip you of your powers nor condemn your eternal soul. You shall return to the Earth."

"Thank you, goddess," Nikki whispered with a sob.

"However, you have killed a Deity," Rhea sighed.

"That was not her choice," Troy spoke up. "I know the heart of this woman, and if I can forgive her, surely the gods can as well."

"Yes, we can forgive her repentant heart. However, she made a very public statement which deserves a public reply. You are to be whipped. The people must see you pay for your crime."

Nikki nodded and, although her eyes filled with more tears, she gracefully accepted her punishment. Her body shook and shivered as if it were going to crumble into pieces at any moment.

This was not fair. None of Nikki's actions were of her own free will. Salina implanted the controls into her mind, using black magic.

She turned an innocent, faithful Shadow Lady into a murderer. Why should Nikki be punished?

Ryse took a step towards Rhea and she held out her hand, knowing he was about to interject. "Thracian, our people know this woman to be a murderer. She killed their Grand Deity in a public fashion. The people will want justice."

"They shall have it when Salina is punished," Ryse argued. "Do not make me rebuke this woman. I find no fault in her."

Nikki turned to Ryse and looked him in the eyes. The strength he saw there was incredible. "No. I will take my punishment. The mother-goddess is right, Ryse. The people will want to see me reprimanded. If I get away with murder in their eyes, the entire system might be challenged." Her voice broke on her last sentence. "This is for the best."

"No," Ryse whispered to her, pleading with her to save herself, stand up for her innocence. The thought of having to whip her weakened his knees and squeezed the air from his lungs.

"Go meditate, child," Zeus commanded of her. His guards escorted Nikki out of the temple.

Ryse wanted to sink into the bench and put his head between his legs. He was light-headed and nauseous. How would he explain this to Avery? He had to give her best friend lashings. It would rip her heart in two. Brenden, oh *gods*; how would he ever face Brenden after this?

The gods listened to the testimonies of soldiers who Salina telepathically poisoned. They were to lose their powers, stripped of Thracian and Olympian gifts and the memory of them, sent into the human world and never to recall the great lineage they came from. For any proud Thracian soldier, it was a fate far worse than death.

That punishment was horrible, but all he could think about was whipping Nikki. His pulse beat loudly between his ears.

As many people as Ryse put to death in his long life, none of them caused such a reaction inside. Hurting Nikki could cause a great rift between him and Brenden. Avery might understand in theory, but what would happen with the first sign of Nikki's pain? How would Avery and Bren react when Nikki's blood spilled?

Avery. She was supposed to be here. He looked to Rhea, desperation in his eyes.

"Ah, yes." Rhea smiled at him. "I have forgotten something of vital importance, haven't I, Master Thracian?"

Ryse knelt down in front of her, looked high up into her clear blue eyes. "My goddess, if it would please you, I beg that you deliver my Grace back to me."

"Take notice, with all of you as my witness." Rhea spread her arms and her power whipped about the room, rustling their clothing and hair. "As the creator of creators, the Master of the universe and ruler of all the Heavens, I give to you, Master Thracian and first born son of a Deity, the gift of your beloved Grace. Avery, who once was dead, will rise again. Her destiny and her life are in your hands." Rhea pinned him with a cold stare. "Take. Care. Of. Her."

"Yes, my goddess. By my honor, I will." His body shivered at the chill of her voice and the whip of her aura.

From the side of the temple, Andreas came forward with Avery on his arm. The smug warrior had a grin that stretched from ear to ear. He wiggled his red eyebrows at Ryse and the two men nearly laughed out loud.

But it was Avery who captured Ryse's attention and didn't let go.

She was perfect, more pleasing to his sight than Aphrodite. Emerald eyes, wild unruly curls that ranged from light brown to dark red, high cheekbones, sensual lips, and the most beautiful smile in all creation.

When he would have run to her, Rhea steadied him.

She whispered, "Unlike you, her body is not in the portal. Her spirit is fragile and must be returned to her body as quickly as possible." Louder, she said to the congregation, "I'm afraid you cannot touch her until both of you have crossed into the earthly realm. I wanted you to see her, to know that I have kept my word. She shall return to Earth in due time."

Avery's eyes broke away from him and settled on Salina. *Did she just snarl?*

"I believe you have something you want to tell her?" Rhea motioned her arm to Salina.

The change in his mate was obvious. She'd held smiles for him, but now her lips curled up, her fists were balled up at her side. Avery took a deep breath, her chest rising, her chin tilted up.

"I killed you. I fucking killed you!" Salina shook her head, her face showing her disgust.

"Yeah, ya did." Avery took a few steps closer to her. "Unfortunately for you, you messed with the wrong farm girl." Avery raised her fist and slammed it down on Salina's jaw. Salina's head whipped to the side, a black burn mark on her face.

A collective gasp went up from the Deities in the room. Hayden's mouth hung open. Even Ryse was shocked. Avery's spirit might not be weakened, but her power obviously was not.

"*That's* for hurtin' my family and friends."

Avery backhanded Salina, jerking Salina's head back around. Another black mark appeared on her other cheek and blood gushed from her mouth. "That's for messin' with my man."

Ryse's chest filled with pride. *Knock her out, baby.*

Avery delivered a flawless uppercut, knocking Salina's head backwards and sending her to the ground. "And *that* is for killin' my damn dogs, you heartless, home-wreckin' hussy!"

Salina pushed herself up and spat blood on the floor. "I'd do it all over if it meant watching you die again."

"Shut the hell up." Avery hit her once more. This time, Salina stayed down.

Ryse saw Charles shaking his head. "No remorse. There's no remorse within her." He starred at the spectacle with his head tilted as if he didn't understand his daughter's coldness.

Athena laughed; actually threw back her head and laughed. It echoed off the temple walls, the only sound in the silent room. Ryse didn't know whether that was amusement or condescension. "That's one way to get a confession. You are fierce, daughter of Rhea. It makes me proud." She reached out and offered a hand to Avery, who clasped her forearm as the soldiers did.

Avery nodded to Athena and then came to Ryse. She kept her distance, but did cast an apologetic glance to Charles. "Sorry. She did kinda stab me to death, though. It warrants a grudge."

"Your actions are more than justified, Lady Avery. Do not

apologize to me." Charles bowed his head. This all must be so difficult for him. It was hard for Ryse, and Salina wasn't his daughter.

"Time to go, lass." Andreas touched Avery's elbow. He nodded to Ryse, his lips pressed tight, hiding his smile.

His heart beat wildly. Was this it? Was this all the time he would get with her here? Was she returning to Earth before him?

"I love you," he said, searching for answers in her eyes.

Avery blew him a kiss and winked. "See ya soon, darlin'. I love you."

Ryse could only nod, his voice gone. They would be together again and it filled him with such joy he could not express it in words.

CHAPTER ELEVEN

RHEA STRAIGHTENED. SHE CLIMBED THE STAIRS TO THE HIGHEST PEDESTAL and held out her arms. "Hear me now, Deities of Earth, and my children. The time has come for the gods to make their presence known once more. Our absence has brought us to this point. The people do not worship as they once did. We have mixed-blood descendants that wander around as humans, never knowing of their lineage. The great Oracles of Delphi have not been consulted in centuries." Rhea indicated the men in the front row. "These Deities bear the burdens of leadership without guidance from the very gods who ordained them. Look; witness what happens when you ignore your creation." Rhea pointed to Salina.

"You have a choice, children. Actively seek out relationships with the earthly Olympians, or I shall eradicate them. I will not have the powers of my blood taken for granted and I will not have a race of unworthy subjects risking our secrecy. It is only a matter of time before the humans detect the Olympians and realize they are not alone on the Earth. Their technology grows at alarming rates and that endangers us all. Humans are not ready for such revelation. I suggest you decide wisely."

Hayden, along with all the other earthy Deities, rose to his feet. "I beg of you to give us a chance to redeem the race! We have not fallen so far that we cannot be saved." The gods looked to him, as did Ryse.

Hayden swallowed hard as his eyes surveyed the room. He gave Ryse an *oh-shit-I-should've-kept-my-mouth-shut* grimace. For all his joking and kidding around, Hayden did not like to be the center of attention in conflicting circumstances.

Proud that his little brother had asserted himself before such an audience, Ryse gave Hayden a slight nod of encouragement to continue.

"Our people need to feel the presence of the gods once more. They're hungry for traditions, they long for the guidance of the Deities and Oracles of old." His voice was shaky, filled with more uncertainty than confidence. Hayden stepped forward in front of his peers, straightening a bit, encouraged by the murmurs of endorsement from the others. "Yes, we have diluted the bloodlines and many have mated with humans. That doesn't mean we are a lost civilization. You, our creators—our source of life and power—have stepped aside for many centuries. We've been left wandering in the dark, guessing what your will is instead of seeking your presence.

"Do you no longer care about our race? Do you no longer wish to rule us as you once did? Have you abandoned us? These are the prayers of your people, the questions you have left in their minds." Hayden pointed to Ryse and the other Deities. "They feel your presence. You speak to them. They know your voices. But who else? Our people are neglected."

Ryse marveled at Hayden's ability to express what an entire populace had struggled to say for years. Admiration for his brother overflowed his heart. Hayden held the gods' attention and, whether he realized it or not, the other Deities were standing behind him, looking for him to be their voice.

Judging by the smirk on Rhea's face, she noticed too.

"The entire population of our Haven in North America gathered when Hermes came for us. For many, it was the first time in their entire lives they had any direct interaction with a god. Some of our people are well into their third, fourth, and fifth centuries of life. And they just *now*, because of this tragedy, beheld the gods they are expected to worship blindly.

"Those people, *my* people, stayed by the portal during the hours after Hermes' first visit. Some of them slept in the grass all night so they wouldn't miss his return," Hayden continued with growing charisma, impassioned, full of conviction that moved Ryse to his core.

"This happened in my country as well," Eekon of Africa spoke up. "My wife and household servants brought blankets and food to the multitude that gathered overnight."

Hayden motioned to the other Deities. "Anyone else?"

The other men nodded. Gabel of Australia mentioned how his people lit candles and sang ancient songs of praise he had not heard in decades.

"Don't you see?" Hayden addressed the gods with fierce desperation. "Our people want to see you. For the first time in many years, my mother walked among the congregation and offered them blessings, prayers, and encouragement. It's been too long since the people came and *asked* for a Deity's blessings."

"Because they don't care." Salina screamed with mocking laughter. She'd gained consciousness with a vengeance. "The people don't care about you because the gods have forsaken the Deities. They're afraid of Ryse, because he'll *kill* them, but they don't give a damn about getting *blessed* by a Deity. You have no gods to back up your blessings. Most of you Deities sit in your Havens, never going outside the realm into the human world like you're too good for the commoner. You think the people don't catch on to that?"

Ryse glanced around to see shame on some of the Deities' faces. As much as he hated to admit it, Salina was right. His parents were proof. Troy and Dynasty were good leaders, faithful servants. But they never left the Haven unless it was a dire emergency. Although there was another Haven in North America, up near Canada, and another near the equator, Ryse alone had visited them. Not his parents, nor his brother. How many kings could say the same? How many Deities never left the safety of the known and thereby forsook the Olympians on the outside?

Salina motioned her head toward the tiers of gods and goddesses who sat on their thrones. "Don't you get it, you fools? They don't give a bloody fuck about us earthlings. They sit, high and mighty on their thrones, basking in their own glory, while your people rot on Earth, living in fear of the pathetic humans discovering us. Go ahead and wipe them out," she yelled at the gods. "It's not like this group of pansies can lead them."

Charles rushed to Salina and backhanded her, flinging her to the marble floor. Ryse quickly pulled him away before he did something unforgivable in the presence of the gods.

"I did not raise you like this. I raised you to love the gods, to respect and worship them. What evil dwells within that you would spew such vile words in their presence?" Charles fought against Ryse's hold. "Have you no dignity? No appreciation for the ones who created you?"

Salina stared unblinking at her father. Blood dripped from her lip and her eyes were dead and hard. "I am done bowing to the gods. Their gifts are curses to me."

The entire room took a collective breath. Ryse couldn't fathom the depravity and sickness that would cause Salina to damn her soul in such manner. Any hope she had was gone.

Aphrodite, goddess of beauty and love, stood and sauntered up to Salina. Her curvaceous, sexy body moved with all the grace of a jungle cat. The sway of her hips and flow of her sleek legs was mesmerizing, almost hypnotic. But the glare of anger on her lovely face sent shivers down Ryse's spine. He urged Charles to back away slowly so as not to attract her attention. Charles didn't fight him. They moved together, slowly, one step at a time. No one wanted to be in the path of an enraged and insulted goddess.

"My gift is a curse to you?" Aphrodite whispered, her temper barely controlled. A fine tremor rippled down her body and her aura burned bright with fury. The walls strained to contain the power. Many in the room pointed their eyes to the floor; some even went to their knees. "You were my creation. I fashioned you to be the most ravishing, lovely woman in the Olympian world. Men fell at your feet. Women envied you."

Aphrodite twirled her wrist and Salina's bedraggled appearance shifted into the woman he once knew. Salina stood before them, unbound, dressed in a fine gown of red silk that hugged her breasts and hips. Her hair shone with golden splendor and her plump lips glistened red.

This was the Salina that Ryse remembered from his youth. There was no doubt who created her. Her beauty was beyond compare. She was perfection personified. Yes, men had fallen at her feet, women strove to live up to her standard. But none compared to the radiance of Princess Salina Avondale.

"My beautiful baby girl." Charles made a sound of distress beside him and Ryse saw the love he had for who his child used to be. Moisture gathered in the man's eyes. Even Salina was taken with herself. She touched her hair, smoothed a hand down her dress.

"And for what?" Aphrodite spit out. "So you can use your beautiful body for revenge, for blackmail, for treachery?" She snapped her fingers in the air and Salina was once again the dirty prisoner, tied up and kneeling on the floor. "I had such plans for you, Salina." Aphrodite used one finger to tilt up Salina's head. The control she had of her tone only made her more ominous, like a motionless snake right before it struck. "Now you curse my gift?"

Salina stared at the magnificent goddess. "Your gift turned me into nothing but a whore, a plaything for men."

There was a beat of silence as everyone in the room held their breath.

"Then I shall take it away," Aphrodite roared like thunder, shaking the pillars of the temple. The finger she had under Salina's chin whipped up her face, her fingernail separating the skin.

Salina screamed as her supple flesh peeled back and disintegrated. Her golden hair turned gray, her arched brows dipped, her high cheekbones sank in, and her skin shriveled up like a raisin. Full, red lips crinkled into the thin lines of an old hag.

Ryse turned his head away, unable to watch Salina's remaining beauty vanish. Charles stood firm, but tears dripped down his face as his child aged before him. His grip on Ryse's arm tightened as his knees gave way. Ryse took him to the bench and made him sit.

"You bitch," Salina cried out as she examined her withered hands and sagging skin.

Rhea peered down at the scene before her. "Salina Avondale, you are found guilty of murder, blasphemy, and a myriad of crimes against the people you were born to protect. You are hereby sentenced to beheading by the hands of the Thracian Master in front of the Olympian population. Your soul shall not enter the afterlife, but is banished to the depths of Hades, where it shall burn with the demons for all eternity. May your execution be an example for all the Olympians of Earth. Take her away. The sight of her makes me ill."

Guards dragged Salina's decrepit body from the temple.

Ryse's jaw nearly flopped open. Rhea was going to make him execute a Princess in front of the entire Olympian race? Stars danced in his eyes. Never in all his years, never in the history of Olympians had such a spectacle taken place.

The room spun. He pulled in deep breaths and tried to wrap his head around the thought. His eyes met Charles'.

Dear gods, he was going to have to kill Charles' daughter. Until this moment, when he looked Charles in the eyes and saw his anguish, he thought it would be such an easy task. That longing for revenge was birthed out of his suffering over Troy. Now, he couldn't fathom bringing Charles and Filene such agony.

"Of all the people who could perform this task," Ryse said to Ares. "Why must it be me? Is it truly the will of the gods that I execute the daughter of a man I call my friend?"

"His daughter murdered your father," Ares stated in a practical manner. "You are the executioner of your race. It's your job to bring justice to those who do evil."

"Then I demand that the gods be in attendance. I will not have my people assuming I carry out this execution out of rage or mourning or revenge. If it is your will, you should preside over it."

"Done," Zeus said.

"What?" Hephaestus came off his throne. "Why should this man be allowed to demand anything of us? Why should we have to endure the earthly plain to oversee him carry out a job he was created for? This is his duty."

Rhea's temper rose and the marble walls of the temple shook so hard Ryse feared they would collapse.

"Silence!" Zeus rose and shoved Hephaestus back to his seat. "It is such attitude that has brought us to this point. Although she has betrayed her title, Salina Avondale was born into a family of royal blood.

It will cause a panic when a Princess is executed. There is already fear brewing because the Grand Deity was murdered. We must show our subjects that we have given Ryse the authority to carry out her punishment. And," he looked to Rhea, "we must show the Olympians that we have not abandoned them or the Deities we've anointed to rule them."

Many of the gods nodded in agreement with Zeus. Ryse noted those who did not: Hades, Hephaestus, Poseidon.

"I believe," Hayden's voice lifted over the murmurs, "that it would be a show of solidarity and strength if all the Deities and the gods were in attendance and if the population of Olympians were witness to this execution. This way, all messages will be clear. The gods stand behind the Deities, the Deities are supporting Ryse, and Ryse..." Hayden looked at his brother, his brows dipped and he sighed. "And Ryse is a man to be feared, that it is his job to deliver your divine judgment."

It was the burden Ryse had carried all his life. People feared the executioner. He was not a man invited to meals, more like an unwelcome guest. No one smiled at him on the streets of the Haven or waved when he crossed their paths. Thracians both worshipped him and feared him. To see Ryse at the door was to see death.

Hayden knew this was his brother's curse and, as much as they both hated it, Ryse was a necessity among their race. He was the iron fist by which all others ruled. He was the oil that greased the machine of their society. Until recently, Ryse had loathed his very existence. But now, he had love. He closed his eyes and imagined Avery's smile shining at him, her green eyes holding such adoration, promising that she would never fear him. With a deep breath and the gift of her love in his heart, he raised his eyes to accept his fate.

"I shall attend, in support of Ryse." Eekon placed his hand on Hayden's shoulder. "I will support the Castilles."

"And I," Gabel of Australia agreed, as did Dimitrios of Asia and Amais of South Africa.

"I shall stand with Ryse and Hayden. I shall stand with the gods," Charles whispered, his voice hoarse and shaking. "This evil has spread from my house, and I will do whatever it takes to make it right."

Rhea glided down the thrones and into the middle of the room. "This matter is settled. Return to your homes, to your world. Hermes will deliver the message to the Olympians of all that shall take place. When the multitudes gather in each Haven, the gods shall descend. All but myself."

Murmurs and protest arose from the gods and Deities alike. Rhea held up a hand. "You must all understand that our people look to Zeus as their highest power. That should not change. The Olympians of Earth are his responsibility and he shall once again lead them as the god they are seeking." She held out her hands to encompass the room. "You, my children, know that when there is trouble in the chain of command, the people see it as weakness. Zeus is your god. I am merely watching over you from the other side."

"You have my word." Zeus took his mother's hand and addressed the Deities. "You will not be alone again." He met the eyes of each man, making a silent promise to guide them throughout their reign.

"What of the Grand Deity?" asked Amais. "And which of his sons will take Troy's throne?" He spoke as if the two positions would surely be separated, as if neither Hayden nor Ryse could fill the seats of both North American Deity and Grand Deity.

Rhea looked to Zeus and something passed between them. He stepped forward and narrowed his eyes at Hayden and Ryse. "As for the Castille throne, I must converse with the Oracles and Troy. I have not made my decision on who reigns as Grand Deity. Each of you are well suited in your own way."

As much as Ryse wanted to be concerned with the fate of his family's throne, he had only one care on his mind. Avery.

"I go to Delphi, to see the Oracles." Rhea lifted her arms up. Wind, fire, and rain swirled about her body. "Zeus and the other gods will listen to any more that you need to address. Be well, my children, until next we meet."

The tornado of lights and flames swirled until Ryse could barely stand. With a clap of roaring thunder, she was gone and all her fireworks with her.

"Now that's an exit," Hayden said with a nervous laugh.

Ryse smirked at his brother. "And not the last we will see, I'm sure."

With her departure, the official meeting adjourned. The gods came down from their thrones and gave the Deities a rare chance to converse and speak to them face to face. It was the first in what Ryse hoped was a long line of opportunities to get closer to the gods who created them.

"You and I have a previously scheduled meeting, Master Thracian." Andreas came up behind him.

Ryse smiled up at the goofy brute. "Yeah, we do."

CHAPTER TWELVE

"**A**RE YOU REALLY GOING TO MAKE HIM WHIP NIKKI?" AVERY ASKED Rhea, her eyes filling with unshed tears.

"Yes."

No explanation, just a simple one-word answer that made Avery sick to her stomach. "Is it possible to blow spiritual chunks? 'Cause I gotta tell you, I'm feelin' like road kill." She bent at the waist and put her hands on her knees.

"In all things there is purpose, child. Trust me." Rhea touched her head and the illness in her gut went away.

"She's such a good person, Rhea. You have to know that."

"Of course I do. Nikki has a destiny, just like yours, Avery. Her journey is not an easy one, but it will make her grow as a person."

"Will I get to keep her with me? As my Shadow Lady?"

"Her title will be stripped, but you may keep your pet."

Anger boiled up in her veins. "What does that mean? Nikki is not my pet! She's a woman with feelings and heart to serve. She is bravely acceptin' punishment for a crime she was forced to commit." She lashed out at Rhea before she even realized it.

A small smirk grew on Rhea's face. "Don't ever lose that passion, Avery." Rhea clasped her hands in front of her. "Shall we check on your home?"

Confused, and obviously not getting clarification any time soon, Avery pursed her lips and nodded. Nikki receiving punishment wasn't fair, but when Rhea made up her mind, there was no going back. She was Master of the friggin' universe, after all.

"I thought you said I was going to the portal? What are we doing in Delphi?"

"Observing."

Avery and Rhea stepped into the temple and the three Oracles of the Pythia came running. *Great stars and stripes, they were naked.* She turned her face away as the women fell at Rhea's feet, kissing her hands, her legs, fawning over her like a long lost lover returned home.

"They're naked," Avery whispered with a shiver, keeping her eyes away from the awkward nudity in front of her. Her voice pitched high. "Very, *very* naked."

Rhea giggled. "Do not be shy. The Oracles are my beloveds. For all their wisdom, they are quite childlike." She smiled at one, ran a hand down her cheek. "Their little lights burn so brightly for a short time, then they go out."

"They die? I thought they were immortal."

"A soul can only handle so much, Avery. The Pythia see it all and are trained not to feel emotions from their visions." Rhea petted the women's hair, their shoulders, their faces. "After a while, it finally – how would you say it? Fries them?"

"Oh my god. Why would you let that happen?"

"Look at them, Avery." Rhea kissed the head of a brunette and the dazed Oracle beamed under the attention. "Think about what kind of a life they would have lived on Earth. Seeing it all and having no protection against the deep emotional impact. Humans would have locked them up; Olympians called them insane. Here in Delphi, they can be of use, have their visions, and when their time is up, I take their souls into me, where they have peace for all eternity. They become a part of me."

"Well, that's…yeah, I don't know what that is, but it's not normal."

Rhea chuckled and then whispered to her sans-clothing fan club. "Come, my pets; show me what I wish to see."

The Pythia led them to a pool where the Oracles sat and stirred the waters clockwise until the water churned into a whirlpool. It finally rose into the air and formed a smooth surface like a mirror. Avery watched everything that happened in the Haven since the moment she left. She especially took interest in the Oracle Lysandra, who Rhea sent to Earth.

"Be of care, Avery," Rhea warned as she inched closer to the pools. "None but the Oracles can enter the water. The unique separation of your body and spirit makes you fragile."

Avery backed away and observed the Pythia as they swayed and bobbed like rag dolls on invisible strings. When the show was over, they waded back through the pool and over to Rhea.

"So this was Lysandra's fate? To live in a drunken fog and finally, *poof*, she's gone?" Avery made an explosion with her fingers.

A blonde with the same drunken glaze in her eyes leaned onto Avery. "Lysandra feels things."

Oh, holy jeez. Avery nearly gagged at the cold clamminess of the woman's skin.

"Lysandra is broken." The brunette kissed Avery's hand before she could pull it back. Her jerking motions didn't hinder the Oracle. She simply rubbed her chest against Avery's legs like a cat.

Avery knew *exactly* who was broken. And it damn sure wasn't Lysandra. These chicks were one egg short of an omelet. *Fried* took on a whole new meaning.

"Lysandra needs to feel love," murmured the other Oracle. Her eyes were so glazed over, the pupils appeared missing, the eyes completely gone white. "All we feel is our goddess. Rhea is all we need." She wound her body through Rhea's legs and leaned her head against her inner thigh.

Weird didn't quite cover it. Nope. Not even close.

The three drunken women all jerked upright at the same time. Their heads snapped around to the waters of the pool.

"Show me." Rhea commanded.

A horrific scene appeared in the waves of the pool.

"Tell me that's not what I think it is." Avery leaned over the edge, her rapt attention on the swirls of smoke and evil that were conjured inside the Haven.

"I'm afraid the situation in your realm is much worse than I antici-pated." Rhea's eyes narrowed, her voice stone cold.

"Is that—Dante?" Avery reached out, as if she could stop him from his actions. She leaned over the water just enough to throw off her bal-ance. "*Ah*," she cried as she went face first into the waters.

"Avery! No!" Rhea reached out for her, but it was too late.

A thousand voices filled her head. Prayers. Thoughts. Fears. Laughter. Tears. Sorrow. Joy. Every emotion and reaction of the human spirit engulfed her, drowning her quicker than the water filling her lungs. Avery screamed, not knowing how to surface, unaware of which way was up. She pressed her hands over her ears, trying to block the voices and emotions.

All at once, she was yanked from the water and laid flat on the marble floor of the temple. Air refused to take the place of water. Vaguely, she felt more than heard, Rhea.

"She must go back. Now."

"But, Rhea, the waters, the pool? Her mind—"

"*Now*. Before her spirit is captured in the afterlife forever."

Avery thought someone was pulling her intestines out of her nose. The pain shooting through her gut was nauseating and wretched until she thought she was being stabbed all over again. As the scorch-ing of her innards intensified, her vision dimmed.

Her world went black.

⚓

Ryse and Andreas clanked two pints together. Naturally, it was the best beer ever to grace Ryse's palette.

"Bloody hell, this is good." Ryse gave him a half-hearted smile. "It's good to see you again, Andreas. I think I can finally have peace now."

"Aye. Now you can entertain that lass of yers. Mighty fine woman she is. Scary lit'le thing when she's riled." He grinned wide, uninhib-ited by the burdens that now weighed Ryse down.

"Incredible. She's…everything." He took another drink and closed his eyes as the ale slid down his throat.

"Ryse, how's my Hanna?" Andreas appeared solemn for the first time. "Is she recovered or moved on?"

With a heavy sigh, Ryse shrugged. What could he say? Hanna had rarely spoken since his death, afraid of what might come out of her mouth. She definitely hadn't moved on or tried to find another man to keep her warm at night. Now that he thought about it, Hanna had become the literal shadow in Shadow Lady. Yet she served faithfully without complaint or resentment.

"She misses you. We both do. But she is loyal and dependable. You should be proud of her strength, Andreas. You rubbed off on her, after all." Ryse clapped him on the shoulder.

"I know it's hard to believe a man would want his woman to love another, but I do." Andreas scowled, his red brows dipping deep. "I don't want her to be alone. I want her to love and be loved."

"Andreas, I won't bullshit you. I don't know if Hanna is capable of giving her love to anyone but you. That woman will be faithful to you until the day she enters the afterlife and is once again in your arms."

Andreas gave him a nod and a ghost of a smile. "There's not much I fret about up here, ya know? But I miss my wife. You've been given a rare gift, lad. Don't forget it."

"*Ryse.*" Hayden ran up, his face pale. "We were at the portal and this woman ran up, talking to the guardian on the other side. There's a demon in the Haven."

The three men raced to the temple where the portal stood, open to their Haven, ready to receive them back.

"You must go. It's time." Andreas nearly pushed them through the portal, but not before he pulled Ryse into a tight hug.

"Wait," Hayden cried. "We didn't get to say goodbye to our father."

"His soul rests with the gods, young Olympian Prince. Have peace for the dead and go tend to the livin'.'"

"What of Salina and Nikki?" Hayden persisted.

"They will be delivered by the gods. You must hurry." Andreas bid them farewell.

Ryse reluctantly stepped through the portal, leaving his old friend behind. The last thing he saw was Andreas smile and wipe a tear from his face.

He didn't have time to feel the loss again as blinding light consumed his eyes and his mind. He tumbled from the portal and onto the grassy knoll, back in the Haven. Behind him came Charles, Hammon, and Hayden. The Thracians took to the woods after the others while Hayden and Charles bolted to the palace to check on the women.

Dear gods of Olympia, how had a demon entered the Haven?

THE
HAVEN-EARTH

CHAPTER THIRTEEN

L YSANDRA APPROACHED THE PORTAL THAT WOULD TRANSPORT HER FROM the Holy City of Delphi to the earthly realm, her fear boxed up deep inside. She could not show any hesitation. If Hermes could go to Earth and collect the Deities with no issues, she could take the one step forward into the portal.

Still, her body shook.

The portal showed her a regal woman with golden and silver hair walking among the Olympian population. This woman was a queen. And she was missing a Shadow Lady. As the queen left her populace to go to the temple to pray, Lysandra edged up to the portal.

A heavy, repressive robe cloaked her body, smothering her in fabric when she'd been hundreds of years without clothing. The soldier guarding the portal went to one knee, bowing until she touched his head and spoke blessings to him in Greek. He straightened and gave her a warm smile. Lysandra tried to return the gesture as she tugged and pulled on the weighty robe. She'd never left Delphi and her hesitancy must have been written on her face. That was not acceptable. She steeled her spine and squared her shoulders. Duty. Duty before all else.

The widowed queen, Lady Dynasty, knelt down and willed the single candle to flicker to life. Lysandra listened to her prayers.

My gods and goddesses, creators of this world and the next, holy mothers and father of our universe, I come humbly to beg for your guidance. The souls of my entire family rest in your care and I find myself more alone than ever. My Shadow Lady must guard Avery and, without her by my side, I feel as though yet another piece of me is missing. The people notice. What shall I do? Guide me, oh lords. Show me the will of the gods and give me the courage and strength to follow you. I am so afraid. Without my husband and my sons here, my daughter in a state of deathless-life, the troubles between my household and that of the Avondales, and all the Deities being gone all over the world, I fear for my people. I fear what might happen in my sons' absence. Show me, lords, show me what I am to do to banish this fear and lead the people as you wish me to. I am your vessel. I sacrifice myself to your will. Help me, please.

Her last three words were whispered with such earnest desperation, it nearly brought tears to Lysandra's eyes. She stepped through the portal, crossing over from the Heavens to the temple on Earth. Electricity sliced through her body for a split second, but she shook it off.

Lady Dynasty wiped her cheeks, the tears falling freely in this sanctuary. When she had gathered her strength, she stood and turned to leave. She stumbled when she encountered Lysandra.

"Who are you?" Dynasty asked.

"Lady Dynasty, faithful servant of the gods, you prayed to the gods for help and they have sent me." Her voice was musical, smooth, and as hypnotic as she could make it. "Many fears you carry, Dynasty. I am here to relieve such burdens. My name is Lysandra. I am from the Holy City of Delphi."

Dyna gasped and went back down to her knees, one hand clutching her chest. "You are an Oracle?"

"I am in line to join the Pythia, to be an Oracle of Apollo. But the gods have seen the need for me here. Your son's mate is resting in this place, yet her spirit has entered the Heavens, correct?"

"I don't believe you have been correctly informed. My son's mate was murdered." Dynasty did her best to lie, but she was not in the presence of a mere Olympian.

"You need not fill my ears with tales, wise one. I have seen the truth as given by the gods."

Dynasty nodded. "No one is supposed to know. How—"

"Oracle." Lysandra's lips twitched slightly as she tapped her temple. How long had it been since she'd used humor? She'd thought herself incapable. But here, in this place, it was her first reaction to diffuse the tension of the queen. "I am here to watch over her and conceal her existence. Meanwhile, your Shadow Lady may be free to resume her duties and avoid suspicion." Lysandra covered her head with her cape so that only her long braid could be seen. "Let's go."

Dyna hesitated. "You will have to convince the Elites of who you are."

"Worry not." Heaven knew Lysandra was doing enough fretting for the both of them, no matter how controlled she appeared on the outside.

She'd grown up on legends of these warriors. Thracians, as a rule, were huge in stature, quick to action, and swift to kill. The Elites were rumored to be the worst of the Thracians and yet the best the race had to offer. They killed first and asked questions later. Meeting these men face to face gave her a chill of fear up her spine.

I am a holy messenger of the gods, she kept telling herself. No one could deny her the task appointed to her. Lysandra turned and followed Dyna. The Oracle walked with sure footsteps around the temple and through the passages that led to the palace. When they reached the outer entrance to Dyna's private chambers, they were met with Thracian soldiers. *Heavens, they are massive.* Their eyes studied the cloaked woman, and then the queen.

"Let us pass," Dyna commanded. The two soldiers exchanged glances, then moved. Dyna ushered Lysandra into the outer hall. Then she was faced with a soldier who had been present in her visions. He was fairly tall with hair so short it was nearly nonexistent. His eyes looked her up, then down. The black robe she wore covered her entire body except her hands and bare feet, which caught his eyes.

"Yankee, dear, I need you to gather the Elites." Dynasty kept her voice calm and even.

His eyes stayed on Lysandra, no doubt wondering what was under the hood. "What's up, Your Majesty?"

"It is imperative I speak to all of you."

"Who's your friend?" He crossed his arms over his chest.

"Son, you would be wise to do as I ask. Now." Dyna was getting upset. Sure, the soldier had his reasons for being protective. But—

Before Lysandra could react, Yankee pinned her up against the wall, a gun pointed at her exposed forehead. Her cape fell to the floor. *By the gods, he is fast.* Dynasty gasped and tried to step in between them. Lysandra stood calm and still as a statue—and completely nude. She didn't so much as draw breath. Not that she could. Fear was a living, breathing dragon in her stomach.

"Stop this," Dynasty cried out. Two more soldiers came running to the door. "Brenden, make him stop."

"What the hell, Yankee? Holy Zeus, she's *naked*." A blond soldier with deep blue eyes and a kind face tried to intervene, but Yankee pressed the gun more firmly against her skin. "Why are you naked?" He looked from Lysandra to Dynasty to Yankee. His voice pitched high. "Why is she naked?"

"State your name, woman."

"I am Lysandra, an Oracle from Delphi. You are Samuel, known as Yankee."

"No shit, Captain Observant. Tell me something I don't know. Like what the hell you're doing here and why you have my queen so damn upset." He paused and looked her over. "And why are you naked?" His eyes went to her chest. "Not that I'm complaining."

"*Yankee.* This is entirely inappropriate," Dynasty whispered so the exterior guards wouldn't hear the commotion.

Lysandra spoke evenly. One would never know she was in peril but for the slight shiver in her skin. "I was sent here by the gods to aid in your cause."

"And what cause is that, exactly?"

"To hide the body of Lady Avery until her soul returns from the presence of Rhea."

Three Thracian soldiers turned their piercing gazes to Dynasty, who held out her hands. "I didn't tell her."

Now Lysandra sighed and shook her head. Her nudity didn't bother her as much as it seemed to bother the lady and two of the three soldiers. "Did I mention I was an Oracle? I could have sworn I did. You do comprehend the powers of an Oracle, do you not?"

The three men nodded at one another and Yankee slowly lowered the weapon.

Dynasty nearly collapsed with relief. "I need to sit."

Lysandra would have followed, but a giant warrior bent to pick up her robe and aided her in dressing. Eyes the color of sand met hers.

Dearest mother-goddess, what masculine beauty. She was instantly held in his gaze, his prisoner…his prey.

It was quite a shock for Dante to exit the room and find Yankee holding a gun on a naked—*fantastically* naked—woman. Her creamy white skin and perfect curves stopped him in his tracks. Black hair hung in a braid as wide as his arm down her back. He imagined that once the mane was loose, it would be a thick curtain about her lovely petite body. That lovely piece of her artful perfection would be burned into his brain for all his days.

The Oracles of Delphi were sacred. Apollo's temple housed the Pythia, the three lead Oracles. But many young women had surrendered their lives to the service of the gods by becoming priestesses in the temples. Their souls left the Earth to join their sisters in the Heavens.

In all his history classes, Dante had never heard of an Oracle coming back to Earth for any reason. However, these were uncertain times. Gods came to Earth, the Deities were summoned to the Heavens, and a soldier of Zeus stood in the knoll outside, guarding a portal to the Heavens. Why not an Oracle from Delphi?

Dante lifted the cloak and gently placed it on the shoulders of the Oracle as Lady Dynasty began to wilt. Yankee ushered Dyna to her room, but Dante stood planted in the hall, his eyes locked on those of the Oracle. The two stared at each other, caught by the intensity of the other. He was over a head taller than Lysandra, yet he felt like he was on his knees before her, unable to breathe without her permission.

His world shifted. Inexplicable tingles and electrical signals went off in his brain.

Mine.

It wasn't enough to call her beautiful. The word did her no justice. Lysandra was...*ravishing*, brilliant, mesmerizing in every way.

Brenden cleared his throat, breaking their trance. Lysandra ducked into the room.

Her thick, black braid swung over her shoulder as she knelt to take Dynasty's hand. Ruby red lips were in contrast with her pale skin. Her eyes were large, innocent, a shade of gray he couldn't place. Unique eyes—like his.

Those eyes shot up as if he'd said her name. "Mighty warrior, will you please close the door until the other Elites arrive? We would not want anyone to see our Lady in such distress."

Dante fought the urge to look around to see who this *mighty warrior* was, but he was the only one standing by the door. Snapping out of his confusion, he obeyed. He then moved to the other side of the queen so he could watch the Oracle. If love at first sight was real, this might be a shining example. His heart beat as loud as a timpani drum in his chest and he feared everyone in the room would hear it. He kept his aura locked tight. All he needed was for the other Elites to pick up on his infatuation with their new guest.

"Thank you, I'm fine." Dynasty accepted a glass of water from Hanna.

Yankee knelt down by Dyna and touched her knee. "My lady, you are not fine. Don't sit there and lie. A lot of shit has gone down in the last couple days and it's cool if you need to rest."

"Samuel." Dyna rested her hands and cup in her lap and narrowed her eyes. "I'm not too tired to wash your mouth out with soap. Or even better, sic Hanna on you. Keep that in mind," she threatened in a motherly fashion.

Yankee huffed out laughter and patted her knee before rising to his full height. He mumbled about it not working the first time and

Dante suppressed a grin. Lady Dyna might be the only person on the planet other than Ryse who could control Yankee.

That was when he noticed the Oracle watching him with curious intent. Their eyes met, then her gaze skirted away. It was enough. He caught the flash of fire in her gaze. When Yankee brushed by her, she recoiled as if he carried the plague. Guess he had that unnerving effect on everyone. Satisfaction blossomed in Dante's chest. *He* was her mighty warrior, not Yankee the Untouchable.

Moments later, the Elites remaining in the Haven were assembled. Cutter, Philippe, Yankee, and Brenden stood in a semicircle while an unflinching woman held her own against their questions.

"The gods sent me to look over the body of this woman." She indicated to the other room where Avery's body lay. "I foresee that she will be in this state for a while. The queen and her Shadow Lady cannot be separated too long; people are already asking questions. Hanna must be presented with her mistress and Dynasty must be accessible to the public. Therefore, I shall stay here and tend to the mate of the prince."

"Why one of the Pythia?" Brenden asked. "Why not a soldier?"

"Guards she has. I am not one of the Pythia *yet*. It is my duty to serve the gods where necessary until then."

Dante made a mental note of the way she clarified her status with a frown. Was something that weighed heavily on her? He had a deep desire to find out.

"How we know you not spy?" Cutter asked.

Lysandra's gray eyes focused on him. She spoke in Chinese and Dante didn't understand what she said. Judging by the way Cutter's eyes widened for a fraction of a second before he regained control, it was probably best Dante didn't get involved. When she was finished, Cutter put his palms together and bowed, speaking in his native tongue.

Lysandra returned the gesture, then addressed the group. "The gods also revealed that when Avery awakens, she will need my assistance. Her Shadow Lady is—"

"Careful," Brenden growled.

"—indisposed," Lysandra said, casting him a sidelong glance. "Avery will need me."

Her eyes settled on Dante and he felt the heat of her gaze from across the room. "All of you will need me."

Dante swallowed the lump in his throat. The type of need he felt at that moment had nothing to do with the gods and everything to do with the exquisite woman with ruby lips and gray eyes.

CHAPTER FOURTEEN

ASHTON JOGGED OVER TO HIS INTENDED TARGET. DANTE WALKED DOWN the street that connected the training center and the palace. The bastard had avoided him for the last couple days, but there was only so far one could go in this Haven. Persistence was key.

"Hello." He gave a cheerful smile. "Dante, right? My goodness, you've changed since I saw you last. What was it? Twenty years ago?"

The color of his eyes was eerily similar to Xavier's. For a moment, it caught him off guard. This is what Xavier might have looked like in his first century. Odd, he'd never really thought of Xavier as the sexual type, but this Thracian boy was proof that the old man had shagged someone at some point.

"Prince Ashton," Dante said, his tone tight and strained. He gave a formal bow.

"Relax; no need for all that." Ashton shoved his hands in his khakis. "Let's take a walk."

Dante glanced to the training center. "I was actually on my way to—"

"Five minutes. Please? I really should explain Xavier's behavior; apologize even."

Dante's eyes narrowed and he took a deep breath. Indecision was written on his face. His duties awaited him, but a well-trained soldier would not ignore a prince.

Ah, you want to hear this, though. Don't you?

Dante nodded. "What can I do for you, prince?"

Ashton guided their steps away from the training center and the palace, into the side gardens. "I realize that you and I are connected and yet we barely know each other."

"Yes, prince." His automatic, bored response was an insult.

Ashton clapped the warrior on the back, noting how he flinched away from his hand. "Dante, call me Ashton. Please. I know what's going on here."

"Oh?" Dante's face and emotionless tone were a trademark of his father. The apple didn't fall far.

"Your father left your family to tend to mine. That couldn't have been easy on a young man. It's not easy living in my father's shadow and he does his best to spend time with me when he can. Xavier, in contrast, is ever the soldier. Cold. Hard. *Abrasive.*" He leaned in and whispered the last word with a wink.

"Yes, prince." Dante's faint smile was enough.

"You and I have much in common. Both of us growing up at the feet of legends, striving to be like our fathers and missing the mark completely."

Dante's head whipped around and Ashton knew he had him.

He chuckled, kept a smile plastered on his face. "Don't look so stunned. Even I have tried to walk in Charles' steps and faltered. Why do you think I choose to blaze my own path? It's hard to live up to men like that. We must be different, you and I, if we are ever to stand out and achieve our own greatness. Don't you agree?"

"Yes, prince."

Ashton stopped Dante with a hand and faced him. "I want you to know, I think it's quite an accomplishment to be accepted into the Elites. They are legend in their own right. You must be proud. Deep down, I know your father is too. He's just, well, he's shit at showing how he feels."

The two men shared a chuckle. The seed was planted.

"I know things are hectic right now, especially for an Elite. Any time you need a break, come find me. We can go riding or hunting. Looks as if I'll be here a while. I look forward to getting to know you. Maybe we can rise above our fathers' shadows together, eh? You're already on your way." Ashton held out his hand and, with only a second of hesitation, Dante clasped it.

"Thank you, prince."

Waving him off, Ashton smiled widely as Dante loped back down the path to the training center. Yes, the seed was planted and, even better, the ground was fertile.

CHAPTER FIFTEEN

B Y THE FOURTH SUNRISE ON EARTH, LYSANDRA SETTLED INTO A DAILY
cycle of cleaning, tending to Avery, fixing food for the Elites, and
reading books on the last thousand years of their people's history.
Often, Lady Dynasty and her Shadow Lady, Hanna, joined her in the
evenings and they read together.

This world was so different. Nothing felt right. Although Lady
Dynasty provided her with clothing, it didn't fit comfortably. It had
been too long since she'd been cinched up in long gowns. They had
finally fitted her with a modern style Hanna called a maxi-dress. The
gowns were long but sleeveless, their material light and loose. Lady
Dynasty assured her she was both modest and fashionable. Not that
she cared about the latter.

Lysandra did enjoy the running water—*hot* running water. She
stared at the steaming flow that came forth from a silver decorative
tube. Lights that illuminated at the flip of a switch, a handheld device
called a cell phone that allowed people to communicate over any distance, television, refrigerators, electric ovens, ironing board, washing
and drying machines; there was so much to marvel at.

So much to learn…

The Holy City of Delphi was primitive in comparison. Then

again, what did she require hot water for up there? They did not eat, sleep, wear clothing, watch the animated television boxes.

On this planet, she was human again. For the first time in nearly a thousand years, Lysandra felt hunger, exhaustion, the need to empty her bladder—praise the gods for toilet tissue. She bathed daily. It appalled her to think she might smell. Some of these necessities frustrated her to no end, but the first time she tasted a warm chocolate chip cookie and soaked her body in a hot tub of floral scented water, she quit internally complaining about how the ovens didn't cook food like a fire.

Thus far, all of the warriors she'd tended to were polite and kind, with the exclusion of one. Cutter visited and she thoroughly enjoyed speaking with him about his familial heritage. Philippe was distant and quiet, but polite. Brenden carried a tremendous emotional burden that she wanted to free him of. Most of his visits ended up with him confiding in her.

In contrast to the others was Yankee. Flirtatious and crude, he had a mouth like the back end of a donkey. If not questioning her virginal status or the nudity in Delphi, he stared at her with predatory eyes.

Then there was Dante.

From the first moment she laid eyes on him, she was under his spell. To call him anything but fierce and strong and handsome would be an insult. His body was muscular and wide; his shoulders were like great stones, round and bulging, the body of a noble Thracian warrior. Unlike the others, he seemed almost shy. He could barely look her in the eyes, yet she often caught him staring. Lysandra couldn't help but flick her gaze to him every few minutes. Their eyes would meet, connect for a heartbeat, then dance away.

She loved those heartbeats when they were connected.

On her second day, she'd tried to engage him in conversation by mentioning how glorious the roses smelled. The windows were open and the breeze carried their aroma from the gardens below right into the room.

"The flowers in Delphi do not carry scent. Did you know that?"

He cleared his throat and shook his head, unable to look at her.

"Everything that would appeal to the senses is muted. The flowers are pretty, but not radiant. They do not feel real. The texture is poorly replicated. I think I'll ask Hanna to bring me one, so I can compare—"

"I can." He shot to his feet.

"Oh." Her hand went to her chest. "Do not bother yourself, mighty warrior. I am positive the books you study are much more important than—"

"It will only take a moment."

Dante retrieved a most lovely bloom. The white and pink rose overjoyed her. She bragged and bragged about the scent, the softness, the colors. She even made him touch and smell it. The blush of his cheeks sent her heart to fluttering.

It broke some of the tension between them, for which she was grateful.

"Are you good here?" he asked as she placed the flower in a vase.

She didn't understand the question so he rephrased it. "Is everyone treating you kindly?"

"Yes. Lady Dynasty and Hanna are very sweet. Almost all the guards have been cordial."

"Almost?"

"Not to speak ill of him, but Yankee is," she searched for the right word, "difficult."

Dante laughed. "Don't be offended. He is a jerk to everyone. If he didn't like you, he would shoot you."

Lysandra gasped. "Do you mean that in the literal sense?"

"Given his initial greeting, what do you think?" He shrugged, drawing her eyes to his firm, round shoulders.

She pinched her lips and nodded.

"If Yankee thought for one minute you were a threat, he would send you right back up to the Heavens, Oracle. Consider it a compliment that he remains in your presence at all."

The next time Dante came to sit with her—no, with *Avery*—he brought a different flower, a sprig of lavender. The next day, it was an orchid. He would hand her the flower, accept her thanks, and then retreat to his books. Unless she asked him a direct question about how something functioned, he was quiet.

Lysandra asked as many questions as she could think of. He had explained every contraption and mechanism in their palatial suite twice.

On her fifth day, Lysandra accepted another rose bloom graciously. "These are my favorite." She smiled at this kind warrior, wondering how he could be as brutal as a Thracian soldier was famed to be. His power must be immense, so frightening that their legend alone would strike fear in the heart of the enemy.

In an effort to get him to engage her, she asked.

"My gift?" he questioned, his eyes darting away from hers and back to the book that lay open over his leg.

"Yes. I am aware of the others' but not yours. Yankee has great strength, Brenden is a shapeshifter, Cutter is a legendary swordsman, and Philippe controls the elements. But I do not know of your skills, warrior."

Dante rubbed the back of his neck and fidgeted. "Well, I…" He looked up at her from his seated position. "I block Olympian gifts." Once again, his eyes went to the floor and the blush rose on his face.

Lysandra took the seat next to him. "I am afraid I do not understand."

Dante flinched away at her proximity. He leaned over on his knees and popped his knuckles; she'd noticed this action before.

"Why do you do that to your fingers?"

"Nervous habit." Dante shook out his hands and inhaled deeply.

"Are you nervous?" She tilted her head in inquiry. "I admit I am. I have not been in the presence of a man in a long time, much less a mighty warrior such as you. I am afraid I have forgotten the protocol. Should I kneel before you?"

"No." Dante jerked back as if she'd slapped him, held up his hands to halt her movement towards him. "You're fine just how you are."

"Do you not care for my presence?" As much confidence as her question held, internally, she feared he would say he didn't. Odd, since she'd not ever cared what a male thought of her.

"It's nothing like that." The red on his angelic face deepened. "I've heard of the great Oracles, but I've never actually met one."

"I've heard of the great Thracian Elites, but I've never actually met one." She couldn't help but grin at him.

"I'm only an apprentice."

"I'm only a priestess."

They shared a mutual understanding and a smile. His silken lips curved up and Lysandra mirrored the action. *Holy gods and goddesses*, he had the most sensual smile she'd ever beheld. It created heat deep in her gut.

"Here is a promise, mighty warrior; if you will accept me, I shall not reject you."

He nodded. "It's funny, only a few days ago, I had nearly this same conversation with Avery. She was raised in the human world, had no idea about what she was. She's a hugger." Dante chuckled. "She didn't know what a big deal touch was to many people, including Ryse."

"What transpired?"

"Brenden was raised in the human world too and they have that touchy-feely thing in common. Then Yankee referred to her as hot."

"Hot? Because she manipulates fire?"

Dante cleared his throat. "No, uh, hot as in attractive, sexually."

Lysandra's eyes widened and she gasped. "He should not say such things about another man's mate."

"I asked her if she was comfortable with him being so familiar in his language, and she said that she didn't know the stinkin' rules." He imitated Avery's accent and Lysandra giggled. "Then she told me that I could speak freely with her."

"And you did?"

He looked into her eyes. "Yes. I instantly trusted Princess Avery, long before she ever told me I could."

"Why?" What did a woman have to do to earn Dante's trust? And why did she suddenly want it so desperately?

"The first time we ever saw each other, she walked up and stuck her hand out for me to shake it." He demonstrated, thrusting his hand out in the air, then placed it back in his lap. "Most people who are aware of my gift guard themselves around me. When I touch someone, I create a boundary. No Olympian magic can exist within it, not even that person's gifts. That didn't stop Avery. She was being polite, uncaring of anything else. Even after she knew, she never shied away."

"You seem quite taken with Avery." Jealousy, evil and angry, rose up her spine. The emotion caught her off guard. The icy tone of her voice tipped Dante off that something was amiss.

"It's biology, nothing more," he said quickly. "Thracians are drawn to Divine Graces as nature's way of insuring we will protect them with our lives, claimed or not. It's nothing more than that."

Didn't she feel foolish now? "Of course, warrior. I should have remembered such."

"I confess, biology or not, Avery won my loyalty by not acting crazy about my gift."

"Show me how it works."

"What?" Dante shot to his feet to put distance between them. He shook his head and huffed.

"Show me what Avery did to earn your trust. I know it will not be painful."

"No, of course not. But you don't need to experience it. Take my word on this." Again, he stepped away.

Lysandra stood to face him. "I'm not afraid," she assured him with confidence that this man would never put her in harm's way.

"I read that Oracles don't like to be touched." He crossed his arms over his chest, but not in defiance or to ward her off. It was more protective-looking. And she did not skip over the fact that he was reading about her kind.

"Typically, they do not. Touch often stimulates visions for Oracles. If I understand you correctly, that shouldn't matter in your case. Please, I would like to learn of your unique gift." Lysandra held out her hands, palms up. She smiled warmly, hoping to encourage him to trust her.

Dante sighed. "If you insist." Dante covered her hands with his. The warmth from his body invaded her arm and soaked into her bones. His aura changed, lighting up upon their connection.

"I feel nothing." That was only a half truth. The things she felt had nothing to do with his gifts and everything to do with the way his rough hands covered hers or how his clean scent invaded her mind, stimulating her senses.

"Try to have a vision."

Lysandra closed her eyes and reached deep within to the sacred place in her soul where she was joined with the gods. She sought out the link to their divine presence and…

"Nothing. I can't feel the gods within me."

Dante dropped his hand and put distance between them. "There you go. Now you've seen the extent of my gifts."

His tone, the quiet sadness therein, hinted that her lack of reaction was nothing new. Was he disappointed with this power?

"Tell me, warrior, how have you used your gift? You must have stories." She turned to the couch and sat down, patting the seat next to her.

He remained standing, but leaned against the fireplace to relax. "Oddly enough, the best stories I have all revolve around her." He pointed into the next room, where Avery lay sleeping.

"I wish to hear."

"I thought you were an Oracle? Haven't you *seen* everything?" His lips twitched and his eyes crinkled with amusement.

There was a fluttering in her stomach when he smiled again. Her pulse quickened and her cheeks heated. "You tease me?"

"Maybe." He looked down at the floor, his foot twisted at the heel.

Bashful. This huge beast was *bashful*. She took delight in this revelation.

"Tell me your point of view, warrior. I can see events but not the individual thoughts or emotions of the people playing them out."

It took him a moment to decide he would speak to her. When he did, Lysandra sat still as death, listening to his every word. Watching his lips move gave her a warm sensation in her core. What was this feeling? Why was it so strong around this male in particular? Brenden, Philippe, Cutter, even Yankee, in his own way, were all handsome men. Brenden's heart belonged to another, but the other men were not mated. She didn't have this reaction to them. Dante, only Dante turned her upside down.

When his tale was done, she had a hand over her chest and her pulse pounded beneath. "You highly underestimate your role in this situation, warrior. Without you, Avery might have done something tragic or the teleporter might have taken Salina away. You were a vital part of Princess Avery's survival."

Dante ran a hand through his blond hair and the shining strands fell back around his ears. "I have a lot to learn about real life or death situations. The preparation in the training center is adequate, but I plan on speaking with Master Ryse when he gets back."

"Your insight would be of great value, I have no doubt."

"Thank you, Lysandra." The way he said her name made her breath catch. His tone, so soft and kind, was laced with what she hoped was affection.

Wait. This could not happen. What was she doing? She'd vowed her life to the service of the temple of Apollo. That vow required her body and mind to be pure, not allowing lustful thoughts or unclean acts. These intimate moments with Dante were a violation of those rules. The more time she spent with him, the more she fell under the spell of his voice or lost herself in his eyes, the closer she came to a cliff. This was a slippery slope. One wrong move and she would endanger her position in the temple.

"You're welcome, warrior." She intentionally used a title and not his given name. Names were linked to relationships, and relationships were out of the question for a priestess of the temple. "I must get back to work. Do enjoy your book."

⚊⚊ ⚬⚬ ⚊⚊

There was a very high probability of Dante losing his cool. He sat in the conference room with Bren and Yankee, going over the week's schedule. Everything was fine until Yankee opened his mouth about Lysandra. Things had quickly gone downhill.

"Give it a damn break, Yankee," Brenden sighed as he threw his head back against the office chair.

"Seriously," Dante agreed with a shake of his head. "Have some bloody respect."

Yankee laughed, his eyes no livelier for the action. "What? She's a fine piece of ass. Lysandra is prime flesh. You saw her naked. I know you didn't miss those tits." He held up his hands as if fondling the subject of his obsession. "They were perfect, ripe for the picking."

"Enough." Dante slapped his pen on the table before he broke the thing in half. "I'll not have you speaking of the lady in such barbaric terms. She is an Oracle and you should—"

"Keep my hands off your woman?" Yankee arched a brow and puckered his lips to make kissing noises at Dante.

"No. Of course not. I mean, yes, you should keep your paws off her—"

"Little Brother has the paws."

"—but she is not my woman."

Brenden shot Yankee the finger for the reference to Bren's inner beast, but it didn't faze the jerk. It was a low blow from Yankee. Bren was considered a mutt among Olympians, able to shift into many animals at once creating a gruesome creature.

"She's got the hots for you, Ken Doll. Asked me why none of the Elites were mated, if it was against some rule. She was especially interested in you. I'm telling ya, give it another week and she'll find a new excuse to spend time with you." Yankee kicked his boots up on the table and folded his arms behind his head, knowing he'd struck a nerve.

"Leave it alone, Yankee." Brenden rubbed his temples. "She's sworn to the temple. She's off limits. Can we please get back to this schedule? You're giving me a headache."

"I agree with Brenden. You're wasting valuable time." Dante took a deep breath and studied the rotations for the next week. They couldn't have a pattern of who watched Avery. They all had duties outside of that task that needed to be accomplished so no one grew suspicious.

Yankee leaned over the table and eyed Dante with a hard stare. "You know what's a waste of time? Picking a fucking flower every day before you go to see her."

Dante stilled.

Brenden popped his head up. "You *what?*" His face wrinkled up into an expression of disgust.

"Tell him." Yankee waved his arm. "Tell Brenden about how you bring her a rose every day, how she keeps them in a vase next to her bed. Not out in the open, but by her *bed.*"

Brenden let out an exasperated sigh and dropped his head, his chin resting on his chest. "Are you insane? C'mon, man. I thought you were smarter than that. For Ares' sake, Dante, that girl is basically married to Apollo. Besides, don't you see the situation I'm in with Nikki? Why the hell would you want to follow that path? Don't bring her gifts and don't get cozy with her. Nothing good can come of it."

"I'm not getting cozy with her. I understand and respect her vow to the gods," Dante argued. "She enjoys flowers but never gets to go out in the gardens. In case you haven't noticed, she works nonstop, all day. It's a small token of thanks for her many hours pent up in that room."

Yankee rolled his eyes. "Pfft! It's a token of you wanting to tap that ass. There's a thought, the two virgins losing it to one another. You want to pop her cherry?"

"You're a bastard." Dante stood and shoved the piece of paper towards Brenden. "Put me down for whatever. I need to get out of here."

"She's getting to you, Ken Doll. Be careful, women are a bad addiction," Yankee called to his back just before Dante slammed the door to the conference room.

What did that crude, arrogant ass know about women? To Yankee, all women were sexual toys and nothing more. Gods, what he would give to see Yankee turned upside down by a woman. Wouldn't that be a sight?

It would never happen. He was too full of anger and vengeance to let a woman soothe him with love and tenderness. Dante blew off his ramblings and concentrated on avoiding his father and continuing his studies and duties.

Yankee continued to be a pain in his side, leaving reminders of their conversation everywhere. Dante entered the suite a couple days later to see Lysandra nibbling on a bowl full of cherries as she folded sheets. *Bastard*. Every time she slid one of those red drops across her lips Dante's pants tightened. The innocent woman had no clue what lustful thoughts played in his mind.

"Would you like a cherry? I can share mine?" Lysandra asked, holding out the bowl.

"Oh, dear Zeus." Blood drained from his head and rushed to his groin. He clenched his jaws and focused on anything in the room but those red lips.

A couple of days later, the palace chef brought up a freshly baked cherry pie for Dante, compliments of Yankee.

"Sonofabitch," Dante muttered when he saw Valarie holding the sweet-smelling treat. Her face dropped until he kindly thanked her and accepted the pie.

Dante took it right to the wing of the palace where the Elites' quarters were. He picked the lock on Yankee's door and slipped in. Pulling back the sheets, Dante smeared the pie all over his pillow and bedding.

"Dream of that, jerk."

Yankee's cursing could be heard all over the palace.

CHAPTER SIXTEEN

DANTE COULDN'T HELP BUT WATCH LYSANDRA—NO, LYSA—OUT OF the corner of his eye. She'd asked to be called Lysa, since it sounded more modern. For the last three weeks since her arrival, she'd been more than attentive to Dyna, Avery, and the Elites.

She prayed with and for Brenden who slipped further and further away with each agonizing week of waiting. He feared with the passing days that Nikki would die, but Lysa reminded him that earthly time and heavenly time moved at different speeds. The gods would need Nikki to testify against Salina, they would not let her die. Brenden was taking her word for it. He still kept to himself and came to talk to Avery often.

Yankee continued the cherry references and poor Lysa was none the wiser. She thought he had a weird obsession, nothing more. Thank the gods.

Dante, however, felt a ping of joy when it was time for his shift. For three weeks, he had dreamt of her body. The image of her standing naked and strong, like a true goddess, was burned in his brain. He could recall every hill and valley of her torso, the sweep of her hips, the curves of her modest breasts. The memory tortured him relentlessly. If the gods had sent her to test his strength, they picked a perfect specimen.

"Eat your dinner, warrior," she said softly. "You need your strength."

"Do you imply that I am lacking?" Dante retorted, desiring to see a beautiful blush spread across her ivory cheeks. She was so innocent, so pure, and a bit naive. He forgot everything else when he was with her.

Her eyes widened. "No. I would never insult you in such manner."

Ah, there it was. "But you would insult me in other manners?" It was almost cruel to tease her, but he loved it so.

"Of course not. I would never mean to disrespect a great—" She noticed him grinning and narrowed her eyes. "You antagonize me? Why?"

Dante had spent hours researching the Oracles of Delphi. The humans had their stories of women high off chemicals, but that was not what the Olympian histories recorded. In fact, the gods respected the Pythia. Their guidance to Deities of Earth was priceless—back when the Deities consulted them. A woman such as Lysa would be taken into the temple and adopted into a family of all women who resided there. Humans would compare them to monks. They take a vow of celibacy upon joining the temple and their bodies became vessels of the gods. No men were allowed in their sanctuary so as not to compromise their purity.

He knew he should feel guilty, thinking of her the way he did when she was promised to the gods, but she'd become the brightest part of his days. No matter what crap his father gave him, or how Prince Ashton bothered him, or how Yankee teased him relentlessly; all he had to do was step into Lysa's presence and all his stress melted away.

She learned quickly how to adjust to all the changes, including dealing with him.

"It is good for you," he answered her question.

Her eyes darted away. "I'm sure you are correct, warrior."

He went back to reading his book and she folded clean sheets for Avery's bed. Her soft humming turned into singing. It centered him and he closed his eyes to listen to the melody for a moment. Her voice was high and light, almost like bells. The clarity of her tone could put a man in a trance if he let it. Lysa could truly calm the beast that ran through his Thracian blood.

"Are you tired, warrior? I can be still so that you might rest."

"No, no. I enjoy your singing. Your voice is pleasing to the ear." Dante once again lost his breath when she turned her shy face away from him and pushed her black hair behind her ear. His experience with women was next to nonexistent. But he enjoyed their tennis match of flirtatious glances.

Lysa sat down in a chair. Her nearness caused his body to stiffen and his heart to accelerate. "I remember my parents always had music in our home." She stared off into space, her mind in another time. "My mother had a voice that would've made Apollo jealous. My father played the harp. He was gifted at stringed instruments. We danced and sang almost daily." Her shoulders fell, the light in her eyes dimmed. "When I joined the temple, I mourned the loss. They do not sing that often in Delphi and they do not dance at all."

"You have found your songs again, here on Earth?"

"Yes." She smiled. "Lady Dynasty sings with me. I thoroughly enjoy it."

"As I enjoy listening."

Lysa moved closer and Dante shifted in his chair. The scent of roses lingered on her skin. Images of Lysa naked in a tub with floating petals filled his mind until he couldn't concentrate. *Dearest gods, give me strength.*

"Can I confess something to you?"

"Of course." He leaned in, eager to hear her secrets. Her dove-gray eyes captured him at once.

Breathe, breathe you fool. You cannot pass out in front of her.

"In the city of Delphi, there is abundant beauty. The flowers never wilt, the soil never dries from lack of rain. The sky is a canvas of painted art, the clouds set in place and flawless in their shape. When Rhea does make it rain, it's a perfectly synchronized orchestra. Each drop lands in a designated spot. Everything is beautiful, but everything is dull. There are no vibrant colors; they are all muted. The entire atmosphere is designed for optimal comfort and no distractions. Things are so different here."

He ached to touch her and he clenched his fists in resistance. Why the hell did she have to be so tempting, so irresistible?

She swallowed and took a deep breath. "You mustn't tell anyone what I'm about to say. Do you swear, with the gods as your witness?"

Dante gave in. He touched the back of her hand and leaned in closer. His heart beat wildly in his chest as he met at her intense stare. "I swear, milady. You can confide in me."

"I'm not like the others," she whispered. "Rhea sent me here because I did not adjust well to Delphi. My soul did not enjoy the muted colors or the synchronized rains. It was as if I was muted as well. For centuries, I've longed for the vibrancy of life again." Her face crumpled and she looked down at where their hands lay together in her lap. She trailed her fingers absently over the lines of his knuckles. "That's why I've never become one of the Pythia. I'm grateful to be of service to the gods, and I have tried. Oh blessed Zeus, how I have tried. But I have failed."

"No." Dante cupped her cheek, the soft skin like silk under his massive hands. Her eyes met his and everything else in the universe faded away. All he wanted was to be the man who fixed her broken spirit, to be the man who made her feel worthy and happy. He wanted to be the man she confided all her secrets in and turned to when she was lost. Hell, he just wanted to be her man. "You have not failed. There is no sin in wanting a different life. Not everyone is destined to live as the Pythia do. You've sacrificed a piece of yourself for the gods. I know they are proud with your efforts." Dante dropped his hand from her cheek. "I'm sorry that you view this task as a punishment."

"I don't," she replied quickly. "I, I simply..." Her shoulders slumped; she touched her trembling lips and closed her eyes. "That is a lie. My mission here is important, I know. But I feel caged in this room. It is like a punishment, to have the world just beyond these walls, but not be able to touch it, feel it." Her eyes met his once more. The building moisture nearly killed him. "The roses you bring me, they are a most treasured gift. They are my taste of the outside. I can never repay you."

"Did the gods instruct you to never leave Avery's side?" Dante questioned, his mind turning with a possible solution to her problem.

"Not exactly. Why?" She straightened, her chest moving with deeper breaths.

Dante recalled all too quickly how her breasts fell and rose when she stood naked. He mirrored her position, his chest puffed out and his breath coming faster.

"If Brenden will come sit with Avery, you can slip out the back of the palace and right into the woods behind the stables."

"It's not possible."

"Why not?"

"What if I am caught? What if someone asks questions?"

Dante pursed his lips, going over all the places in the Haven Lysa could go and be safe. The only problem would be getting her there.

"What if I can make this work? Would you try?"

"Will you take me?"

His mind misfired and, for a moment, he forgot all about going outside. He wished her offer were something far more carnal. Air left his lungs in a rush and she picked up on his reaction. *Damn it.*

"Outside, I mean. In the woods?" She closed her eyes and placed a hand over her mouth. Those creamy white cheeks pinked with blush again. "Let me rephrase; will you come with me?"

As aroused as he was by her innocence, he took that statement straight to the gutter too. *Gods!* What he would give to come with her, to watch her climax while she pushed him over the edge with her. *Oh, sweet rapture.*

Dante cleared his throat and nodded, unable to form the right words.

To his own humility, he realized he was as inexperienced as she was. Once people learned of his gifts, they had little to do with him. Women appreciated his visual appeal, but none had ever made advances once they knew he could block their Olympian gifts. He dared not go into the human realm to find lovers. His sand-colored eyes would have quickly labeled him as different.

He shook off the negativity and set out to find Lysa an ounce of freedom.

"You must be bat-shit crazy," Yankee scoffed when Dante consulted Lady Dyna and a couple of the Elites.

"Language, Samuel." Dyna shook her head. She addressed Lysa, "I'm sorry that I have overlooked your needs, dear one. Truly, if I had to stay in this room every minute of every day, I would go crazy. Forgive me for not picking up on your distress sooner."

Lysandra knelt in front of the queen. "You are not to blame, Majesty. I do not wish to be a distraction or hindrance."

Dyna lifted her by the shoulders. "You are neither. I have a solution. Come with me." Dyna led them into the closet of her sleeping chambers. Behind a rack of clothing was a hidden door complete with a number key pad. Dyna typed in four numbers. "This tunnel was built centuries ago; very few know of it. It seems like you need in on the secret." She smiled and pushed open the door. "Down the stairs and there is another door." She rattled off a four-digit key pad number. "Follow the tunnel to the right. It will lead you far into the mountain wilderness. It is far from the village, on the very edges of the Haven. No one will see you. Take your time."

"Thank you, milady." Dante took a flashlight from the interior wall and turned it on.

"Just for the record," Yankee said, his arms braced on the frame of the closet door. "I still say this is a stupid idea."

"We'll be careful," Dante assured them.

"I hope so. You sure you don't want to pack some cherries to snack on?"

"Leaving now." Dante gave Lysandra a gentle push through the door. He heard Dyna ask why on earth they would want cherries. Yankee snickered.

At the bottom of the stairs was a short hallway that housed a massive metal door like a vault entrance. He typed in the four numbers and the door swung open silently.

Of course, the tunnel was clean; it was created by magic and guarded by magic. He could feel it rippling on the walls. This series of tunnels was an emergency escape route for the royal family.

"Can you see adequately?" Lysandra whispered.

"Yes."

"Good. Because I cannot."

Her hand touched the small of his back and clenched in his shirt, barely missing the weapons tucked into his belt. Instinctively, he reached around and took her hand in his.

"I have you, milady."

"I know you do."

He caught the soft hint of a smile in her voice and his heart flipped in his chest. Her small hand was warm and snugly tucked into his. It felt…natural, right. And it shouldn't have.

As they reached the exterior door, Dante released her hand and immediately felt the absence.

Focus.

"I'm going to go out first and scout the area." He handed her the flashlight. "I want to get a feel for where we are. The perimeter of the Haven is heavily guarded right now. I want to make sure not even another Thracian will find us."

Lysa nodded, her eyes wide, her hands gripping the flashlight for dear life.

Stairs led upward to another massive metal entrance. The vault door was hard to open and he had to push a foot of moss and debris out of the way. The tunnel flooded with natural light and he blinked to adjust his eyes.

"Don't be too long." Lysa's lips narrowed in a strained smile.

"Fear not; I won't let anything happen to you."

His assurance allowed her to smile to soften into something real.

Knowing she was afraid, even if only a little, Dante took spare minutes to jog around the area, studying the layout, and finding the roof of the palace and Thracian Training Center further down the mountain, the village nestled in the opposite side of the valley.

Assessing the area as safe, he opened the door and held out his hand to help Lysandra up the stairs. She willingly came, her face alight with joy. Dove gray eyes sparkled and ruby lips stretched wide. Pink touched her cheeks and he could all but feel her excitement. Her aura rippled with happiness.

Dante feared he would bend every rule to see that incredible smile on her face. Damned if he would ever admit it, but Yankee was right – women were addictive.

Lysandra could no more contain her enthusiasm than the clouds could contain the rain or the sun could contain its heat. It poured out of her. The moment she stepped out into the forest, she took a deep breath.

"Ah," she sighed. Leaves were wet from a recent shower. Dirt, stirred up by small animals. Pine needles. Rainwater dripped from the leaves high above. A nearby creek trickled down the slope. She walked deeper into the trees, touched their rough bark, and heard the crunch of the forest floor beneath her feet. Hidden among the leaves and moss were wildflowers. Not many, but enough that she had to bend down and examine the delicate yellow petals. The color was so vibrant, so happy that her soul sang out in praise.

When she turned around to find Dante, he was leaning against a huge trunk, arms crossed over his chest, smile crossing his face. He watched her with open amusement.

He did this for me. The thought hit her hard. Dante had made this possible simply for her own enjoyment. Did this mean that he cared? Were his smile and his twinkling eyes a sign of affection? She truly hoped so.

"It seems silly to you, doesn't it, my obsession with the outdoors?"

"No, I'm envious of your carefree love of the Earth. Are you sure you're not part Gaian?"

She laughed and buried her fingers in the moist soil as if to anchor herself to the moment. "Funny you should say that. My father was. My mother was the one with visions."

"That explains a lot." He pushed off the tree and motioned with his hand for her to follow. They hiked uphill and to the southeast for several minutes. The trickle of the creek became the steady flow of a stream.

Twice Lysandra had to scurry to catch up because she stopped to look at a flower on the ground or upwards at the pattern of sunlight streaming through the trees. Greens, browns, blues, reds. The colors were incredible. The intricate patterns of leaves and the texture of the tree bark, all of it called to her, begged to be explored. When they stood on the bank of the stream, Lysandra breathed in the scent of the water, fresh and cool.

Perfect. It was all so perfect. Not the illusion of perfection as in Delphi, but real, touchable perfection. The type of natural wonders that sparked all the senses. Her chest contracted and she felt a funny wetness trickle down her cheeks.

Tears. She was actually crying. Joy overflowed her heart.

"Thank you…*Dante.*" She whispered his name for the first time, her voice laden with emotions. "This means so much to me." She laughed and wiped one of her cheeks, but the tears kept coming.

Dante reached up with a tenderness seeming at odds with his giant body and pushed back a loose strand of hair. His eyes were soft, so unique in their color and intensity. "It is my pleasure, Lysandra."

He tucked her hand in the crook of his elbow. They stood in silence and listened to the water. This was what she missed in Delphi. Companionship, touch, the intimacy of having another person to stand with. She leaned her head against his arm and sighed.

CHAPTER SEVENTEEN

Taking Lysa into the mountains became one of Dante's favorite activities. Like everything he did, they kept the visits sporadic, so as not to draw attention. Sometimes they were in the mornings, sometimes they would have lunch by the creek.

This was their first evening trip. Brenden volunteered to stay close to Dyna's suite while they ventured out.

Lysa stepped out of the dressing area and Dante nearly swallowed his tongue. Even Bren froze.

"I've never worn pants before." Lysa fidgeted with her new pair of jeans. The suckers fit her like a second skin and accentuated every curve. She ran her hands over her stomach and tugged at the teal button-up shirt. Another first for her, as were the hiking boots on her feet. "It might take me a while to adjust." She cast her eyes to Dante, but he was busy trying to keep his tongue in his mouth and the drool off his chin.

Bren saved him. "You look very modern, Lys. Just like the girl next door." He smiled widely and Lysa blushed under his compliments.

Lys? That snapped Dante out of his lustful stupor. Lys? Brenden had a special nickname for his—*oh boy*. She wasn't *his* anything, now was she? Lysandra belonged to Apollo and if Dante had a damn brain in his head, he would remember that.

"Ready to go?" He pushed through Bren and snagged her coat. The nights were cooling off and if Master Ryse didn't hurry, it would be winter by the time he and the others returned.

Before Dante and Lysa snuck out the private exit, Brenden grabbed his arm and pulled him aside. "You're headed down a dangerous path, bro. Don't fall for her."

Dante blanched. "What makes you think that I'm—"

"The same way y'all knew I fell for Nikki." One blond brow rose and his lips thinned. His southern accent was so much like Avery's.

"I appreciate your concern, Bren. But you need not worry."

"Funny, that's what I said." Bren glanced down the staircase where Lysa beamed up at him.

Knowing his secret was out, Dante nodded and went down the staircase to join Lysa. He couldn't deny the physical attraction; the woman was his personal version of perfection, a real life Snow White. Even now his body stirred as he descended the staircase and saw her waiting by the door. Her porcelain face turned to him, her eyes sparkling and her smile stretching wide. She loved their escapes.

They scurried out the exit and deep into the woods behind the palace. He marveled at the way she danced over the exposed rocks, her light footfalls barely heard on the leaves. Perhaps she really was an angel.

Lysa stopped and took in a deep breath. Her eyes closed and her shoulders moved up and down, her chest expanding as if she could capture the entire forest with one inhalation.

Merciful Zeus, he needed to get a grip on his hormones. He was a soldier and he needed to act like it. This wasn't simply a joy ride. He scanned the area and made sure no one had followed them. The only sounds were the forest creatures and the wind rustling the leaves in the tall trees. He didn't sense another aura for nearly a mile.

"Do you feel it? The winter is coming," Lysa whispered. "The animals are preparing and the leaves cringe at the thought of the cold. I've never seen such a beautiful place as this." She glanced back at him. "Have you been in this part of the world long?"

"About five years. Before this, I lived at the Haven in Rome with my family."

"Your father is a guardian of the prince. Have you spent time with him during their visit?"

Dante clasped his hands behind his back and looked down at the ground, noticing how the moss grew on the rocks. "My father did not care to spend time with me until I grew into adulthood and my gifts developed. Even then," he sighed, "it was very little. Now, it is a strain for us both."

"That saddens me."

"Why?" He tilted his head up at her, curious as to why she would care.

"My parents were devoted to me. I was blessed with the most loving family. My mother doted over me and my father treated me like a little goddess. I can't imagine a childhood without them. They were proud of me when I joined the temple. My mother cried because it meant that my body and soul would be separated, a technical death. But they were proud that I gave my life to the service of the gods."

"May I ask how long you've been with the Oracles?"

Her face fell, her eyes lost their luster, and her brow furrowed. He instantly wished he could take the words back.

"Long enough to watch my parents live on this Earth, die, and ascend to the Heavens."

"Don't you see them?"

"Delphi is separate from Olympia, where the souls of our people spend eternity. No one but the highest of gods enter Delphi, mainly Apollo. Rhea alone can set foot in our temple. It is a very solitary life." She gingerly sat down on a boulder, then perched on the edge of a lightly trickling stream. "We see everything and everyone. The pools of the Pythia are full of faces and events. Every ripple is the birth, life, and death of one of our people. But we are so far removed from it all."

"Did you know that going in? Before you surrendered your life to the gods, did you realize how isolated you would be?" Dante stood close to her and watched the water weave through the rocks, over the dips and curves of the land. The warmth from her body reached his leg, although he didn't touch her.

"One never knows what they might get into with the gods." She chuckled. "It's not as if they have ever sent an Oracle back to Earth." Lines formed between her eyes and Dante wanted to lean down and kiss them away. She truly believed she was shamed somehow by coming here.

"Their secrets are vast and their knowledge is immeasurable. Make no mistake; there are those of the gods who simply tolerate mankind and the Olympians of Earth. If the decision were handed to them, they would rid the universe of us all and start over. Then there are those gods and goddesses who adore us. They fawn over our achievements and ache when we ache. Rhea was once like this, until she lost her connection with her children."

Dante knelt down, perched his weight on one knee, and picked up a smooth, rounded stone. "What do you mean?"

"She allowed Zeus to take over. This is why our people consider him our ultimate authority. In most circumstances, he is. Even Zeus answers to Rhea. As do Hades and Poseidon. The fact that she created Avery, sent her to Earth, and revived her after death is incredible. It could be the beginning of something wonderful."

Dante stared at Lysa. He couldn't help it. Her knowledge of the gods and the Heavens was impressive and enlightening. When she turned her eyes on him, he looked away. If he allowed himself to indulge in her innocent stare, his obsession would only grow. Instead, he thought of the obvious reasons they couldn't be together. They were both bound to the service of the gods.

"I've often felt blessed that Avery chose me," he confessed in a quiet tone. "Until she picked me out of the crowd, I was less than a leper. I had few friends in the training academy and there were times when I know they hesitated to shake my hand." Holding out his hands, he examined the scars and calluses. Warrior's hands. Not the hands of a gentleman who could delicately stroke the cheek of the beauty beside him. "So many nights I've wondered what the gods could have in store for me. What was my purpose? Why do I have such a rare and fear-inspiring gift? Could they not have given me something that would…"

"Make your father proud?" Lysa picked the words from his thoughts.

"Humph." Dante shook his head and stood, tossing a rock into the flowing stream. "I've come to the conclusion that unless I become Master Thracian, I cannot live up to what he wants me to be. Even then, he would resent me for gaining more favor with the gods than he has. He's angry with me now because I am an Elite. He might deny it, but I have achieved something he coveted for many decades."

"Do you long for his approval so desperately?" Lysa's question was birthed from her genuine concern and he could sense it in the way she looked up at him.

"I did. Until I saw the truth. He is a mighty man in his own right and his own mind. I've caused a great rift in our relationship by becoming an Elite. Yet, I finally discovered my purpose. My mistress is a kind woman and my Master is an honorable man. They have each given me more approval than I could have ever desired. I have the Elites as brothers. It is a far better gift than that of my father's acceptance." He held up his hands. "And none of them shy away from my touch."

Lysa smiled, her ruby lips stretching wide. She held up a hand and wiggled her fingers at him. "Your assistance, warrior?"

Eagles took wing in his gut as he reached down and slid his palm against hers. "Milady."

She closed her fingers around his much larger hand and pulled herself up. "Mighty warrior, I shall never shy away from you either. It does not take a vision from the gods to see why Lady Avery chose you." She bowed her head to him and he returned the gesture. They stood, staring at one another, their hands clasped.

What was he doing? He couldn't fall for her, he just couldn't. It was impossible, irresponsible, and a lot of other words that end in -ible.

"Thank you for helping me." Lysa released his hands and started back. She was two steps in front of him before he gathered his courage and called out.

"Lysa?" He cleared his throat as she turned to face him. He clenched and unclenched his fists, then wrung out his hands. "Would it be, uh, might I have permission to…" He swallowed hard. "May I hold your hand while we make our way back?"

⚊⚊ ⚬ ⚊⚊

Lysandra was momentarily stunned. He wanted to hold her hand? As courting couples did? Or perhaps this was a warrior's way of keeping his charge close. Perhaps she should clarify?

There were already so many emotions that bubbled up inside when it came to Dante. Oracles were not supposed to feel so much. They were trained, *she* was trained, to view the world with neutrality and dispassion.

Oracles didn't take sides, they didn't judge right and wrong, they didn't make assumptions. They simply interpreted the visions they received. One of the Pythia told her that they were heartless. They must be. Lysandra couldn't imagine the heartache they witnessed. It was best to distance themselves from the emotions of their visions.

Dante, however, tipped the scales. The way her body reacted to him was a surprise. The way her mind connected with him was a treasure. The way her heart desired him was like nothing she'd ever experienced. But…what did a woman such as she know of love and matters of the heart?

On the other hand, Lysandra wasn't in Delphi any longer. Rhea had admitted that Lysandra was different from the others of the temple. Maybe, just maybe, she should attempt to understand these abundant new emotions.

"I have to ask. What does this gesture mean to you?"

She was delighted at the way he stumbled and stammered over his words. "Well, um, it means, it's a way of…I-I would enjoy the connection as we walk." Red washed over his face and his smile was shy, reserved.

The bashful beast. Such a contradiction, this man. The thought of him desiring her was preposterous—but possible, judging by his current nervous fidgeting.

Lysandra held out her hand. "As would I."

Dante smiled, his sand-colored eyes glimmering. He took her hand in his and tucked her arm close to his side until they had to walk in sync lest their hands be separated. It was a most pleasant sensation. Their thighs brushed and her body rested against him.

"Dante, will you tell me about your duties to Avery? When she awakens, what will you do?"

"Bren and I will both be at her side. Truth be told, I'm not sure. Avery and Ryse are not like other royals. There might be a dinner party every now and then, but I have a feeling guarding Avery will be much more adventurous." He chuckled.

Precisely what she feared. The excitement in his voice told her all she needed to know. He was proud of his station and ready to follow Avery to the ends of the Earth—even outside of this Haven if necessary.

"These are uncertain times, though," he continued. "All I know is that once she awakens, she has to be my first priority. It is the fate of all Thracians to be at the service of the Olympians we protect." He stopped walking, lifted his face to the darkening sky, and took a deep breath. "I've been waiting for this all my life. To have a purpose, to protect those under my care." He turned his eyes to her. "Avery has to be my first priority. Do you understand what that means?"

Even as his words shattered what hope she might have had, she lifted her chin and squared her shoulders. "Of course. It is no different from my vow to the temple of Apollo and the other gods. My life is theirs, my body is theirs. They are my first priority."

Dante's jaws clenched. "As it should be."

They continued to the palace tunnel in silence. She didn't know what he was feeling, but she didn't think it could be any worse than the loss of what could have been. They were both chained—voluntarily— to their appointed tasks. Their respective vows brought them together and they were the exact things that would keep them apart.

CHAPTER EIGHTEEN

H E SPIED ON THE YOUNG THRACIAN AS HE WALKED THROUGH THE gardens of the palace. Ashton was curious as to why Dante came here daily and picked a single rose. They had to be for Lady Dynasty because he always took them to her suite when she tutored him.

What was the boy's angle? Was he simply trying to please the widowed queen or perhaps he was overly fond of her? That could be the ammunition he needed to bring the Elites down.

Ashton would find out.

"Dante." He forced a wide grin that put people at ease around him. Dante's body went rigid for a split second before he returned the greeting.

"Beautiful day, isn't it?" Ashton ran a hand through his blond hair as it whipped about in the breeze. He looked to the skies as if he didn't have a care in the world, save soaking up the sun.

"Yes, prince. It's a perfect day for a walk." Dante brushed his hair back, the strands of gold falling in his face.

"I've always enjoyed the gardens here. When I was a child, this was my favorite place to play with Sa—" He swallowed, his eyes darting away as he played the role of lamenting brother. "With my sister. The castle was full of children then. Ryse, Hayden, Evander, and so many screaming little girls; it would drive us all bonkers." The two men shared a chuckle. "It's different now."

"Troy's death has cast a shadow here," Dante observed. "It's as if the walls mourn his passing."

Ashton nodded and shoved his hands in his pockets. "I agree. But there will be a time of rejoicing soon enough. We are Olympians. We never mourn long."

Dante nodded his head in agreement but said nothing. After a couple weeks of this mindless chatter, Ashton had to change tactics. Dante must've been warned off trusting him, but giving up wasn't an option. If he could get even the slightest bit of information from Dante, it would be worth it. He merely had to find a weakness. Xavier mentioned Dante took after his mother and was close to his family, especially his sisters.

"Your father told me something today," Ashton said. "Did you know that your sister wants to come visit you?"

"Really?" Dante's brows rose high on his head, the first true emotion he'd shown. "Which one?"

Shit. Xavier had twelve daughters and, for all their years together, he couldn't recall ever giving a damn enough to memorize all their blasted names. Seriously, twelve kids? How did Xavier even remember with that many ankle-biters running amuck?

Ashton pinched his lips and looked down at the ground as if trying to recall the conversation. "Bloody hell, what did he say? I was so preoccupied with my mother I was only half listening. He said you two were very close."

"Ariabella?" There was excitement in Dante's voice and his eyes gleamed at the thought.

Ah. Here was Ashton's chance. He snapped his fingers. "Yes, Ariabella. You didn't know?"

Dante's face went placid again. "No, I can't say I did."

"Oops! Maybe it was supposed to be a secret." He shrugged. "I wanted to tell you, though. I know it's been so long since you've seen your family. You must miss them terribly."

"I do. Especially Ariabella. I'd like to see her." He spoke absently, distracted enough to show his weakness for his sister.

Before Ashton could make promises he had no intention of keeping, Dante spoke. "I'm afraid I will have to discourage her trip. I don't believe it's a good time to be traveling."

"Do you think the Haven is unprotected?"

"The Havens are supposed to be on lockdown. I don't imagine even a daughter of Xavier could get through. It's simply not a good time for our people. The kings are gone. The rogues attack young Olympian women. She is safest at home. Sadly, I would be a distracted host right now, anyhow. I should talk with my mother and ask her to postpone the visit." Dante headed into the palace with Ashton hot on his heels.

"Don't worry yourself with it. You have so much to do and I've already taken up too much of your time. I'll relay the message." He waved it off. "Tell me, Dante, what will you do now that there is no position for you in Avery's service?"

"My position is secured," Dante said.

Ashton nodded, his lips curving upwards. "That's a shame. I would've liked having you in my ranks."

"I'm honored, prince. But my place is here, as an Elite."

Ashton stood in front of him, looked him dead in the eyes, his grin fading. "There's going to be a day when the Elites will no longer be as," he searched the air for the right word, "*legendary* as they are now. If you're only staying here because you want to be a part of that legend, then you need to understand something." He stepped closer to Dante and whispered, "Thracians in Europe hate them, Dante. I'm only telling you this because I believe you have a greater future ahead. But the soldiers in my country, they loathe the Elites and the way they have no regard for rank or regulations. It would pain me to see you fall into that category. I would hate to see your career as a Thracian compromised because of your affiliation with them.

"If you want to come home, Dante, to see Ariabella as often as you like, you can have a place with my guard. It's not too late to secure a respectable position in my court."

"I cannot work with my father, prince."

Not a full rejection of the idea. Hmm. Was he considering it?

Had Ashton finally hit a nerve with the promise of reuniting with his family?

"Then don't." Ashton shrugged and chuckled. "I'm going to be the Deity of my region one day, Dante. I can place you in any position you wish. All I ask in return is your loyalty." He slapped the Thracian on the shoulder and smiled warmly. "Think about it, lad. Surely you want to see your family more than once a decade. I know young Ariabella would like that, as would your mother."

Dante's eyes flickered up to his and Ashton saw the wheels turning. Dante missed his family. Ashton could use this as bribery. It was almost too easy.

"I'll consider your proposal, Prince Ashton. Thank you. I must attend to my duties now."

"We can chat later." Ashton bid him farewell and watched him go back into the palace. "Come out," he called over his shoulder. Maxim, one of his Thracians loyal to his cause, came to his side. "Put a tail on his sister, Ariabella. I want to be able to grab her at any moment if he decides to rebel. She might come in handy."

"I can keep her close to me—"

"No," Ashton said, knowing Maxim' propensity to hurting women. "That's still Xavier's daughter. We only use her if necessary."

Dante hoisted twenty-five hundred pounds of weights over his chest and back down again nearly fifty times before he began to sweat. Brenden spotted him; his eyes were ringed in red and dark circles hung underneath. Both men decided they needed to work off some physical frustration. The ladies asked for privacy while they cleaned Avery and worked with her limbs so she didn't have any side effects from lying in one position for so long. It was unnerving to see the way Dynasty lifted her with magic and made her sit upright or stand up, much like a puppeteer.

The guys ran and lifted weights in the Thracian Training Center gym until the early hours of the morning. A few other students mingled across the gym, but left Bren and Dante alone for the most part, which was great until Yankee joined them and spread his usual vile cheer.

He flopped down on the bench beside Dante, pressing over four thousand pounds without a spotter and barely using his full effort. Dante could almost feel his testosterone levels dropping. As annoying as it was to be shown up by the smaller man, strength and speed were Yankee's god-given powers. He might look smaller than typical Thracians and walk with a lazy gait, but only a fool would believe their eyes. Yankee worked hard to look as casual and non-impressive as possible.

"Your eyes are popping out of your head," Brenden whispered as he aided Dante with the bar. "Let's call this one, 'kay?"

"Yep." Dante strained to speak and breathe until the bar was firmly in place on the rack. He sat up, appreciating the ache in his muscles.

"What's got you ladies all hormonal? Run out of tampons?" Yankee racked the weights with one hand. He nodded with his chin at the gawking Thracian students as if to say, *yeah, you saw that right.*

Arrogant prick.

"Fuck off, man." Brenden rolled his eyes and sighed. "I've had just about all of you I can stand."

"You know, if you need to talk about your feelings and shit, I hear you can bribe Lysa with flowers."

"I'm leaving." Brenden grabbed a towel and headed to the showers. Dante was right behind him.

"I saw you today, or yesterday." Yankee glanced at his watch. "I saw you talking to Ashton. What did he want?"

"None of your business." Dante scrubbed a towel over his sweat-drenched forehead and gulped water.

"I thought we went over this; it's all of our business."

"Let me rephrase so you will comprehend." Dante glared at him. "If Philippe or Cutter has a concern about my interactions with the prince, they can feel free to discuss it with me. It's none of *your* business."

Yankee threw back his head, bellowing laughter. "Wow. Look who got a pair of steel balls all of a sudden. You get one little show of brotherhood over your old man and suddenly, you're fucking Superman. I think I'm going to have to change your nickname."

"I'm tired of your crap, Yankee."

"What the hell did I do?" He threw his hands up in the air.

"That shit with Lysa has to stop: the cherries, the comments, all of it. Leave her alone."

"You know your problem, Superman? She's your Kryptonite. You want her so bad, you can barely breathe."

"I respect her vows to the gods and wouldn't do anything to cause her to stumble. How many times must I say this?"

"Until your actions mirror your words." Yankee got to his feet and stretched his arm over his head, pulling on his opposite elbow. "You're not fooling anyone, Superman. Do yourself a favor and go get laid. I promise, you go down to the village and find some Elite-chasing broad, work out some of your sexual frustrations on her, and you won't be so damn hung up on the priestess who's sworn off dick."

The thought of sex for sex's sake was not his idea of fun. Dante would never admit the truth of his affections for Lysa. It was a dead end road and he had to deal with it. She'd done nothing to lead him on purposefully and took her vows seriously.

"I don't have to work off anything. There's no...*sexual frustration* there."

"We'll see about that." Yankee grabbed a towel off the rack and wrapped it around his neck, even though he hadn't broken a sweat. "Get your head out of your ass, man. You're a sinking ship."

Dante watched Yankee walk through the gym and wished like hell the guy wasn't as observant as he was.

Dante had to put some space between him and Lysandra. He had to cover his tracks better. Ashton had caught him picking a flower this morning and, while he might have a lie on reserve, it was a close call. His affection for Lysa was causing him to slip. None of them could afford to have people asking questions or poking around in Dynasty's wing of the palace.

Once again, he warred with his duty and his deep obsession with Lysa. He had to keep his mind in the game. Avery depended on it.

CHAPTER NINETEEN

L YSA STARED OUT THE WINDOW AND WATCHED THE RAINDROPS splatter on the etched glass. Blurred by the texture of the panes, she longed to see out into the gardens below. What she would give to shed her robes and feel the brisk drops on her skin. Or watch them drip down Dante's chiseled chest. The constant flush he caused in her body was unwanted. Would the rain be able to cool the warmth that flooded her senses when he was near?

She sighed heavily, wishing she could test the theory.

"You're like a caged dog," Yankee said from behind her. "What's the matter, girl? Need to go run and play outside?" He patted his leg and his voice sounded uncharacteristically high.

"I do not appreciate your mocking, Elite." She rose from the window seat and stuck her chin up high. Yankee rubbed her the wrong way and if her visions were any indication, he was not a man she wanted to befriend.

"I think you do, Eight-ball." He winked at her, playing with the glass bottle in his hand. He had a liking for sodas and often used straws to chew on instead of to drink from.

"And I don't like this cognomen that you address me by. I have a given name and a proper title." Lysandra clasped her hands in front of her and stood strong while he listened to her speak. "I know much about your history. We are far beyond pointless interactions."

His eerie black eyes narrowed. They held no spark of life or laughter, only emptiness. "Not even close."

"I know you give people nicknames for the same reason the gods tell Oracles not to use given names. You create distance between yourself and others. You know if you call me by my name, it opens the door for us to eventually become friends."

"You want my friendship, Eight-ball?" He licked his lips and her eyes tracked the movement. Raw sensuality shone on his face. She must keep control of the conversation and not let him know he made her uncomfortable.

"You were once a famed fighter in the human realm. Will you tell me about it?"

"Aww," he taunted with mock affection. "Trying to get to know me better, Eight-ball?"

Lysandra leveled her gaze at him, knowing his intimidations would come. "My curiosity of the human world gets the best of me. Will you tell me about your experience in their realm?"

Yankee stood, set his bottle on the coffee table. "I could show you some things the human world taught me." He pushed up the sleeves of his shirt, baring his forearms and tattoos.

Lysandra pressed further. "I saw your family. Your parents were especially evil, but your sibling—"

"You've been a naughty little spy," he sneered and took an invading step. "I don't like that." His tone changed, deepened with each stalking step.

Their dance backed her up against the wall. She was out of room to retreat. She was now the mouse to a fiercely angry cat.

"Tell me, Lysa, are you tired of being a virgin?" His lips curled up into a cruel sneer. One hand slid up and wrapped around her neck.

"You don't frighten me." A bold lie told by trembling lips. He was close, too close, too wild and unpredictable. There was a streak of cruelty in him; she'd seen it in her visions. Yankee walked a fine line between insanity and loyalty. One had to break through the insanity to earn the loyalty. Lysandra was determined to do just that. But how far was she willing to go? "I don't believe you to be a predator of women."

"Then why are you panting, little rabbit?" Yankee nuzzled her neck and inhaled deep, making her shiver and flinch. "Dante was right; you smell damn nice. Since he's determined to be a monk all his life, maybe I should teach you the pleasures of this world?"

She swallowed hard, sure she'd made a grave error in prodding him. A cold shiver went down her spine. Pushing against his chest was fruitless. He was immovable. "I am priestess of the temple. You should respect my—"

"Virginity?" He pinched her chin between his fingers and gave a humorless chuckle. "I'm going to show you something, all right." He leaned in as if to kiss her, but his head twitched to the side, his ear to the door. "Three…two…one—"

Before he would have planted his lips on hers, his body flew backwards and crashed into the coffee table. Wood splintered and cracked, but her view was blocked by a wall of male muscle and barely harnessed rage.

"Are you out of your goddamned mind?" Yankee complained as he rose from the floor.

Dante's anger pulsated in his aura like a flashing red light. His words came out more of a growl than any human sound. "I should ask you the same thing. How dare you put your hands on her!"

"What's the matter, Superman? Don't like to share?" Yankee laughed—right up until Dante punched him with the force of a wrecking ball to his jaw. His frame, thinner than the warrior protecting her, flew backwards again. It took Yankee a moment to recover and get to his feet. He wiped blood from his lips, studied it on his hands, and glared at her savior. "How did you do that? No one but Ryse can draw blood from me."

"Ryse isn't the only one who can counteract your power. Keep that in mind next time you try to manhandle a woman."

"You'll pay for that," Yankee promised, his eyes narrowed into thin slits and his nostrils flared. "You know damn well I wouldn't actually hurt her."

"Do I?" Dante growled.

"I'm only trying to prove a point, asshole." Yankee swiped at his bleeding lip and shook his head. "Don't say I didn't warn you." With a bow to Lysandra, he exited the room.

For long, quiet minutes, she stood still until she saw the tension slowly ease from Dante's shoulders. *Dearest gods of Olympia.* This was a side of her bashful beast she'd never seen before. Truly, he was a ferocious warrior. The power with which he hit Yankee would have killed a human. He'd come to her rescue, even against one of his brothers.

Oh no. This was her fault. Dante went up against another Elite in her defense. What was she thinking? Rhea would be so disappointed to know Lysa was causing dissent among the warriors.

When she knew her heart wasn't going to explode from her chest, she slid away from the wall and around the furniture to face him. His eyes were fastened on the broken table and his jaw looked tight enough to break.

"Did he hurt you?" he said low and tight.

"I am unharmed. Shaken, but unharmed." She bent to pick up the pieces of wood that littered the carpet. "I do not think he would have hurt me, but for a moment, I did fear." Emotion was thick on her tongue and her voice wavered. She mustn't cry; it would only make things worse.

"Don't. I'll clean up." His great body propelled into motion, gathering up the shards.

He did not speak to her, much less look at her.

"I'm so very sorry. This is all my fault. I antagonized him. Please accept my apology. Do not be angry with me." She swallowed the sob trying to escape.

He went motionless as the dead. "You think I'm angry with *you?*" he whispered, his voice sounding like his throat was full of rocks. The unfamiliar rumble and coldness caused her to step backwards.

"You appear to be. You cannot even look at me. I've angered you and I would do anything to make amends. I know this is my fault."

When he did look, when he raised his eyes and caught her with his stare, she wished she'd kept her mouth closed. A great emotion, something deep and smoldering, lit his eyes and turned them into swirling globes of sand. His pupils were gone; the entire eye was one color. She must have done a most horrible thing to cause this reaction from him.

Lysandra cast her eyes down and bowed her head; tears gathered but did not fall. "I'm sorry, Dante," she whispered, his name spilling out with no thought.

Dante crossed the distance between them and stepped so close to her she was overwhelmed with his body heat and his fresh, clean, masculine scent. Her breath hitched when a soft finger caressed her cheek and tilted her chin upwards.

"You said my name again. I like how it sounds on your lips." One corner of his lips pulled back, but his eyes were still smoldering. Their heat seeped into her bones, melting her from the inside out.

Lysandra gasped and her pulse drummed in her ears. "You do?"

His thumb traced a line across her bottom lip and his eyes tracked the movement. The expression on his face made her blood simmer. Dante appeared...*hungry*. Desire, so unfamiliar and exhilarating, blossomed in her lower stomach. This was what it felt like to be consumed with the need of another person.

"I'm quite fond of your lips. The very thought of someone else tasting them enrages me." His face was so close that his breath tickled her cheek. One hand curved around until his fingers burrowed into the hair at the base of her neck.

"It does?" She could barely breathe. Every rise and fall of her breasts rubbed against him, creating a tantalizing friction she'd never felt before. It was as if he'd electrified her body. She didn't move, didn't raise her hands to touch him. Every nerve was attuned to his movements, his aroma, and his heat. He stared at her lips as his head inched closer. *He's going to kiss me.* Lysa closed her eyes and lifted her lips, awaiting his kiss.

It never came.

"I can't." Dante bolted out of the room, tripping on the table remnants and nearly falling out the door. He couldn't get away from her fast enough.

What happened? He'd been so close, so warm against her. Knowledge of the opposite sex might be in short supply, but she could have sworn he was about to kiss her. What did she do wrong?

His absence left her colder than the arctic winds. She wrapped her arms around her waist and slumped down in a chair. Tears sprang to her eyes and she failed to control them. They dripped down her cheeks and onto her lap. A huge hole opened in her chest and sucked away her air supply. She rubbed at her sternum, expecting to feel the gap.

What a fool she must have looked like. Standing there with her eyes closed and head tilted upward, expectant. He was probably laughing at her even now. Foolish girl. As if she deserved the affections of a mighty warrior, much less his kiss.

If this was heartbreak, she didn't want any part of it. Rhea could take her back to Delphi now. There was something to be said for a world free of emotion and attachment. At least as a priestess, she would never feel the sting of rejection from someone she lov—

"Oh no," she whispered, new tears forming in her eyes. This couldn't be happening. She'd been sent to Earth to take care of a Deity…

Not to fall in love.

⚬

Dante muttered every foul curse word he could think of as he stomped down the hall, hell bent on giving Yankee the beating of his damned life. Blinded by rage and jealousy, he'd almost done the unforgivable. Kissing Lysa would have broken rules set forth by the gods. The Oracle was to remain pure and untouched so that she could serve in the temple. He'd nearly ruined everything for her. Guilt wound around his chest, strangling his heart until he thought he would pass out. Sure, she wasn't exactly backing away, but after it was all said and done, she would have hated him. Gods, she deserved so much better than him.

"Hey." Bren came around the corner and stopped dead in his tracks. "What the hell happened to you? You look terrible."

"I can't stay here."

Once the words were spoken, Dante knew they were true. Ashton's offer was looking better with every encounter he had with Yankee. He could see why the Thracians in Europe hated the Elites, especially if that asshole was the ambassador.

"Okaaaay," Bren said. "Let's go chill at the training center for a while, play some video games, or punch something."

"I don't mean at the palace. I mean here, in this Haven. I'm going back home." Dante pushed by him, headed down the corridor for the wing of the palace where they stayed. He could gather his things and move out of the castle. For now, it would put plenty of space between him and Lysa until Ryse came back.

"Whoa! Hey, hey, hey." Brenden jumped in front of his path and held up his hands. He glanced right, then left to make sure they were alone. "Don't do anything hasty, okay. Talk to me, man. What's up? Is it Yankee? The woman?"

"Both."

Bren groaned. "Ah hell, what did he do now?"

Dante let out a gust of air and clenched his fists. "He made his point. I have feelings for her. I can't get her out of my head. The gods will punish us both if we cross that line."

"You have to give her time. She's been through a lot lately, Dante."

He stared at Brenden's blue eyes, now permanently shadowed with heavy bags. "Wasn't it you that told me to stay away from her?"

The other soldier put his hands on his hips and hung his head. "Yeah. I did. Because I didn't want you pining over a woman you shouldn't even be looking at that way. But I've talked to her, Dante. She might be fragile right now, but she cares for you, even if she shouldn't."

Dante ran his hands through his hair. "This is a bloody mess. We both have vows that cannot be ignored. We are not supposed to be together and yet I don't care. I want her anyway. What do I do?"

Brenden leaned against the wall and rested his head backwards, closed his eyes. "I know what I said. Truth is, I wouldn't give anything for the time I had with Nikki. I'd give up our future together if it meant she lived. At least I have the memory, at least she knew without a doubt how I felt about her." He opened his eyes and turned his head to Dante. "If you love her, tell her. Damn the rules, damn the protocol, damn what anyone says. Take every minute you can. 'Cause when Ryse gets back, you might not ever get the chance again. I don't believe in coincidence. Maybe it took Troy's death for you two to be together. You never know with the gods. Don't pass up the opportunity to be with her." He straightened from the wall. "I'll go on watch until you're ready to deal."

"I don't know if she'll ever want to see me any time soon. I nearly kissed her, then bailed."

"Give her time, man. She's been through a lot. It's a huge adjustment. I'm sure the last thing she expected was to fall for you in the middle of turmoil." Bren grinned. "Bring her more flowers; she loves that mushy crap."

Dante mustered a quick smile.

"You cool? No more deep-end diving?" Bren asked. When Dante nodded, he slapped him on the bicep and sauntered off.

Dante went to his room and flopped down on his bed. Gods, what would Ryse think? What would Avery do? He'd been too hasty in saying he didn't want to be here. Guilt shoved into every crevice of his mind. What was he thinking? He could never leave Avery. His vow as a soldier had been made.

Yet, so had Lysa's. The thought of hurting her was too much. As long as she'd worked for the chance to join the Pythia, she would never forgive him if he acted hastily and blew it all to Hades.

Maybe Brenden was right, though. Maybe the chance to love and be loved was as powerful as any vow. Lysa said before that she didn't fit in at Delphi. What she saw as damaged, he saw as beautifully whole and perfect. Brenden had been prepared to balance a life with Nikki and his position as Avery's head guardian. Could he, too, take such a risk? Did he dare open Pandora's Box and let her into his world?

CHAPTER TWENTY

ASHTON NEARLY DROPPED HIS TUMBLER OF VODKA WHEN HIS MOTHER burst through his door and slammed it shut.

"What in the name of the gods are you doing?" He caught the wildness in her eyes, the frantic way they darted around.

"Leave us," she commanded to the servants and guards. "All of you. Except you, Xavier."

The general exchanged a glance with him before aiding Filene into a seat.

"What has your skirts twisted?"

Filene touched a shaking hand to her lips and closed her eyes. "I overheard something terrible."

"What?" He let out a heavy sigh. For weeks, he'd listened to her pity party about being a horrible mother, about somehow messing up Salina and blah, blah, fucking blah. If ever he wanted to escape his mother, it was worse now.

"I wanted to try to talk to Dynasty. Things are so strained between us and I wanted to see if they could ever be like they were. Even with everything that has happened, I miss our friendship." Filene sighed and put a hand over her heart. "I wanted to make things right."

"Yes, Mother," Ashton said in his gentle "don't break the glass" voice that he always used with Filene. "I know you love her dearly. What did you overhear?" He sat down next to her. The attentive, sensitive son act was wearing on him. Bloody hell, he hoped she had something useful.

"Outside her suite, I saw your son." She looked to Xavier. "And that boy, the blond one with the big blue eyes. What is his name?"

"Brenden? The Elite?" Xavier supplied.

"Yes, yes, the animal boy. Dante was leaving the suite. He was upset about something and Brenden was trying to console him. Dante said he couldn't stay here because he had feelings for a woman he shouldn't. He said the gods would punish them both if anything happened. Then Brenden said that this woman cared for Dante, even though she shouldn't, and something about how she's had a hard time lately and needs time." Filene put her hand to her cheek. "And this is the worst part: Brenden suggested that Troy had to die so that they could be together."

"Holy mother of Zeus," Xavier gasped.

"Did they ever say her name?" Ashton prayed they did. This was too good.

"Well, no. Not exactly. But they *must* be talking about Dynasty," Filene said, her eyes wide and bouncing between Ashton and Xavier. "Who else could it be? If it were her Shadow Lady, why would the gods punish them for being together? They *had* to be talking about Dynasty."

Ashton stood and paced, the wheels in his mind turning. "That's who the roses are for."

"What roses?" Filene asked.

"Every day, Dante picks a flower from the garden and takes it to her suite for their *tutorials.*"

Bloody hell. It all made sense now. Why else would the young soldier be spending so much time in her private chambers? They said she was tutoring him in history, but apparently, they were learning a lot more.

"I'm sickened." Filene shot to her feet. "I'm absolutely sickened. Her husband passed less than two months ago and she's—" She cupped her mouth as if gagging. "This is a disgrace. What do we do?"

"What can you do?" Xavier said. "She's broken no laws. Besides one overheard conversation, we have no other proof."

"True. We need to investigate. If nothing else, she should be held accountable for dishonoring the memory of our Grand Deity. The mourning period is not over, not even close." Ashton would use any excuse to make the Castilles look like fools.

"I can't believe I'm saying this." Filene sat back down in her chair and shook her head. "I'm afraid I don't know Dynasty at all. What if..." Her breath hitched. "Dear gods, what if she did have an affair? What if you've been right all this time, Ashton? What if Ryse really is a product of her infidelity?" She held up her hands and shook them. "No! No. I can't believe this. I can't believe I even said it. She swore on her honor to me centuries ago that Ryse was Troy's son. I can't forget the fact that both boys looked entirely like their father, acted like him. I'm just so confused." She covered her eyes with her hands.

Ashton stood back and observed his mother have an entire conversation by herself. No doubt about it, the woman was slipping into madness. Not that it was a bad thing. Weak minds were easily manipulated.

Even if spotless Dynasty wasn't having an affair with young Dante, she gave the appearance and that was a situation he could twist and use against them.

"Don't worry, Mother. I promise to get to the bottom of this. If Dynasty and Dante are having an unethical relationship, they will have to answer for it."

"What are you going to do?" Xavier asked.

Ashton shrugged and turned his back. "Dante and I have a sort of friendship blooming. Perhaps I can entice him to tell me the truth."

Xavier clasped his hands behind his back and lifted his chin, his words whispered for Ashton alone. "I knew the boy wasn't Thracian material. I just had no idea he would sleep his way to the top. First Avery, now Dynasty."

Ashton sent him a nod and turned back to his mother, speaking to her as if she were a child. "I'll get to the bottom of this. I'm sure it was all a misunderstanding. You should never eavesdrop, Mother. You know that."

Filene relaxed into the chair. "I know." She sighed.

She was so weak. When did his mother get like this? How had he missed her becoming a delicate bubble so easily popped? It only steeled his resolve to guide her away from the fold of the gods and into the future where demons and Olympians ruled together.

CHAPTER TWENTY-ONE

THE DISTANCE WAS PAINFUL. THE SILENCE WAS TORTURE. THE LACK OF roses was disheartening.

Lysa did her best not to make eye contact when Dante was in the room. The passion she'd witnessed was gone. Only a cold, desolate cavern remained. Him on one side, her on the other.

Dynasty and Hanna picked up on the tension and that only added to the layers of silence in the room when Dante was on watch. He'd switched his rotations to mainly night shifts when all three women would be asleep. He sat in his chair by the fire and read until someone relieved him.

No doubt, he was *relieved* to get away from her. And that cut her deep.

One morning, when she went to check who had replaced him, he was still there. Dante's head rested against the side of the tall, winged-back chair. His eyes were closed, his face free from the usual worry lines and creases. The urge to run her fingers through the soft blond hair that fell over his forehead was so strong, she actually lifted her hand but stopped. She didn't have the right to such intimacies. Gods, did she want them, though. Dante was so attractive, more than any man she'd ever seen. What would it be like to kiss his lips and feel the satin of their caress? How would he touch her if she were his lover?

Lysandra shook her head to dislodge the thoughts before they could grow roots in her mind. It could never be.

With a sigh, she moved right in front of him and softly called his name. He blinked a few times and rubbed his eyes.

"Damn it. I fell asleep." He gazed up and focused on her. "Has anyone else been in here?"

"Only me."

"Good." He stood and stretched his arms to the ceiling, exposing his long arms roped with muscles. "Thanks for waking me."

"Are you getting enough rest?" Lysandra asked as she gathered the glass of water beside him to be washed.

"Huh? Oh, yeah. I'm fine."

She nodded, accepting but not believing his answer, and scuttled off to the kitchen. When she returned, he was talking on the cellular phone. "Yeah, I know I'm off today. I think I need to crash for a while. I'm fine, man. Need to clear my head, you know? I can't keep this up."

Lysandra cleared her throat and Dante finished his conversation with brisk efficiency.

"Are you hungry? I can—"

"No. Thank you. Brenden will be here shortly. Have a good day." He righted the decorative pillow in the chair and gave her a mere head nod before he stepped out the door to the antechamber.

Just before he shut her in—or out, as it were—she noticed his book on the table. As her fingers wrapped around the old leather tome, she fell into the chair with a vision.

Two people hold each other. Their bare bodies are close, skin on skin. Heat and friction build. A man looks up, adoring his lover. Dante.

"I love you. I've been yours since the moment I first saw you."

The woman is slowly moving on top of him, their bodies joined in lovemaking.

They are panting together, rising together towards the pinnacle. Their tongues mingle and duel, kissing, stroking. Her body is on fire and getting hotter with every thrust.

"Dante," she cries out, her hands gripping his hair.

He picks up the pace, moves her underneath his massive body. The intensity is too much and light explodes behind her eyes, her body winds tight and springs loose. She's having an orgasm...with Dante! He says her name over and over again, whispering it like a prayer. Finally, he groans, gasps, his body shudders as he fills her with his release. His body relaxes on hers, but his hands and lips never stop their ministrations.

He gazes at her with wonder in his eyes. "I love you, Lysandra. I have to believe the gods sent you for me."

"I know they did." It's the happiest, purest moment of her life.

Lysandra jolted from her vision, her heart thundering in her chest. It had all been so real. But it couldn't be right. Dante could barely stand the sight of her, much less want to take her to bed.

For over an hour, she didn't move. The vision replayed in her mind, a continuous loop of making love to Dante, him wanting her and loving her. What a fantasy. What a miracle it would be if he did love her.

All her visions had a purpose. All of them warned her of events to come or gave her direction and insights. Rhea had filled her mind with the knowledge. Was this too from the goddess? Was this her way of preparing Lysandra for the future? Could she truly be destined to be with Dante after her job with Avery was over?

"Hey. Hello? Lys? Lysandra?"

She snapped out of her trance and looked up to see Brenden standing over her.

"You okay in there?" he asked. His mouth might have curved into a smile, but his eyes were still dim and hollow. Each of his expressions were flat, not quite as lively as they should be.

"I'm fine. Thank you for asking." She rose and offered him breakfast, but he had eaten.

"Can I talk to you for a minute?" He rubbed the back of his neck.

"Of course, warrior." Lysandra motioned to the chairs in the living area. She chose the one Dante often occupied. It still held his scent from last night. "How may I serve you?"

"I know something is going on with you and Dante."

Heat crept into her face and her eyes darted away from his. "I'm afraid you must be mistaken."

"Cut the crap, sweetheart." He sighed. "You two look at each other like love-sick puppies. I'd know that look anywhere. I practically invented it."

"Is that how you look at Nikki?"

This time when Brenden smiled, it held a flicker of life. "Yeah. That girl wrapped me up fast. I'd give anything to kiss her again." His face fell. "You never know what tomorrow holds, Lys. You never know when the person you love might be ripped from your grasp." He leaned over and took her hand, made sure she looked him in the eyes. "Dante is messed up over you, believe it or not. He's too honorable to do anything about it, though. You've got to take a chance on him. Don't give up, 'kay?"

Lysandra blinked away the forming tears. "I'm afraid."

"Love is some scary shit." They grinned together. "But once you grab a hold of it, it's amazing."

"I've never been so…" She couldn't find the right words.

"Vulnerable? Freaked the hell out?" Brenden smirked when she nodded. "Yeah, sweetheart, that's part of the package."

"What if he doesn't find me adequate?"

Brenden scrubbed a hand over his face. "Lys, trust me when I say the boy is crazy about you. I wouldn't steer you wrong."

She smiled and patted the top of his hand. "I know. You've been a good friend to me, B-Brenden."

His face brightened a fraction. "Was it so hard to call me by my name? It's nice."

Heat rose in her cheeks again and she turned away. She finally felt like she had a friend.

Brenden narrowed his eyes and chewed on his bottom lip for a moment. "I know what we can do. He's resting today. I can get you to him without being noticed."

Frantic butterflies winged about her stomach as Lysa made her way to Dante's room that evening. Her body was covered in her black cloak, her aura locked up tightly in her mind. No one would see her ghost down the back halls to where the soldiers had taken up residence. Never in her life had she done anything this bold, this unplanned and rash. But deep inside, she knew that Rhea had sent her here to find love, to find the life she'd been sacrificing for so long during her service to the Pythia. No, she would never be one of the three sacred Oracles. Truth be told, she'd figured that out fairly quickly after joining the temple. For centuries, she'd given it her all, watched others ascend before her. After only a few months on Earth, it was clear she didn't belong in Delphi.

Every time Dante delivered a bloom, she knew in the deepest recesses of her soul she could not live without ever smelling the fragrance of roses again. Every time she walked among the tall oaks of the forest, she knew life would be dull without their sounds and textures. A breeze blowing through their leaves was music to her ears. The roughness of the bark and the softness of their leaves gave them character and life. Her existence would be monotonous without them.

Thanks to Rhea, she felt the joy of life in her veins. Thanks to Dante, she felt the blush of affection on her cheeks.

No plans, she realized as she stood outside his door and lifted her hand to knock. She didn't know what she was going to say or do. All she knew was that her body and soul were driven to his side, even if it meant she'd never join the Pythia. If her vision was any indication, she would find a much greater devotion.

Three taps on his door. Two muffled voices. One, the masculine sound she knew so well. "Get off me."

The other, a high-pitched feminine giggle. "Do you want me to put my clothes on?"

Oh dear gods. Her heart stopped beating and the air was sucked from her lungs.

Dante opened the door, pulling on his button-up shirt, his toned chest bearing red lipstick smudges. The fly of his jeans was undone and he hurried to button it. "*Lysa.* What are you doing out here?" He stuck his head out of the door and looked both ways down the hall.

"Making a terrible miscalculation." Lysa gathered her robe around her and turned to leave. "I'm sorry to interrupt."

"*Stop.* Please wait." Dante grabbed her arm and she jerked away. "You don't understand."

Her heart shattered in her chest when she saw the brunette woman come into the hall, her clothing messed up, lipstick smeared, and hair in disarray. "It costs extra if she's joining us."

"A prostitute?" Lysa bit out and glared at Dante, whose eyes were as round as dinner plates. "I…I can't."

As fast as her legs would take her, she ran back the way she came. Behind, she heard rushed conversation and heavy footfalls as Dante charged down the hall after her, but she didn't stop or slow. Instead of going back to the safety of Dynasty's suite, she ran down stairs and into a utility closet, where a secret door took her into the tunnel. Thankfully, Dynasty had shown her the various hidden passages around the castle. Right at that moment, Lysa didn't want to face the queen, or anyone else, for that matter.

She needed to escape. She needed fresh air and space to deal with all the pain that invaded her heart like a disease. The cancer ate at her very soul.

"Lysa," Dante called from far behind her, just now entering the tunnel, his voice echoing off the rock walls.

Tears blurred her vision as she punched in the numbers on the keypad to the exterior door and pushed it open with all her strength. As quickly as she could, she closed the door and hit the emergency lock button. If he wanted out, he would have to go all the way back to the palace and out the traditional way. It would take him a while to get up the mountain.

She could barely hear Dante's loud cursing from behind the door.

When she thought her legs might collapse, she urged them to run. There was only the moonlight guiding her through the dark night, but she ran in the frigid air until her lungs burned and her muscles ached. Finally, her body couldn't carry her another step forward. She slumped against a tree and slid to the ground.

Sobs racked her frame, tearing emotions from her heart that she didn't know she possessed. Over and over, she pounded her fists into the ground, wishing it was Dante she was hitting. The image of him— bare chest painted with the kisses of another woman, his pants undone, ready for intimacy—burned in her brain. Dear gods, he was perfection and she hated her attraction when she should be concentrating on how he had betrayed her.

How could he do that? After the tender moment they'd shared not so long ago, the way he'd looked at her with hunger in his eyes, he'd turned to another woman to sate his desire. What of her vision? Was she mistaken? Was it the other woman who Dante had made love to? He'd said her name, she was sure of it. Maybe it was all a mix up? Most of her visions were from an omniscient point of view, never in first person where she was a part of the scene. What if her vision of passion and love had been from the eyes of another woman? Did this mean they were not meant to be together after all?

Lysandra sobbed so hard she never heard him approach until Dante knelt down and pulled her into his arms.

"Please, dearest gods, please let me explain. Lysa, I'm begging. I'm sorry. I know how that looked and you must hear me out. Please."

He crushed her to his warm body, gripped her hair, and held her to his chest. His breath was heavy, panting with desperation. Under her ear, his heart boomed like a bass drum.

No matter how good it felt to be in his arms, she pushed him away; the image of the mussed-up brunette was as good as cold water in her face. A prostitute. He'd replaced her with a whore. She hit at his chest like she wanted to.

"Let me go. Leave me. I never want to see you again." She fell backwards against the tree. "I don't care if I have to spend the rest of my existence miserable and alone in Delphi. I don't want be anywhere near you. Go back to your paid woman."

"Lysa, please. Yankee sent that woman to my room. He's a prick and—"

"And he is obviously rubbing off on you," she screamed, swiping at her flowing tears.

"No, I swear, I was *not* going to be with her. She barged into my room and started undressing me, talking crazy because Yankee sent her there. She'd only been there a moment before you knocked. Please believe me." Dante reached for her and they both noticed the blood dripping from his hand.

"What have you done?" Compassion for him battled with her anger.

"Sorry." He tore a piece of his shirt and wrapped it around his bleeding fist. "I had to get to you and I wasn't going to let a damned keypad stop me. Lady Dynasty is going to be upset, but I couldn't go back." Dante met her eyes.

Her breath caught when she saw his tears.

They stared at each other for a moment before he looked away. "I never should have gotten involved with you."

What? He'd chased her out into the cold, beaten down an armored door, and all he could say was *that*? "Am I such a disappointment? That you can't look at me or kiss me or admit that you care? Is it because I'm a virgin? Is it because I'm over a thousand years old, but none the wiser than a child in this era?"

His head popped up. "Dear gods, is that what you think?"

Lysa huddled into her cloak, the cold of the night seeping into her limbs. "I know you must think I'm a failure in my duties to the temple. I'm not what you are accustomed to. I've never been with a man. I've never been kissed or touched intimately. There is so much about this time period that I am ignorant of. I couldn't even figure out the shower." She sobbed again, wishing she could disappear. "It was foolish for me to believe an honorable warrior such as you could ever lower himself to care for a woman like me."

Dante's shoulders slumped and his head fell to the side. "You have no idea how I see you." He stood and pulled her to her feet. "You're freezing. Come back to the palace, where it's warm and we can talk."

Lysa shook her head and dropped her hand from his. "If you have something to say, do it now. I can't wait any longer. If there is no hope between us, then let's get it out now so I can be rid with this insane need of you."

Dante sighed and his brows dipped, taking his time to answer. "I don't want to screw up your chances of ascending to the Pythia. I don't want to ruin your innocence, to scour your purity. You're worth more. But every time I look at you, I want to take you into my arms, into my bed, and love you until even the gods know you belong to me. I want to possess you so fully your every thought is of me, and have you know that I feel the same about you. I have no right, but when I thought Yankee was going to kiss you…" His jaw clenched up and his aura flared with red anger. "I wanted to beat him to a pulp for touching you."

"You weren't angry with *me*?"

"Never. You are my beautiful flower." Dante cupped her cheeks. "I want the right to kiss you, Lysa. I want to be the first man who makes you feel desire. I want to consume you until all you see or feel or taste is my body. More than that, I want to be the man who wakes you with roses every day and showers our children with love and affection."

If she thought she'd been nervous earlier, she damn sure was now. The butterflies were back with a vengeance and Dante was so close, their breaths mingled.

"Do it," she whispered, desperate for the life he'd described. Could there be a greater fantasy? Married to the man she loved, giving him children, and being loved so fully for the rest of her life sounded like Heaven.

"What about the gods? What about the Pythia?"

"I'll never be one of the Pythia. Why do you think Rhea sent me here? I'm not suited for temple life, even after all these decades, and she knows it. If I have my choice, I'd rather spend one night with you than a thousand lifetimes there."

Gathering her courage, she inched up on her toes and closed the distance between their lips. The silk of his mouth pressed against hers, hesitant at first. Her eyes drifted closed and she wrapped her arms around his neck. Dante pulled her closer and weaved his hands in her hair, tilting her head. He nipped at her lips until he chased away the chill of the night.

She couldn't get close enough to him. No matter how much she leaned in, it wasn't enough. Dante held her tight, one hand splayed across her back. He licked across the seam of her lips and, on instinct, she opened her mouth. When he plunged his tongue inside her, they both moaned.

Having never been kissed, much less kissed like this, Lysandra took her cues from Dante. She mirrored his movements, learned the things that made him moan, and did them over and over again.

"You're a quick study," he panted against the wetness on her mouth.

"You're a magnificent teacher."

His kiss-swollen lips kicked up to one side. "I'm not nearly as experienced as you might think."

"Teach me what you know and we can learn the rest together." Lysa smiled.

"Oh, Lysa, how I long to do just that." He smiled so brightly it lit the night. There was nothing so beautiful in all the land of Delphi. "First, I have to get you warm."

"You are doing a fine job at the moment." Unable to get enough of his taste, she kissed him again, gripping his shoulders for dear life. She'd already discovered that there was a direct link from her lips to her most feminine places. The more she kissed him, the hotter she became between her legs.

"Let's head back to the palace. We can go to my room and *learn*."

"You must let me tend to your fist; it's bleeding right through the wrap." Sure enough, small droplets of blood hit the leaves of the forest floor. "Will your *visitor* be gone?" She arched her brow as she kissed the back of his hand, ashamed that his injury was her fault.

"Gods, I hope so. Otherwise, I'm going to rip off Yankee's testicles. I swear he's trying to get rid of—" He sniffed the air, his brows furrowing deep. "Do you smell something?" He shifted into warrior mode, his eyes hard and cold, his jaw set.

Lysandra lifted her nose to the night breeze. Sulfur and smoke, acidic and revolting. "Is something on fire?" she whispered.

"That's not simply a fire." He took her hand and tucked her close to his side. "Stay near me. Walk quietly."

She obeyed, scared to make a sound. They snuck through the forest towards the smell. Through the trees, they could see the faint glow of a fire. Not a campfire, but a ring of fire. Standing in the middle was a—

"Holy Zeus!"

Dante spun her around and clamped a hand over her mouth when she was about to scream. "Shh."

She nodded against his palm. They crouched behind the nearest tree.

A demon! Dearest mother-goddess, there was a demon in the Haven. Its ghastly form danced about the fire, the flames and smoke blurring the image. What she could see of the beast was far more than she could handle. Red skin, cracked and crinkled, as if it had been burned a thousand times over and reformed over the scabs. Black talons stretched out like daggers. Its head was of a beast she'd never seen, nothing she could name. It had three pointed horns atop its head, the extended jaws with rows of teeth and dripping toxic drool. The black caverns where eyes should've been haunted her the most. If she stared hard enough, she could see the souls of others, screaming out in eternal agony.

How did it get there? They were banned to Hades. How could a demon have possibly crossed the barrier to the world of the living? Especially one as fully formed and solid as this one. This was not its first visit.

"Who is that with it?" she whispered when she saw the figure of a man cross in front of the fire. She could only make out a silhouette.

"I can't see his face."

They stayed close to the ground cover and strained to hear.

"I've given you enough," snapped the demon, a serpentine-like tongue flickering out of his mouth.

"I need more. There's something going on here and I have to find out what it is." The crackling of the flames muffled the man's voice, but Dante's body went rigid.

She got close to his ear and whispered, "Do you know that voice?"

Dante stared her in the eyes. His face turned glacial. The line of his clenched jaw was sharper than usual. A shiver went down her spine. He nodded once.

"Get back to the castle, Lysandra. Warn the others."

"What about you? You are unarmed, Dante. Don't be foolish! You cannot fight a demon with your bare hands. It will kill you." Her heart drew up in her chest at the very thought.

Dante pulled a wicked knife out of his boot. "I'm always armed."

"What can you do to a demon with a knife?"

"I have to try."

"You have to live," she pleaded, grabbing his collar. "Think. Don't be rash. Come back with me. You know who that is; we can gather soldiers and apprehend them."

"I am thinking," he said, grabbing her hands and prying them off. "I have to distract them so you can get down the mountain safely. Leave, Lysandra. I'll not risk your life. Run, while their focus is on me. I'll hold them off as long as I can."

Tears once again streamed down her face. Dante was willing to sacrifice himself so she might live and that meant everything to her. But she couldn't lose him, not now. How could she live when he held a piece of her heart?

"I love you," she whispered. "Please don't make me leave. I love you."

He gasped at her confession and sat in silence for a heartbeat before he pulled her lips to his. She thought he'd given her passion before, but this kiss was unbridled and raw. It was the kiss of a man saying goodbye.

"Because I love you with every breath, I will not let you die." He pushed her away. *"Run."*

CHAPTER TWENTY-TWO

I T KILLED HIM to watch Lysandra slink off down the mountain. But Dante had to give her credit—she was quiet as a mouse. Neither of his adversaries noticed her run for safety. He took a deep breath.

Damn it. What the hell was he going to do against a demon? And *Ashton*. Ryse was going to blow a gasket when he found out that bastard was in league with demons. Was the whole Avondale clan evil? Was Lady Dynasty truly safe with Filene in the palace?

Dear gods, was his *father* aware of Ashton's affiliation? The thought knocked the air out of him better than a kick to the gut. Ramifications of this spread far and wide. If Xavier was in bed with demons, what would that mean for his family? His poor mother; what would she do?

Ashton and the demon kept talking; negotiating, if he had to judge by the back and forth. He crept up closer, staying low to the ground. They were so involved with their debate, they never noticed him inching closer until he could hear them clearly.

"You do not dessserve more of my blood," the demon hissed, drawing out the *s* like a snake.

"Bloody fucking hell I don't. It's only because of me that Salina hasn't spilled her guts about everything. Do you think she would have kept your secret all this time if not for my power over her? Hades would end you if she'd confessed the truth."

"When her sssoul gets to Hadesss, we ssshall sssee what sssecrets were kept. It isss only a matter of time before Hadesss intervenes..."

"Then give me your blood so I can work quickly. If I take down the Castilles, the others will domino with them. Now is the time to strike at them. The Thracians are stretched thin, and they are so focused on the rogues abducting women, they have no idea what's going on behind the scenes. But I need more blood to keep our tracks covered." Ashton held up a sparkling vial.

Dante tried to recollect from his studies what material would be strong enough to contain demon blood. He came up blank. Then again, this had to be the first demon to make his way into a Haven. The only other recent demon problem they had was at Avery's home in Texas, part of the human world.

If he made it out of this alive, he had to warn Ryse that the rogues were the least of their problems. Traitorous Olympians hunting women for sport was a terrible crime against their people, but demons invading and taking over—that meant the end of their world and exposure to humans.

"Thisss isss the lassst you ssshall be given. You weaken me. I'm not ssstrong enough to fully crosss over yet."

Ashton took out a knife and the demon extended his claw. Right before he sliced the red scales of his palm, the demon pulled back. His head thrashed about in the air. He lifted his snout to the air and inhaled. "I sssmell the blood of a Thracccian."

Shit. Dante looked down at his knuckles. They had bled through and blood dripped to the ground. There was no hiding his presence now.

A wailing cry broke through the air. Dante looked up to see Ashton slashing the claw of the demon, collecting a vial of his black, oily blood.

"You'll pay for that," the demon threatened.

"I doubt it. You need me. Now go." Ashton broke the solid line of fire by kicking dirt into the ring, breaking the seal that held the demon. With a hiss, he vanished.

Maybe Dante couldn't use a simple knife to kill a demon, but he sure as hell could use it to kill Ashton. He stepped out from behind the tree trunk and into Ashton's line of sight.

"Why, Dante, you're exactly who I wanted to see."

"Save your pretty words, Ashton," Dante growled. "I know the truth now." He readied himself for a fight.

"You know nothing." Ashton shrugged, a smug sneer on his face.

"You're the one behind all the attacks on the women. You're using the demons as cover."

Blond eyebrows rose on Ashton's face. "Well, aren't you a sharp little student. I'll have to tell your father you're not as stupid as he thinks you are."

Dante let the comments roll right off him. Ashton thought to strike at his weakness, but the need for his father's approval was long gone.

"What do you plan to do, Dante? Turn me in? Arrest me and take me to your band of Elites?"

"Exactly. You don't have to be living, though."

Ashton laughed. "Your threats don't scare me, boy. Do you know what this is?" He held up the vial. Black demon blood overflowed the tube and dripped over his hands. "Most people think it's toxic, poison to Olympians." He stuck one bloody finger into his mouth. "In large quantities, it is, which is why you need a diamond container to store it. But when you ingest a tiny bit of it…"Ashton's eyes changed from blue to black. "It actually gives you amazing strength and power." He licked at another bloody finger. "It enhances the body and, with a gift like mine, why, it's like adding accelerant to the fire."

"We'll see about that." Dante charged at him, ready to kill this bastard before he could infect others. He jumped, raised his fist, and came down on top of Ashton.

He hit the ground.

Ashton moved—*fast*. Too fast. Could he be right? Could the demon blood really enhance an Olympian? He spun around to face his opponent.

"Easy there, brute." Ashton said and laughed. "You wouldn't want to stumble." Ashton flicked out his wrist and Dante's body crumpled to the ground.

His muscles cramped up, his limbs bunched up and refused to straighten. Pain shot through his head.

"You and I both have secrets, don't we, boy? Not many people know that I can control the brain. They labeled me a Paean when I was young." He sauntered up to Dante, who lay helpless, writhing in agony on the ground. "The thing is, Paeans train to heal people. I trained to manipulate people. The brain is an amazing thing. Every nerve, every muscle, every organ—all dependent on it."

Dante tried to speak, but his voice came out as a groan, his jaw locked shut.

"I'm sorry. Does it hurt?" Ashton's black eyes shone. He enjoyed Dante's misery. "Here. Better?"

Instantly, his limbs relaxed and he gasped at the relief. If he could only reach Ashton, he could neutralize his powers. It took all his strength to roll over onto his hands and knees.

"No, no, no. No touching." Ashton shuffled backwards. "You're a sneaky one. It's a shame that Xavier turned his back on you so early on. You would have made such a good ally. He doesn't see the value in you, Dante. But I do."

Ashton held up his hand and Dante stood, fully controlled by the prince's will.

"If you're going to kill me, just do it. I'll never help you," Dante spit out through clenched teeth.

"Yes, you will. And to make damn sure you will, I'll tell you a little secret. My friend Maxim has a man trailing your little sister even as we speak. Ariabella has no idea she's a breath away from a painful death—"

Dante lunged at Ashton, nearly had him around the throat, when his heart and lungs seized. It was as if Ashton had his hand inside his chest, squeezing his organs. He fell to the ground, desperately trying to suck in air. Black spots danced in his vision and he knew he was about to die. If he couldn't touch Ashton, his powers and strength were useless.

"I'm really trying to work with you here, Dante. But when you act savagely, I'm forced to remind you who is in control of this situation. Now, can we talk civilized or do I need to kill both you and your sister?"

Dante reached for something; his arms flailed around as he tried to get purchase of anything that might end the suffering. Even in the face of his own death, a lifetime of regrets and fears came flooding in. He wished he could see his family one last time, make sure Ariabella was safe. He wished he had the chance to be with Lysa. Not just physically, but to claim her as his mate, join with her in the sight of the gods, watch her carry their child and hold that baby in his arms. He wanted a life with Lysa and he was certain he wouldn't get it. At least with Ashton's attention solely on him, she could get to the palace. He closed his eyes, resigned to take his last breath as long as she could live.

As quickly as his body had seized, it relaxed. He pulled in a deep gulp of air and his heart beat once again.

"Let's try this again," Ashton said softly. "You will do as I ask. If you do not, I will kill your sister, I will kill you, and I will let the entire world know that you're having an affair with Dynasty."

"What?" Dante coughed, both because the idea was ridiculous and because he still needed more oxygen.

"Don't be foolish. I've figured it out. That's who the roses are for. That's why you spend most of your time in her suite. You're right; the gods should punish you both for such horrid activities. Her husband is barely cold and you've already got your foot in the door to take his place."

Dante frowned. Dynasty? Ashton thought he was having an affair with the recently widowed queen? *Good Heavens, must all villains be so stupid?* He thought for a minute to use this to his advantage. Ashton couldn't know of Lysandra. No matter what lies Dante had to tell, he had to keep her existence a secret. Her exposure was a direct link to Avery's.

"It's not Dynasty." He bent over, his hands on his knees, and finally tried to straighten without blacking out. "It's Hanna. I'm courting Hanna."

It was the perfect out. Hanna and Lysandra both had jet black hair. Lysa was taller and a bit thinner, but Hanna could easily pass for her at a distance. More importantly, if Ashton went after Hanna, he would be taking a lioness by the tail. Hanna only needed to speak to take care of Ashton.

The prince seemed genuinely shocked by this confession. "The Shadow Lady? What is it with you Elites and the bloody help?" He shook his head. "Either way, I'll kill that bitch too. Now are you willing to hear my offer?"

"I don't think I have a choice."

"You're right. You don't." And that made the prince as haughty as ever. "You will get me the information I want on the Castilles. You will be my eyes and ears in their world. I want to know everything."

Dante swallowed hard. "What makes you think I know anything?"

"Don't play me, boy. I know you're a class favorite."

Dante and Ashton both turned their heads at the sound of heavy footfalls coming up the side of the mountain. *Finally.* Back up had arrived. Brenden called out his name, but he couldn't reply.

It was a perfect distraction. While Ashton's focus was on their incoming party, Dante attacked. He launched himself at Ashton's chest, his knife positioned to strike the heart. Just before contact, Ashton swiveled and the knife grazed his left shoulder, leaving an angry, bleeding wound. Dante knocked him to the ground, rolled, and went to his feet, scrambling to strike again.

"You fuckers don't know when to quit." Ashton threw out his hand and once again had control of Dante's bodily functions.

"I'm a Thracian," Dante said, his voice strained. "Only death can stop me."

"So be it." Ashton took the knife and slathered it with demon blood.

With one thrust, he buried it in Dante's abdomen, twisted, and pulled it out, shredding his body open.

"I'll be sure to tell Ariabella all about how honorably you died, right before Maxim has his way with her."

Ashton took off faster than any Olympian should have been able, leaving him to die.

Dante fell to the forest floor, gripping his middle, his blood pouring out around his fingers.

"Brenden," he screamed with the last ounce of energy he had.

The world faded away.

CHAPTER TWENTY-THREE

LYSANDRA RAN, NOT TO THE PALACE, BUT TO THE PORTAL. THERE STOOD a soldier of Zeus, a warrior who could destroy demons. Fear coursed through her body, filling her with adrenaline. She nearly fell on top of the guardian when she reached him. It didn't matter that she could be exposed; all that mattered was saving Dante.

"Please, you must help!" She pulled herself up by his garments.

His eyes never flickered to acknowledge her presence.

"Guardian of Zeus, please. There is a demon in the mountains. He has been conjured."

This got the soldier's attention and, for the first time in weeks, the statue moved. He looked down at Lysandra, his brow furrowed.

"Are you sure of this, Olympian?"

"I am an Oracle, sent from the Holy City of Delphi to reside here in secret until the goddess Rhea sees need of me elsewhere. You must believe me, guardian. I have seen this evil with my own eyes. Right now, there is a Thracian facing it alone. If you do not aid him, he shall surely die. Use your gifts; you will see that I am telling the truth."

The guardian turned his face to the mountainside and his eyes glowed with the white light of the gods. He drew his sword and Lysandra stumbled backwards to keep out of the arch of his blade.

"Return to your mistress, Oracle." His voice boomed like thunder across the knoll. "I shall see to this."

The guardian charged off into the night, his sword drawn and glowing. To the sky he bellowed, "Thracians!" A ripple cut through the air, like throwing a stone in a pond, his voice expanding to cover the entire Haven.

Lysandra ran back to the palace and was nearly trampled by the Elites and a dozen warriors who answered the call.

"What are you doing?" Brenden demanded as he gripped her shoulders.

"Dante… Dante is trying to battle a demon. He had only a knife, Brenden. Go to him."

He took off running faster than all the other Thracians, nearly overtaking the guardian.

Lysandra covered her head and went inside to Dynasty's suite. Yankee guarded the door, ready for battle. He ushered her inside and slammed the door.

"What the hell is going on out there?" Yankee demanded.

With all the strength she had left, Lysandra backhanded Yankee. She wanted, no— *needed* someone to blame and he was the right person to handle her anger. "You bastard. If you hadn't sent that woman to his room, none of this would have happened. We could be together right now. He might be dead. You selfish, heartless bastard."

In the many days since her arrival, she'd never seen Yankee react until that moment. His eyes widened, his nostrils flared, and he stepped back. He blinked rapidly and ran his hand over his nearly bald head. "Sonofabitch." Yankee left the room just as her energy left her body.

"Lysandra!" Dynasty caught her before she collapsed on the floor. "She's freezing, Hanna, get blankets and stoke the fire; she needs warmth."

"Oh, dearest gods, protect him. There was a man," she cried, tears falling down her face. "He's alone. Please, gods, save him." Lysandra leaned into Dynasty and Hanna covered her with a blanket. Until she felt the warmth, she hadn't realized how very cold she was.

"Bring tea, Hanna. We must get her temperature up. Her lips are blue." Dynasty helped Lysandra to the large hearth of the fireplace and they sat as close to the flames as possible. "What were you doing in the woods this time of night, Lysa darling?"

"Do not be angry, mistress. Please do not be upset."

"I'm not, child." The queen gave her a gentle smile. "You may speak openly to me."

"I love him." Lysandra started crying again. Dynasty looked to Hanna and mouthed the name of the man in question. "I didn't mean to love him, but I do. I had a vision of us together and I went to him. There was this other woman, so I ran. He followed me out of the palace and we ended up in the woods. We saw the demon—"

"Demon?" Hanna and Dyna said in unison.

Hanna handed her a cup of tea, but Lysandra's hands were shaking, so she helped her drink.

"A man was there, conjuring the demon, speaking to him. Dante told me to run and he would distract them. I didn't want to leave him. I was so scared. I ran to the guardian of the portal. I knew if there was a demon in the Haven, he could intervene. He called the Thracians and they charged into the woods."

"Oh my." Dynasty shivered, fear showing in her eyes. "We will pray. We must have faith in Dante's abilities as a Thracian soldier and pray that he has the protection of the gods." She took Lysandra's and Hanna's hands and together they petitioned the gods for strength and protection for Dante.

Over a thousand Earth years she'd been alive. Countless times she'd seen blood and war in her visions. Countless times she'd known of injustice. In all that time, Lysandra had never once felt terror—raw, bone-deep terror like she felt as she waited to hear of Dante's fate. In the short time she'd known him, barely over two months, he'd become a beacon of hope and kindness in her life. Every day, he greeted her with a smile and beautiful flowers. He read to her, played games with her, listened to her sing, taught her about the world, and sent her heart soaring with every gentle touch.

If the gods allowed, she intended to be with Dante forever. He had a piece of her heart and she prayed that piece wasn't dead in the cold woods.

Commotion in the antechamber brought all their heads around.

A man entered, one she hadn't formally met yet. He clasped forearms with Yankee and they exchanged words before he turned to the women.

"Hayden!" Lady Dynasty ran to him. Their embrace lasted a long moment before Dyna planted a kiss on each of his cheeks. "My goodness, you look different. You've been touched by the gods. I can see it in your eyes." She hugged him again and the prince laughed.

"Mother, please. I wasn't gone that long." He smiled, and Lysa could see how a woman could get snared by the attractiveness of it. Dark hair flowed to his shoulders, framing a handsome face and dark eyes. He was tall and lean, a fair physique, if she did say so. But compared to her Dante, he was a bit on the narrow side. Then again, the prince was no Thracian.

"Two months. You were gone over two months."

His brows rose high on his forehead. "Are you kidding? It felt like a couple hours at best. Everything was a mad rush." He put his hands on her shoulders. "I saw him. Father. He's at peace in the presence of Zeus." Hayden pushed Dynasty's hair off her cheek. "Everything is okay, you know. He's whole and happy and acting as counsel to the gods on how to move forward with our people. I was able to tell him goodbye properly. I wish you could have been there."

Dynasty cried openly and took his hands in hers. "It is enough that you bring me this message. I, too, can have peace now. Oh, my son," she said as she pulled him to her again. "The gods have blessed me with so much. I cannot mourn any longer for what I have lost." She held his face in her hands and they smiled at one another.

Lysandra was so lost in their reunion, she didn't know she was crying again until her sniffles drew their attention.

Dynasty took Hayden's hand. "Come, you must meet someone very special."

Lysandra knelt down as Prince Hayden approached. "Sire, it is a great honor to meet you. I am Lysandra, Oracle of Delphi."

"Dear Zeus, an Oracle? I should be bowing to you. Please rise." Hayden helped her up. "What brings you here?"

"I was sent to aid your mother in the care of Avery's body."

Hayden had the standard questions: Are you one of the Pythia?

How long will you be here? Is Avery awake yet? Thankfully, Brenden's arrival interrupted his onslaught of inquiries. She waited patiently while he greeted the prince and received confirmation that Nikki was alive.

"Brenden?" she said, clearing her throat. She had to know. Her heart could only be patient for so long.

He turned to her, his shoulders dropped. His lips pinched together.

"He is not dead," Lysandra whispered. "He cannot be dead. Please," she begged as Bren took her by the hands.

"Lys, he's barely hanging on. I don't know if the Paeans can save him."

With those words, her face crumpled and sobs escaped her body. She couldn't lose him. After over a thousand years of existence, she'd finally found love. To give that up so soon, she didn't think her soul could bear it.

"I need to see him. Please, Brenden."

"Take her," Dynasty said. "She might be the only one to make him hang on."

"Thank you, mistress." Lysandra bowed and kissed the queen's hands. She followed Brenden down to the bowels of the palace, where a secret corridor opened into a make-shift medical room.

"We didn't want him in the Thracian Training Center like this," Brenden said. "He's made some of the students very jealous and Thracians are a rather competitive bunch."

"Will he get the proper treatment here?" she asked as Brenden opened a door for her.

"Nothing but the best, Lys. I promise."

Brenden stepped aside and Lysa stopped dead in her tracks. A man—no, a giant stood over Dante's bedside, hand resting on his shoulder. He turned to the door and met Lysandra's stare. A lump rose in her throat and she tried not to choke on it.

He favored Prince Hayden. The familial resemblance was there: dark hair, dark eyes, strong jaw. But this man was twice Hayden's width, twice his mass, and had predatory eyes like those of a wild animal. Those all-too-observant eyes seared her, narrowing at her entry to the room.

"Who are you?" he asked, his lips pulling back in a snarl.

Lysandra stood frozen, swallowed again, but couldn't form words. This man scared the hell out of her. Her instincts told her to run but her heart was drawn to Dante.

"Uh, Master Ryse," Brenden said. "This is Lady Lysandra, an Oracle from Delphi. Rhea sent her after you left. She's uh, well, she and Dante are sort of, uh, *together*." Brenden cast her an apologetic glance.

Master Ryse. This was the Master Thracian. *Oh dearest mother of Zeus.* She could see how his presence alone would intimidate any civilian who crossed his path. The warrior had death written all over his face. He spoke with the confidence of a man used to being in command, the final rung in the chain of authority.

"Together? What the hell has been going on here since I left? Someone conjured demons, my warriors are sneaking out of the palace in the middle of the night, and now some Oracle is *together* with my apprentice?"

Only when Ryse turned to them did she even notice the other men in the room. Philippe and Cutter stood with a fierce-looking man with gray hair and another man with ebony skin and eyes. She'd been so dumbstruck by the Master, she'd missed every other person in the room—including Dante and the Paeans who worked around him. The healer's hands hovered over his body, light emanating from their palms as they tried to fix the damage.

Forgetting everyone else, Lysandra ran to his bedside.

Dante was still as the grave. His entire torso was covered in gauze and bandages. Sweat beaded on his forehead, his skin far too pale. Each breath was shallow and labored. Paeans covered him with a sheet and backed away when she approached.

"We have done all we can for him," one woman explained to Ryse. "We've repaired the organs as much as possible to keep him alive and closed him up. Poison from the demon's talons prohibits our powers from healing him any further. We'll monitor him throughout the day for infections. His fate is in the hands of the gods now."

Brenden thanked the healers, but Lysandra couldn't take her eyes off Dante enough to acknowledge the other people in the room. She hesitantly reached out and ran her fingers through his hair.

He stirred, a soft moan crossing his lips. He mumbled her name.

"Shh, my love," she whispered in his ear, pulling up a chair by his side. "I'm here, Dante. I won't leave you."

"Lysa," he whispered, the action taking great effort.

"Hush now. I'm here." Even though she was on the verge of a mental breakdown, Lysandra leaned her head next to his on the bed and closed her eyes. She hummed songs that he liked and slowly ran her fingers through his hair over and over again. His body finally relaxed and he went into a deep sleep.

"I don't suppose you can get a vision of what happened by touching him, huh?" Brenden whispered into her ear.

She shook her head. "Not with his powers. Possibly his clothing or even the place where it happened."

Brenden pointed to a disposal unit. "His clothing is in there. We are going to have it processed as evidence. Only touch what you have to."

Together, they lifted the lid and the smell of Dante's blood nearly made her wretch. She touched the clothing on a small, clean corner and closed her eyes to concentrate.

Blue eyes, full of menace. The attacker's arm was injured. Dante's knife covered in black sludge, plunging deep into his gut. Exploding pain. Dante's fear of leaving her. His deep love.

Lysandra opened her eyes with a gasp. She had no idea he cared so much for her. And she knew that no demon hurt him.

"This was not a demon," she said. The images were nothing but quick flashes. The more she focused on the male, the fuzzier the images became. "Whoever was there, whoever conjured the demon, they're blocked from me. I can't make out anything but blue eyes. I'm sorry." She closed the lid on the receptacle and washed her hands before returning to Dante's side.

Ryse nodded to Brenden before he left the room. "Good enough. I'm going to my mother."

Lysandra stared at his retreating back. "Is he angry with me?" she asked once the scary Thracian was gone.

"No, he's just walked into a giant clusterfuck after being through a mess of heavenly proportions."

"I wish I could have seen more, helped more. I'll do anything to save him."

"That's more than we had. Thanks, Lysa." Brenden leaned down and kissed the top of her head. "Hold on to him. We can't lose our boy. Avery will be madder than a wet hen."

"Pardon?" Lysandra questioned his slang.

Brenden's mouth quirked up. "It's a Texan thing." He closed the door softly behind him and Lysandra rested her head next to Dante's. She couldn't lose him. Her every breath had slowly begun to revolve around him over the last two months. If she lost him now, she might not recover.

Ever since childhood, she'd remembered the love and affection between her parents. Never had the world seen two people so devoted to one another. Even when they disagreed, they did it with respect for each other, never dredging up old hurts or speaking harshly. Her mother gave her father encouragement and support; her father reciprocated tenfold. When they looked at each other, Lysandra could see the desire and love in their eyes.

It was the same way Dante looked at her.

Great god Apollo, she prayed. *Please do not take Dante from this world. I beg of you. I am thankful for every day we have shared, but I beseech you for more time with him. Let us have the chance to grow together, following your will and doing your work in this realm. Forgive me for straying from the path I have walked for so long. Lead me soundly on this new journey and please, please let me walk it with the man I love.*

CHAPTER
TWENTY-FOUR

Dynasty, Hanna, and two Thracians—Titus and Gabrele—made their way down to the medical room to check on Dante and Lysandra. Dynasty was quite fond of both guardians and hoped, when this was over, they could find sanctuary in each other.

Titus, her personal Thracian guardian, normally didn't follow her every movement around the palace. However, Ryse had insisted on it until the demon, and the person who conjured it, were found. Titus was very proficient at being around at all times, but hardly ever seen. It was a trait the queen appreciated. He respected her privacy, yet never took her safety for granted.

Gabrele had been the guardian of her husband. Since Troy's death, he'd shifted his duties to the queen. The murder of his Master was especially hard and Dynasty insisted he take leave for the last couple months to mourn and be with his family. Now, he was called back by Ryse to serve alongside Titus. The two men were well versed in working together. They had done so for over three hundred years.

"I want to stop by the kitchen and have Valarie fix a meal for Dante and Lysandra. Remember," she said to her entourage, "no one knows of Lysa's presence here."

Hanna, Titus, and Gabrele nodded their understanding.

In the kitchen, Valarie prepared a huge basket of food, assuming she was feeding the four people in front of her. Dynasty thanked her as they left.

Filene and Ashton approached from the opposite side of the hall. Dyna stopped, determined to say a kind word to Filene.

"Did Charles return along with Ryse and Hayden?" Her smile was soft and somewhat genuine.

"He did."

Dynasty noted the clipped tone of her voice, the way her shoulders squared, and her chin lifted.

"Did they find the demon?" Ashton asked. "I can't believe a Haven as secure as this one is having so many problems of late. Maybe the Thracians need to stop their *training* and start actually guarding something."

The two men behind Dynasty shifted their feet, but gave away nothing in their expressions.

"I can assure you, Prince Ashton, my son is doing a fine job preparing these young men for their future assignments. Each soldier is unique and must be attended to with care and diligence."

"You would know all about that, wouldn't you?" Filene sniped.

Dynasty caught a nervous twitch above her eye. "Are you feeling well, Filene?"

"I know what you're doing." The blonde woman stepped close, her infuriated blue eyes boring into Dynasty's. "You should be ashamed."

"Mother, don't," Ashton warned softly, his monotone indicating that he was bored with this conversation already.

"Would you like to have a private conversation? My people can step aside." Dyna never took her eyes off Filene. A wild anger brewed inside her old friend and she intended to address it now.

"No. I think your Thracian guards should hear about what you're doing behind closed doors. Or perhaps they already do."

Dynasty spoke calmly and slowly, in contrast with the way Filene raised her voice so all could hear. "You seem to be able to see through walls, Filene. Is this a new gift from the gods? Do tell us what it is you think you've witnessed."

"You're having an inappropriate relation with that boy, Xavier's son."

Dynasty sighed. Her friend had passed delusional and gone straight to vengefully fabricating lies.

"I know he picks you flowers and goes to your room each night. It's shameful. Troy has barely been dead a couple months and you dare to seek out another; and one so young and naive at that."

"Oh for Heaven's sake, Mother," Ashton said, rubbing a hand down his face. "He's courting the Shadow Lady."

"What?" Filene snapped at her son, clearly upset at not finding out until now.

Dynasty clasped her hands in front of her and turned her head to Hanna, who, after so many centuries of service, could assume what her mistress was about to do. Dante must have used Hanna to cover his tracks with Prince Ashton. "May I enlighten them?"

Hanna narrowed her eyes at Filene and Ashton, but nodded, playing her part.

"The young soldier is courting her under my supervision."

Filene looked Hanna up and down, her lips curled up with disgust. "I don't believe you."

"I don't give a damn what you believe." Dynasty laced her voice with cold steel. The whip of her words cut at Filene and her eyes widened. "You are clearly under duress and not in your right mind. This once I will forgive these outlandish accusations and your display of blatant disrespect of my Shadow Lady and her privacy. Hear me now, Filene. I will not tolerate such betrayal of centuries of friendship again. I highly suggest you meditate on the true source of your anger. No doubt you will find you have lashed out at the wrong person. Now if you will excuse me—" Dynasty hesitated, a feeling in her gut telling her not to expose where she was going. "I have not eaten today and I hope your vile words haven't ruined my lunch."

She turned on her heel and headed in the direction of her chambers. They would have to take another way to go see Dante.

"Lady Dynasty," Ashton called, jogging up to them without his mother. "Please forgive her. She's not in her right mind. Events of late have caused great stress on her."

"That does not excuse her behavior. One should know the facts before publicly denouncing someone else. But thank you for trying." She turned again, but Ashton caught her arm.

"Milady, one more moment, if you will?" He smiled and Dynasty was nearly convinced he was the bright-eyed, innocent boy she'd watched grow up. Nearly.

"How did anyone find out about the demon? I heard the guardian by the portal took off into the woods. Did he sense it?"

Again, a small voice in the back of her mind told her to lie. "He knew it had entered the Haven. The gods sent Ryse and Hammon back to search it out. Why do you ask?"

"Xavier is worried because Dante seems to be missing."

She sighed and forced a fake smile. "No matter what your mother believes, I don't have a connection to the man except that I tutor him in history. Hanna? Have you heard from your *friend* today?"

Hanna shook her head, looking Ashton straight in the eyes. "He could be anywhere. Xavier could start at the training center."

Ashton's eyes narrowed slightly. "I'll let him know. Enjoy your lunch."

Dynasty made sure he was far out of hearing range before she whispered, "I don't trust that boy."

"Nor do I," Hanna replied.

"Gabrele, was Xavier in the woods searching for the demon last night?"

"No, milady."

"Were there any of his men searching?"

"No, milady."

"Does that seem odd to you?" She looked up at the Thracian.

"Yes, milady. When the soldier of Zeus summoned the Thracians, we all felt the call as a command in our heads to seek out a fallen soldier. Only Yankee resisted so he could stay with you. Brenden expressed that the need to find Dante was so branded on his heart he could think of nothing else, as if under compulsion."

"So why didn't the boy's own father feel the pull?"

"Interesting question," Titus said. "I believe someone should ask him."

"I'll do it," Gabrele said. "I'm interested to know if he's looking for his son at all."

Dynasty touched the soldier's arm before he walked off. "Give nothing away."

"Not a problem, milady. I've been away from the palace for a while now." He shrugged one shoulder. "I simply need to reconnect with the general now that I am back at work."

Dynasty grinned at his cunning and nodded for him to be off.

Down in the chamber in which Dante rested, Lysandra lay sleeping. Her head next to his, her body leaned against the gurney. The poor child couldn't be comfortable. Dynasty asked that a cot be brought down for her to sleep properly. No doubt she wouldn't leave Dante's side.

Dynasty touched her shoulder and Lysandra sprang away. "Mistress! I'm so sorry."

"Hush, child." She ran a hand over her black hair. "We brought you food."

"Thank you, but I'm not hungry." Lysandra looked back to Dante, ran her hands gingerly over his hair.

"You must eat. Imagine how upset he will be if you do not take care of yourself."

Lysandra sighed and took the fruit and sandwich from Hanna. She devoured the meal and, blushing, asked for seconds. By the time Dynasty left, Lysandra was full and had fallen back asleep on the cot next to Dante's bed, her fingers laced with his.

"I think young love is a beautiful thing," Hanna observed with a longing expression.

"Any love at all is a beautiful thing." Dynasty took Hanna's arm and held it in hers. "Do you ever think about finding it again?"

Hanna shook her head. "I had my soul mate. His memory can carry me until the gods call me home and we might be together again."

"That's how I feel as well. Perhaps we should start collecting cats? Isn't that what the humans do?"

Hanna smiled widely and shook her head. "No thank you, mistress."

Dynasty's heart pinged with loss once again. There were

reminders of her dearest Troy in every room of the palace. He left his fingerprint on every memory. Each day she missed him, but each day she found a reason to keep going.

And Filene's accusations, how absurd? How insulting. Did the two women not know each other at all? She never would've believed Filene capable of thinking so low of her, much less of saying anything. Even worse, for her to cast out such an accusation in front of witnesses. What was the matter with her?

One thing was clear, the Avondales and their guards were watching close enough to pick up what was going on. They were going to have to be more careful until Avery woke up.

⸻

Ashton paced in his chambers. Dante should be dead. They should have found the body. That blow to his gut should have left him bleeding out before anyone could make their way up the mountain to help him. Even the soldier of Zeus would have taken more time to realize—

Unless someone warned him. Unless Dante wasn't alone and someone ran for help.

Bloody fucking hell.

He wasn't alone, which meant there was a good chance that someone else knew Ashton was out there and Dante might be alive.

Hanna. It had to be Hanna. Why else would a man be out in the woods on a cold night if not for a woman? He had to find out what she knew.

What was even more worrisome was his father's sudden passion about changing the Olympian world. Their reunion last night had been one full of more tears from his mother. Filene was ready to leave this place, but Charles had informed them that the gods would be at Salina's execution and they must stay. Filene had all but stomped her foot in defiance.

"I cannot watch that monster kill my daughter," she'd yelled.

"He isn't murdering her in cold blood, Filene. She practically begged the gods to punish her. You should have seen her. It was horrifying. Her damned mouth sealed her fate with her mockery and downright hatred for the gods. I wouldn't think it possible had I not seen it with my own eyes. She is not our daughter, Filene. She is something unholy, something purely evil."

"She is my *child*," Filene sobbed as she fell into a chair. Ashton about rolled his eyes with the dramatics of it.

"Salina has made her choice. And as hard as it will be, I will stand with him."

"Father." Ashton blanched. "Are you saying you support Ryse executing her?"

"No. I'm supporting Zeus's judgment after hearing the blasphemy coming from her lips. Your sister damned her soul and I pity Ryse for having to bear this burden. Even now he is in the temple, praying and meditating." Charles sat down and put his face in his hands. "I pity him."

"He doesn't deserve your pity." Filene came up out of her chair. "He deserves your hatred. He was created by the gods to kill his own people. That is his sole purpose, Charles. The gods created him to murder Olympians. He has no other reason for living. Do you know how many of our people have died at his hands?"

"Every one of them had it coming," Charles yelled, standing to meet his wife face to face. "He is not a monster, Filene. He is cursed with the task a lesser man couldn't do. It would break me to have to fill his shoes. Even though those he kills are criminals, their blood is on his hands. A weak-minded man could not carry those stains and still be as honorable as he is."

"I can't believe you are siding with the Castilles over your own family."

"I'm siding with the gods. You should consider who you are really up against here, wife. Because I have witnessed their power. They threatened to wipe us all out if we do not change."

Filene gasped and held a hand to her throat. "They wouldn't dare."

"They don't need us, Filene. Zeus wants us, loves us, but they do not *need* us. We were created to love them back and we've royally botched it up. They have blessed us with gifts humans could only imagine and we've spat in their faces. No more," he swiped his hand through the air. "No longer will I sit back and watch my people fall deeper into pits of arrogance and greed. I will follow the gods. I will devote the rest of my days to their cause and their worship. And you are either with me or you are against me. Search your heart, Filene, because the day is soon coming when the judgment of the gods will rain down and I hope you're standing beside me." Charles pinned Ashton with a glare. "And you as well, son. You are to rule one day, but my faith in you is lacking. Make your stand."

Ashton intended to do just that. Charles missed one key point. The gods were thinking only of the Olympians. They didn't count on the demons making a stand also. The only thing in the demon's way was the Thracians. Normal Olympians couldn't fight demons and live. Only a Thracian had the strength and power to kill one. Which was why the demons wanted to invade the very heart of Thracian territory, the training center. Wipe out the next generation of warriors, and clear the way.

For now, he had to make sure loose ends were tied up. If Dante was alive, he had a problem.

CHAPTER
TWENTY-FIVE

RYSE BENT DOWN AND KISSED AVERY'S SOFT CHEEK. WHY HADN'T SHE awakened yet? Didn't Andreas escort her to the portal? She should be here, with him.

Where are you, baby? Come back. I need you now. I need to have you beside me as I prepare for what's to come. Please. Dearest goddess, please bring her home.

He had to trust the gods' timing. More than ever before, he had faith that they knew best. There was something about having to face this execution alone that caused a sickness to settle into his gut.

"I need you, Avery," he whispered to her as he sat on the edge of the bed, his elbows resting on his knees. It was easier not to look at her beautiful face when he spoke his next words. "I'm dreading this more than any other task I've faced. I fear the aftermath. Will Brenden hate me when he sees me whip Nikki? Will you? My mother and Filene are already at odds with one another. Will it destroy their friendship forever when I have to," he swallowed the lump in his throat, "when I behead Salina? And Charles. Dear Zeus, I can barely look the man in the eyes as it is. He says his faith and loyalty rests with the will of the gods. But will he still feel that way when the blood of his daughter stains my blade?" Ryse sighed and pushed his long hair off his face, absently thinking he should trim it. "I fear I might lose my mind before this is all over. And truly, it's only the beginning of a long journey to get our people back to the old ways."

He stood and paced the room, continually speaking out loud. He nearly tripped over his own two feet when he glanced over at the bed and saw Avery looking up at him.

Ryse froze.

Emerald eyes, pure and shining with life, tracked his movements. Her face remained pensive, fearful.

"Avery," he whispered, his voice catching.

"That'd be me. Who the hell are you?"

Oh shit.

"Mother," Ryse called in to the next room. He didn't move, even when Dynasty and Hanna came rushing in.

"Avery!" they exclaimed, going to her side. Dyna picked up her wrist and checked her pulse, felt of her forehead. "How do you feel, child? Can you move your arms, your legs?"

Avery stared wide-eyed at them both but didn't speak.

"Avery?" Dynasty whispered, looking into her eyes. "Do you understand what I'm asking you?"

"I gotcha. I'm just tryin' to move my arms and it ain't workin'." Her eyes misted over. Her face softened and she turned into a vulnerable little girl right before them. "I feel like I should know you. Do I know you?"

Dynasty cast Ryse a glance before turning back and speaking very slowly to Avery. "My name is Dynasty. This is my friend, Hanna. This is my son, Ryse. Does any of that sound right to you?"

Avery's breathing deepened; her aura was wild and out of control, swirling with a mixture of fear, desperation, and pain.

"Ryse?" She took in a jagged breath. "It hurts my heart to look at you. Why? How do I know you?"

He forced himself to shake off the terror of the moment and slowly approach the bed. He smiled, even though he wanted to shake her awake. "You've been through a lot, Avery. I'm sure it's normal for things to be mixed up for a while."

But to forget *him*, her husband and soul mate? This couldn't be right. No, this was all wrong. They had known each other in the

Heavens. What had changed? He'd expected a happy reunion full of tears and kisses and wrapping up in each other's arms. Not this. Gods, *anything* but this.

"Why don't we see to your physical needs?" his mother suggested in her gentlest voice. "Are you hungry? Thirsty?"

"I know how to cook," Avery said. "I'm a good cook."

"You are. Very good, darling." Dynasty touched her cheek. "Can you remember anything else?"

"Frank. Where is Frank?"

The room went still. Avery didn't remember the tragic events that led to the death of her best friend and Ryse bringing her to the Haven. How were they going to explain it without upsetting her?

"Are you thirsty? Hanna can bring you water."

"Please." Avery was temporarily distracted. She turned her eyes to Ryse's and stared at him. Even as she sipped the water, she stared.

"Do you think you can walk?" Dynasty asked.

Avery opened her mouth to speak, but nothing came out. Her eyes were glued to Ryse and he couldn't look away either. By the gods, she was so beautiful. Every feature of her face pleased him, her emerald eyes and high cheekbones, luscious lips and slightly upturned nose. He loved the way her mass of unruly curls formed a deep red wreath around her head and cascaded down her back. The recollection of their lovemaking flooded his memory and he could still feel those soft curls against his naked skin.

Avery took in a sharp breath. "What were you just thinking?"

Ryse stuttered and stammered. If Avery could read his aura, she would know. His mother surely did, guessing by the way her cheeks colored.

"Ryse, son, why don't you come around to this side of the bed and try to help Avery stand up?"

He nodded and the ladies cleared the way for him. He leaned over and slowly peeled back the blankets so he could move her feet to the floor. The moment his hands touched her skin, a zing of electricity shot through him. He flicked his eyes up to meet hers.

"My dang legs don't remember how to work." Avery laughed

nervously. "They feel all tingly, like I've been sitting too long. How long has it been?"

"A little over two months," Dynasty said.

"Holy crap. No wonder."

They moved her feet to the floor and gave her time to sit up and adjust.

"We've worked with you every day, darling. Moving your arms and legs, sitting you up, and making you remain vertical for at least a couple hours a day. I'm hoping your muscles have not suffered too much."

"I feel weak." Avery sighed.

"Let me help you." Ryse reached for her waist and she tentatively touched his arm. "It's all right, baby." They locked eyes again. His entire world, his every breath focused on her. As he guided her to her feet, she clenched her hands around his arms, her legs and hips shaking.

There was a moment when time froze. The clock never ticked. No one drew breath. In that heartbeat, there were only Ryse and Avery.

It was like they were seeing each other for the first time. His heart beat like a snare drum in his chest and he could feel her rapid pulse against his body. Her eyes traced the lines of his face and, when she stared at his lips, his blood nearly boiled over.

Out of the corner of his eye, he could see his mother and Hanna retreating to the other room. *Thank the gods.*

Ryse bent his head and gently pressed his lips to Avery's. He swallowed her gasp, using her slightly opened mouth to swipe his tongue against hers. Even though her body went rigid, her mouth was pliant and cooperative. She tilted her head and ran one hand to the back of his neck, pulling him closer. *Perfect.*

Sweeping her off her feet, he held her against him while he sat down on the bed and kept her in his lap.

"I'm in love with you, aren't I?" she asked before devouring his mouth again.

Ryse smiled at the way her accent thickened with frustration. "You're my wife, Avery."

Her head popped up and wide eyes met his. Her lips were beautifully swollen from their kissing. "Wife?" she whispered.

"Yes, baby. We were recently mated not too long before you—fell asleep."

"That's why I'm so drawn to you? It's like I can't get enough. That's pretty bat-shit crazy, given my current state of *what-the-hell*." She tried to smile, but he could see the fear in her eyes.

"Listen to me," Ryse said and touched her cheek. "Don't worry about a thing. We'll handle this one day at a time. Just know that I'm here for you and I love you with every beat of my heart."

Her eyes narrowed a fraction. "I believe you."

Ryse's shoulders relaxed and he pressed his face into her neck. "I do. Gods, how I've missed you, how I've needed to hear your voice and hold you again."

"Shh," she comforted him, a strange twist of roles. "I'm awake now. Don't know if I'm worth a darn, but we'll figure it out, right?"

They held on to each other for a long time, soaking up the nearness. Something settled in Ryse. They would be okay. He knew the gods would take care of them. It was a solid faith he hadn't had in many, many decades.

Avery's body was jelly. *I guess two months of sitting on your ass does that,* she thought as she tried to walk. Needles pricked her skin and every nerve tingled. When she raised her arms over her head to remove the shirt she wore, her fingers went numb. She had to sit down twice because she was lightheaded.

"I'm really sorry," she said to Dynasty as the woman caught her and set her on the edge of the tub. She wanted a bath so bad she couldn't stand it. Unfortunately, she wasn't strong enough to tend to her own body.

"It's nothing, sweet girl." Dynasty kissed her forehead, her eyes full of tears that were ready to overflow. "I'm so glad you're home. I've never been so relieved." She blinked and took a deep breath. "Forgive my emotions; I'm quite overwhelmed."

The other lady, the one with black hair who never spoke, handed Dynasty a tissue.

"So, let me get this straight." Avery slid her legs into the warm water. "You're a queen." She pointed to Dynasty, then Hanna. "You're her—"

"Shadow Lady," the quiet one said.

"And that's like a helper-maid-person?"

She nodded.

"And Ryse is a prince...that I'm *married* to...and he has a little brother...but his father was killed before I...went to sleep. Right?"

"Yes."

Avery hugged her knees and leaned her chin on them. Being nude in front of two semi-strangers should've bothered her. Then again, they had dressed and bathed her for the last two months while she... *slept*. That pretty much killed all modesty between them.

While Dynasty washed her hair, Avery thought back to the man with the brown eyes and delicious lips. Damn, he was hot. Not simply *hey, he's cute* but *pick your tongue up off the ground and wipe your drool* smoking hot. Tall, dark, and sexy...and married to her. If she was dreaming, this was the best damn dream *ever*. Ryse was pure muscle from head to toe with shoulders as wide as a barn door. When she'd held on to his arms, she'd nearly made a fool of herself. It was like grabbing rock. Yet when he held her, his body was giving and curved perfectly to fit her frame. *It's like he was made just for me.*

"I have to say, well done on creating Ryse. Solid eleven on a scale of one to ten. Wow."

Dyna and Hanna chuckled. "Thank you. You should have seen his father." Dyna paused and her face fell again. "Avery, can you tell me the last thing you remember?"

"Um, I remember going the café and Izzy was talking about some cute blond she'd met." She took a breath. "Things get fuzzy after that. Like a dream."

"Do you remember going to the dance hall with Frank?"

Mentioning the event brought it to mind. Yes, she remembered. She'd been nervous, so very nervous because..."Ryse was coming. I wanted to look good for him. Jerry was acting weird and he left. Then I danced with Frank and...Ryse. Yeah, I do remember that." The memory of being in his arms brought a smile to her face.

Dynasty rinsed out her hair and sat on the edge of the tub. "I know this might be very difficult for you, but you're doing great. I'm going to see if we can't jog your memory a bit."

"I don't like missin' pieces of my brain."

"It's nothing to fret over, child." Her smile was warm and kind, welcoming. This was a woman who genuinely cared and Avery trusted her. "After the dance hall, you went home and waited for Ryse to arrive."

Even as she said the words, the memories came back. "He didn't come. It was...oh god. It was Jerry. Jerry came and he hit me and he tied me up." She breathed deeply, trying to handle the fear and pain that came with the memory. "He did terrible things. To me and Frank, my parents. God. I remember." She started to cry and noticed the water in the tub was boiling.

"Avery." Dynasty stood slowly. "Calm down, darling. You're safe now. You're safe here with me. Jerry is dead. He can't touch you anymore."

Two strong hands lifted her from the boiling water. Ryse wrapped her in a towel and cradled her to his chest on the floor. "I'm here. You're safe, baby." The deep rumble of his voice instantly soothed her. He stroked her hair and held her tight until she could think again. His scent flooded her mind, his warmth covered her and created a protective barrier from the cold memories.

"What's wrong with me?" Avery whispered. "I know I've dealt with this, but it feels raw, like I'm living it again for the first time."

"You've suffered a loss. It's natural to mourn." He looked at his mother, whose eyes filled with tears. "We all have to mourn in our own time."

Dynasty covered her mouth with her hand. She shook her head and stood, exiting the bathroom.

Avery watched her leave. Guilt pinged in her chest. "I upset her."

"She's a strong woman, just like you. Everyone is running on fumes right now, baby. We could all use some rest."

"Don't leave me."

"Never." He kissed her hair. "Never again, baby."

He helped Avery dress and flashes of déjà vu hit her. "We've done this before." She narrowed her eyes at him, remembering snippets of a small room, her body covered in blood, and a quilt. "After Frank was killed. You helped me, but I was angry with you."

Ryse's lips twitched. "You didn't mind showing it, slammed a door in my face."

"A couple times."

"And slapped me."

"A couple times."

Ryse's full smile melted her insides until she was lightheaded again. "You do have a temper." He kissed her bare shoulder. "Even then, I couldn't help think how beautiful you are. Like now. The gods created a work of art when they made you."

"Rhea," Avery whispered. She closed her eyes, desperately trying to see the image of the woman in her mind. The goddess was a blur. "She created me. Other gods helped, but she created me."

Ryse nodded once, allowing her to think.

"She created me for you and you for me. We have work to do."

He stared at her, letting her verbally work things out. But the memories were done revealing themselves for the moment and she felt exhaustion settle into her bones.

"There is much more to this story, isn't there?"

Ryse held her shoulders and furrowed his brow. "I wish I could tell you that it's a pleasant story, Avery. I can't. Much has happened and the effects of those events are about to come to fruition. You're going to have to be strong."

Avery nodded, not knowing what to say. Fear of what she might remember hung over her. As she rested her head against Ryse's chest, she prayed she was strong enough to deal with whatever happened. If not for herself, then for him.

CHAPTER TWENTY-SIX

LYSANDRA FELT DANTE STIR. HER HEART LEAPT. HE'D BEEN STILL AS DEATH for two days and it worried her. Dealing with all these human emotions had worn her out. She couldn't eat, couldn't sleep, and couldn't stand watching the only man she'd ever cared for suffer. Being in Delphi had made her so numb to fear, anger…love. As she traced the lines of Dante's jaw with her finger, she wondered how she'd lived—no, existed—so long without knowing the excitement of love, the flutter of that first eye contact, the tingling sensation on her lips after a kiss. Was it worth the sacrifice? Was it worth putting her heart on ice to perform a job that had become so antiquated that even the gods questioned the necessity for it? Couldn't she do so much more good here on Earth, serving the Deities who ruled?

"Lysa?" Dante whispered, his dry voice snapping her out of her thoughts.

"I'm here." She took the hand he feebly tried to raise. "Be still, my love. Everything is going to be fine."

He swallowed, his throat hoarse. "I feared I'd never see you again."

"Shh. I'm fine. You saved me. You did well. I love you, my darling. Rest and heal. I'm right here."

This was all he needed to hear before he slipped back into sleep.

She hadn't realized she'd begun to cry until her tear dripped down onto his face.

"He awake?" Yankee asked as he stumbled into the room. "I heard voices."

Lysandra stiffened. She wiped her face and turned to him. "He spoke for a moment, then drifted off again. I don't think he will heal swiftly. The demon blood still courses through him. He's lucky to be alive."

Yankee nodded, his bloodshot eyes bouncing around the room. There was so much hostility inside him. His aura was stained with it. He smelled of alcohol and his body swayed.

"Are you intoxicated?" she demanded.

"It's possible. You going to take me over your knee for it?" He reached out to brace himself on one of the beds and missed, sending him forward into her arms. "Ah shit."

"You are. You're drunk." Lysandra struggled under his weight. She urged him onto her cot. "You blasted fool. Sometimes I have to wonder how a cretin like you made it to the ranks of Elite. Compared to Dante, you're, well, you're a prick. That's what he calls you anyway."

"Oh, Eight-ball, don't get your granny panties in a wad. Your Prince Charming is mad because I made him face the fact that he wants to pop your cherry." His words were slurred and his arms waved in the air wildly as he spoke.

"Pop my *what*?"

Yankee tried to roll over and nearly fell off the cot. "Your cherry, steal your virtue, take your *virginity*." He drew out the syllables on that last word and chuckled. "He wants in your pants, or should I say, up your skirt." He belched and swatted the stench away. "But he's all noble and shit. Another fucking Boy Scout. He and Brenden make a damn fine pair. It's practically a bro-mance with all their uplifting, encouraging, patting each other's ass and shit."

Lysandra pushed his shoulders back down. "Watch your mouth. Your words are nearly as foul as your breath. Now that I comprehend the cherry references, I can honestly say you are a pig."

"You know what pisses me off more than any fucking thing?" His eyes crossed and he opened them wide to straighten them out again. If she weren't so angry with him, she might have laughed. Dearest gods, what had he ingested?

"I don't really care, but I have a terrible suspicion you'll share with me anyhow." Lysandra rolled her eyes.

"They *are* better than me."

His confession took her by surprise.

"Those two punks are good to the core. They're not like me. I hate people. I hate everything. Fuck, I hate my own reflection." He chuckled and sighed. "They've both found women, good women. Even if one is a murderer and one is a virgin."

She had nearly felt pity for him until that comment.

"You love him?" Yankee asked, watching her with eyes that were suddenly intense and focused.

"More than I thought possible."

"Then stick by him. He needs someone to give him that. No one has ever backed him up. Not until recently." Yankee took a deep breath and let it out through his mouth, sending a waft of alcohol-tainted air her direction. She cringed. He closed his eyes and put his arm up over his face. "He's a good man, Eight-ball. A damn…good…man…" Yankee was quiet for a moment.

Then he started to snore. Loudly.

Once again, pity and disgust warred for her reaction. Watching him sleep, his face finally relaxing from its permanent scowl, he appeared vulnerable and young.

I hate my own reflection. What a terrible thing to say. What a terrible way to live. She reached down and grabbed a blanket, stretching it across his chest. With lightning speed, he gripped both her wrists, his eyes piercing hers, their noses only inches apart.

A vision came to her quickly, flashing images into her mind.

An angry little boy hid under his blanket. Screaming. Crying. Another child, a girl. Her shrill screams tore at his heart as their father slapped her. Blonde hair stuck to her face with blood. He couldn't take it anymore. The little boy rushed his father, pushing him down. "Go!" he screamed at the little girl. "Never come back!"

Blood mixed with her tears, her hazel eyes wide with fear as she reached for his hand. "Sammy!" But they never touched. She disappeared into thin air. The father beat the boy until he went unconscious.

The vision skipped ahead many years.

A tall woman with long, black hair and onyx eyes smiled down at Yankee. Her fingers touched his lips. "You can't save the world, Sammy. Not until you save yourself." She kissed him, her heart full of love. And for the first time in his life, Yankee felt hope.

Lysandra blinked and focused on his face. Maybe he wasn't attractive to her, but the woman in her vision found him to be so. It reminded her that even a drunken, filthy-mouthed Thracian was lovable to someone.

"Rest, warrior. I shall protect you for once." She slowly bent to place a sisterly kiss on his rough cheek.

His hard features softened and he turned his face away from her, covering himself with the blanket.

She backed away and went to sit on the other side of Dante, facing the door. Before taking up her post, she bent to Dante's ear and whispered, "I love you and I shall always be your greatest admirer. I'll always have your back," she promised, smiling at the phrasing Yankee used.

One day, Yankee would find love too. Hopefully, he wouldn't sabotage it like he did every other relationship. Now that she understood, Lysandra let her heart soften to him. Yankee hadn't been trying to run her off or keep Dante away from her out of jealousy. He simply didn't know how to handle love. In his own—rather messed up—way, Yankee had been trying to protect Dante from getting his heart broken. What he didn't understand was that love, true love, the kind people devoted themselves to and fought for, was also unconditional. It meant daily setting aside selfish desires and pursuing the best for the one you loved. It meant making a choice to overcome emotional circumstances and trudging through hard times.

Dante and Lysandra had a way to go before they were ready to be mated. But she knew with all her heart that he was her choice, the only man she would ever truly love. Together, they could overcome anything.

She smiled as she remembered the woman in her vision. She had to be strong to deal with Yankee, the poor girl. He would fight her the hardest. But if that was his love, the gods would make a way.

A soft knock on the door hours later caused her to startle. She'd fallen asleep sitting upright in her chair. With the queen and Hanna came a woman that took her breath away.

Although she'd tended to Avery daily for the last couple of months, there was a vast difference in seeing her awake and alive. Her aura was shining of white light, pure and brilliant. Brenden held on to one of her arms and she supported herself with a cane.

A smile spread across her face. "Lysandra," she said, excitedly whispering so she didn't wake the soldiers.

"Milady." She bowed low.

"Get up, darlin'. I'm pretty sure since you've bathed me, you and I are practically old friends."

"It was an honor to serve you."

"Ha!" Avery covered her laughter with her hand. "I'm pretty sure scrubbin' my armpits was no honor. But you're a doll for sayin' so. How's our boy?"

The concern on her face as she approached Dante made Lysandra instantly gravitate to her. Anyone who looked on Dante with open affection was golden in her book. Avery leaned over and kissed his forehead. Then she cast a glance at Yankee. "Was he hurt too?"

"No, milady. I believe when he awakens, he's going to be slightly hung-over."

"Oh gosh." Avery sighed and shook her head. "Dumbass. He deserves it. Still, Brenden, can you get him some meds and a glass of water?"

"Dante woke for a moment earlier. I am prayerfully optimistic that he will recover."

"Of course he will." Avery rested her entire hand over his forehead and closed her eyes. "Hmm." Her brows dipped, her lips pinched together.

Everyone in the room watched her.

"Evander should take a look at him," Dynasty suggested.

"He will. But he can't get this crap out of him." Avery opened her eyes and pulled her hand away.

"What did you see?" Lysandra asked, not like being kept uninformed when it came to her love.

Avery's emerald green eyes lifted towards hers. Their depths sparkled just like the jewel. They were mesmerizing. "There is an evil taint to his blood. The Thracian side fights it. It's a miracle, really. He should've died." Her smile widened. "You kept him alive, Lysa. He's fightin' for you."

"I don't want him fighting for me. I want him to heal."

"He will, darlin'. You can take that to the bank. I should've figured when my Ken Doll fell, he'd fall hard."

My Ken Doll. Lysandra didn't know what rubbed her the rawest about that comment. The fact that Avery seemed to think she had a prior claim on the man she loved or the fact that she had no idea what a Ken Doll was and therefore did not understand the moniker.

"Hey?" Avery reached out and touched her arm. "Your aura went off the charts. You okay?"

Lysandra took a deep breath. "I'm fine. I wasn't aware you were so…familiar with Dante."

"She's *familiar* with everyone." Yankee gingerly sat up and rubbed at his temple with his palm. "No need to piss on trees, Eight-ball. Our Southern Belle likes to get all comfy with the soldiers."

"Hello, jackass." Avery slapped him on the shoulder and they both nearly fell over. She'd said the words loudly and Lysandra wanted to explain that he wasn't deaf, only fighting a head—*Oh.*

"Glad you're awake." Yankee rose and stretched his arms over his head, wincing. "This place has been a wreck without you."

"I hear you've been causing some trouble of your own."

"And I hear you have CRS."

Lysandra tilted her head so Yankee explained. "Can't Remember Shit."

"Funny, she remembered you're a jackass," Lysa said, not trying to be comical.

Avery, Dynasty, and even Hanna laughed. Yankee spread his arms wide, his look smug. "Some people are simply unforgettable, Eight-ball."

"You're full of crap." Avery rolled her eyes. "I think Ryse is having some kind of meeting. You might want to go check in."

"You remember where, or did you forget that, too?" Yankee asked.

Avery sighed and swiped a hand over her face. "Everybody's a comedian."

Dynasty chuckled and reached for Yankee's hand. She pressed her palm to his cheek. The healing was visible. His bloodshot eyes cleared up, his shoulders relaxed, and he took a deep, deep breath. "You shouldn't do such things to yourself, Samuel. We need you at full capacity."

"Don't worry, even hung-over, I'm better than all those guys put together." His eyes flickered over to Lysandra for a split second before he left. His bravado was back, but she remembered his intoxicated confessions.

*They're not like me...*No, they weren't. Where Dante and Brenden wore their hearts on their sleeves, Yankee's was buried but there nonetheless.

CHAPTER
TWENTY-SEVEN

"I T's TIME."

Ryse spoke the words to a room filled with anxious people. The Avondales, Charles, Filene, Ashton, Xavier, and three of his soldiers took up one corner of the room across from his family. Dynasty, Hayden, and Hanna were flanked by Titus and Gabrele. The Elites—Hammon, Philippe, Cutter, Yankee, Brenden, and General Falcon—were also behind them. A few other top-tier soldiers and Thracian teachers were there as well. Their scrutiny was daunting. Ares came to him and told him when and how the execution would take place. Ryse conveyed this to the group.

"The gods will be appearing throughout the world. Zeus will be here, with Poseidon, Ares, and Athena. The other gods will branch out to the other realms. They are going to allow each person to see the execution as if they were here, in our Haven, in our arena." Ryse swallowed. He would be killing a princess in front of their entire world. "We will actually be in the arena. Salina, her followers, and Nikki will be delivered by Hermes when the time comes."

"We don't get to see her beforehand?" Filene said. Tears formed in her already red-rimmed eyes. Her lip quivered. "I should be allowed to tell her goodbye."

"You may take it up with the gods," Hayden answered for his

brother. Ryse had already informed him of how Ares wanted things. Due to Salina's behavior in the Heavens, the gods were not going to allow her to infect anyone else. She would be delivered to Earth right before Ryse executed her.

"Should we return home, Ryse?" Charles asked. "Would it be easier if we were not here?"

Filene's eyes nearly popped out of her head. She gasped, and her mouth hung open. "You want to make this easier for *him*?"

"Yes," Charles growled at his wife. Red crept up her face from either anger or embarrassment.

"You must remain, I'm afraid. Ares said that Zeus will bring Avery back and the gods want your family to see it for themselves." The lie was necessary. Ryse hated it, but it was the will of the gods.

"I do not doubt her resurrection is of the gods, Ryse." Charles leaned over the table towards him. "I saw her spirit in the Heavens. I saw her with Rhea. If she returns to Earth, it will be a true miracle. I believe."

"We know you do." Hayden smiled, sending Ashton and Filene a glance.

"Will the maid die too?" Filene asked. "She's a murderer. Will you kill her too, the way you're going to kill my child?"

A deep bass growl vibrated the seats and table. Glasses of water vibrated. The one closest to the source of the rumble nearly spilled. The air was thick with tension.

"Bren," Ryse snapped at his Elite. The growling ceased. He speared Filene with a hard look. "I will carry out the punishment as the gods have decreed. Nikki is to…" He hadn't told any of this to Brenden yet. *Shit.* He hadn't wanted Bren to find out like this, but there hadn't been enough time to get him alone. "Nikki will be whipped, according to the judgment of the gods, for her involvement in the murder of my father."

Brenden froze; their eyes met. His aura went cold, dark, and angry. Its power swept through the room like the wind. His lips curled up into a snarl.

"This is an outrage," Filene cried out, rising to her feet.

"You're damned right it is," Brenden agreed, but for very different reasons.

"Hold your tongue, you monster. If my daughter must die, so should her accomplice."

"Nikki's the real killer," Ashton said.

"Nikki wouldn't hurt a fly. Your bitch of a sister brainwashed her."

An argument began. The room erupted into chaos. Filene and Ashton yelled across the table at Brenden and Yankee, who had jumped in to restrain his fellow soldier, but then opened his big mouth. Charles had his wife by the shoulders, trying to calm her down, but wasn't doing a good job in the slightest. Ryse, Hayden, and Dynasty exchanged frustrated glances.

Ryse stood, opened his arms, and felt the power of the gods flow into his hands. From his palms a bright light burst forth, flooding the room, blinding those who were not paying attention to his actions. His family had closed their eyes, covered their ears.

"Enough," he bellowed, power making his voice reverberate throughout the room. Those standing staggered under the weight of his command. Charles stumbled back into his chair and watched Ryse with wide eyes. Filene and Ashton had been pushed back against the wall. Brenden and Yankee had crouched down beside the table. Only Hayden and Dynasty remained unfazed and sitting properly in their chairs.

"Are you children ready to hear the rest of what my son has to say? Or would you like for the gods to permanently silence your bickering?" Dynasty asked, her eyes focused on Filene.

The other woman lifted her chin and smoothed down her skirt. "Fine." Ashton held her hand and helped her into her chair. She brushed him off.

Ryse, however, noticed the way he glared at Brenden, then turned his eyes to Ryse. Ashton's nostrils flared and his eyes narrowed a fraction. "Way to scare a defenseless woman, barbarian."

"Filene is hardly defenseless." Ryse leaned over the table, face to face with the sonofabitch. "Her *mouth* has been quite the weapon of late." He waited for Ashton to spit out a retort. None came. "Sit," Ryse growled, tired of this nonsense. He stared each of them down, his patience gone. "Tomorrow morning, we gather. The gods will be here at sunrise. Until then, I suggest we all retreat to our rooms and try to get some rest. The Thracian students have been instructed on preparing the arena. I'm declaring a Haven-wide curfew at sunset. The soldier of Zeus still stands by the portal and will remain there until the gods leave. He has been instructed to enforce my rule."

"Is there a reason for this curfew?" Charles asked mildly.

Usually, in this mood, Ryse wouldn't have taken the time to justify his actions to anyone. He could implement whatever system, laws, curfew, or ban he wanted. He was the son of two Deities, blooded warrior of the gods. He'd been given a task most people in this room couldn't even fathom and the authority to do whatever necessary to achieve it.

Had it been anyone but Charles, Ryse would have reminded them of this.

"We have a soldier fighting for his life from a demon attack. Tonight, we are taking him to the portal so that Apollo and one of our healers can look at him. I don't want anyone interfering."

"Is it my son?" Xavier, who had been silent up until now, stood from where he leaned against a wall.

"Yes."

Ryse noted the way Ashton's face paled slightly. He quickly covered his reaction.

The man seemed to sag with relief. Odd, since he could barely stomach the boy. "May I be there when Apollo examines him?"

"No." Ryse stared the man in the eyes. "You will accompany General Falcon on a mission to secure the perimeter of the Haven."

"He's my son." Xavier grit his teeth.

"You should have appreciated that fact long before now. If he asks for you, I might reconsider. Until then, I don't want anyone around who might cause him stress."

"He will be a valuable asset to finding the demon, will he not?" Ashton spoke up.

"Yes. So will our other witness," Ryse informed him, watching his face for his reaction. Ashton's jaws clenched.

"Other witness?" Xavier asked. "You mean to tell me someone was with him? Did they leave Dante to die?"

"This investigation is still ongoing. I'll send you the report when we have more concrete evidence." Ryse closed out the meeting, sending everyone to their respective stations for the night.

He wasn't sure what to do with himself. Truth be told, he wanted to take Avery back to their bedroom, get her naked, and lose himself in her body. After tomorrow, she might look at him differently. It was one thing to talk about what he had to do, who he had to kill. It was all abstract thought. When the sun came up, Ryse, not someone else, would have to put those words into action. The abstract would solidify. Real blood would spill. Real hearts would break, real families would be torn apart, friendships broken.

"*Ryse*," called out an angry voice.

He closed his eyes. He knew this was coming, but it still didn't make it easy. Brenden stormed down the hallway towards him.

"When were you going to tell me? What the hell?" Defying all rationality, Brenden shoved his shoulder. "Way to give me the heads up."

"I refuse to talk to you if you don't calm down."

"Save the Yoda calm bullshit for someone else. Why the hell didn't you tell me that the gods were going to punish Nikki? She didn't want any of this. She was forced. Did you even try to advocate for her?"

"Of course I did!" Ryse stepped up into his face. His extra height had him looking down at Bren. "Even my father begged the gods for mercy on her."

"It was Hayden, wasn't it? This is his fault." Brenden had lost all semblance of self-control. In his right mind, he never would have challenged Ryse like this. "Where is that pretentious bastard?"

Using very little strength, Ryse raised one arm and pinned Brenden to the wall, his elbow up under his chin. "Let's get one thing straight," Ryse growled, feeling more feral than usual. Bren's face glowed as the power of his birthright made his eyes turn white. "You may be one of my Elites, some might even call us friends, and you might be distraught about Nikki, but if you think I'm going to stand here and listen to you say one negative word about my brother, you've highly overestimated how much I like you. Hayden, Father, and I did what we could for her cause. Nikki chose to take her punishment so that the people would feel as though justice was served. You think I'm going to enjoy hurting her? You think I wanted to come back here and face you, face Avery, knowing that I was going to have to watch Nikki's blood spill? For one damned moment, why don't you think about the bigger picture, Bren? Quit being so selfish. Have you thought about how this will affect Avery? That's the only friend she made and now I have to—" He sighed, his eyes brown once more. He moved his arm and Brenden fell to the floor, gasping for breath. "This isn't easy for any of us, damn it."

"I don't understand why," Bren said and choked. "Salina made her do it."

"We all know that, even Hayden. We have to have faith. There is a purpose for this, Bren. If I'm going to go through with tomorrow, I have to believe that. And you have to trust me." Ryse stretched out his hand.

Bren hesitated, then allowed Ryse to pull him up. Whatever arguments Bren had, he kept to himself. Instead, he nodded and walked off.

Come to me...whispered a feminine voice in his head. He would know that southern accent anywhere.

In his mother's suite, Avery stood in a long, navy blue velvet gown that was straight out of Greek history. Her ethereal beauty still knocked the breath out of his lungs.

"This is a new look for you," he said, clearing his throat. "It's a good look."

Avery smiled up at him. His breath caught and his heart lost its natural rhythm. In her eyes shone a desire he'd seen only once before. "I remembered something today."

⮜ ⋯ ⋯ ⮞

Even with the latest memory solidified in her memory, Avery couldn't believe this man was her husband. He was too good to be true. Ryse's dark brown eyes studied her; he licked his sensual lips, and her body melted.

"What did you recall?" His voice turned husky and she could sense the change in the air. Her body responded, growing tight and heated in dark places.

Avery, feeling much braver than she had hours ago around him, looped her arms around his neck and pressed her body as close to him as she could. "I remembered making love to you."

His swift gasp and widened eyes gave her great satisfaction. Wide, strong arms tightened around her waist. "Did you enjoy this memory?"

Avery pressed a kiss to his neck, then another a bit higher. "Immensely," she whispered into his ear. "I believe we need to make more memories like this."

"Avery, my beautiful love, you have no idea how wonderful that sounds. But are you suggesting that we, uh, make memories when you're still trying to remember who I am?"

"I know exactly who you are. You're my husband."

He sighed. "Yes, but do you remember everything that has happened between us?"

Avery captured his face with her hands. "I know that somewhere in this castle, we have a bedroom. I may have a few blank spots in my memory, but I know we have barely spent time in there alone. I would like to go to bed with my husband—in the literal way. And we can see what else happens." She smiled, willing him to comply. Her gut said tonight her husband needed to be distracted by something right and sacred. Although she didn't know the details of what would come tomorrow, it was going to be crap all the way around. Tonight, she wanted to love him.

"We will have to take the passages. You're not supposed to be alive."

"Alive?" Avery stepped back. This sudden, new word had a bit different meaning than asleep. "There's a large gap between alive and asleep. Are you sayin' I...died?" She slipped into a chair, needing support for her jelly-like legs.

Stunned silence was her answer.

"No wonder everyone is so shocked—except Yankee. He was, well, he was Yankee."

"Don't be upset, Avery." Ryse knelt in front of her. "But yes, you were murdered. Rhea kept you alive. Your body was here, your spirit was in the Heavens. No one knew except those who had to take care of you. Tomorrow, Zeus is going to officially present you to the people, so they know you live for a purpose, that your life has been ordained by the gods."

"Right." Avery nodded, some vague memories coming back. "Yeah, okay. This is sounding familiar. I understand." She stood once again and gathered herself. What he said felt solid, felt right. "We stick to the tunnels."

Ryse stood too, and put his arms around her again. "Are you sure? We can rest here tonight." He looked around his parents' suite.

"I don't want to worry about your mama catchin' us makin' out," Avery said. She bit her bottom lip and giggled.

"That would be awkward," he whispered back, a grin tugging at his lips.

Avery remembered their bedroom the moment she stepped into it. Everything came flooding back: their first night together, the brutal poisoning of her dogs, the shower they'd shared, the times they ate on the patio. She immediately went to the curved wall of windows and pulled back the curtains, revealing the night sky.

"You know our time is limited. I have to take Dante to the portal. You can stay here if you wish." Ryse was already taking off his shoes as he sat on the edge of the bed. "Why don't you try to sleep? I'll stay with you until I must go."

Avery reached for the zipper of her gown and tugged it down. "Then I guess we should hurry." The gown slipped to the floor and she stepped out.

Ryse's mouth hung open. "Dear gods, you are incredible."

"I'm fast too." Avery laughed as she pounced on top of him, his laughter filling the room.

They wasted no time peeling off clothing and tossing it across the room. Energy and desire raced through her veins. She'd never felt more alive. It didn't matter what little gaps were missing in her memories, she knew everything she needed to about Ryse. Their love was destined, their souls matched by the gods.

Avery kissed him deep and hard, her hands exploring the ribbed planes of his chest and stomach. The man was a living Greek demigod and was built to make his ancestors proud. Her hand slipped into his briefs and gripped his erection.

"Oh god." He threw back his head and gasped. "You're not wasting any time, are you, baby?" He panted in time with her stroking hand.

"Nope. Our time's too precious, too fleeting. Tomorrow will be hell, but tonight, we can be together and I'm not going to throw away one second with you." Avery devoured his kiss. She sucked and nibbled on his lips until she thought she might explode with the desire building inside.

Ryse disposed of her panties and bra; his own briefs he simply ripped off, the fabric shredding under his strength. Now nothing separated them. Avery settled her legs on either side of his hips and let him guide her down.

The sweet pressure of him sliding into her made her head spin. When he was buried to the hilt, her body stretched to the limits, she let out a shaky breath and moaned. "Perfection."

"Yes, you are." Ryse's voice was deep and husky, layered with his passion.

Avery smiled down at him, her hands roaming his chest and up to his neck. Her hips began to move and he groaned. Every one of his muscles was tight, his control hanging by a thin wire.

"You don't have to hold back, Ryse. You can love me as wildly as you wish."

"I don't want to rush. I want to take our time. I want to worship your body the way you deserve." All the while, their bodies moved in sync, the tension building.

She wanted nothing more than to take a slow, luxurious ride on Ryse. But tonight wasn't that night. Tonight, she needed to give him the escape he desired, the distraction he needed. Ryse's Thracian blood was all about dominating, controlling, claiming. For him, she could put aside fantasies of sweet lovemaking for another time.

"Worship me later. Enjoy me right now." She knew the moment he gave in. His hands clamped over her hips and he took control. Their tempo increased, the wild rush of ecstasy and desire giving them both the release they needed. Avery threw back her head and gasped his name as pleasure twisted inside of her and she plummeted off the edge of sanity.

Ryse roared, the muscles in his neck straining as he gave in and let go, filling her body. He held her against his chest, both of them panting and shivering with aftershock.

"Well," he exhaled with a gust. "That was…embarrassingly quick."

Avery sighed, her body melted butter on top of his. "It was just what you needed."

"Did I ever." With each deep breath, his massive body moved her up and down.

"I forgot what a huge guy you are."

Ryse chuckled darkly. "Are you talking in general, or about a certain part of my anatomy?"

Avery laughed and rested her chin on her hands over his chest. "C, all of the above."

"You southern girls sure know how to sweet talk a man." Ryse held on to her and rolled them to the side. "I love you so much."

"I love you too." Avery smiled. His brown eyes reflected the warmth and affection she felt for him.

He lifted his hand to trace the lines of the tattoo over her heart. The sword matched his, but hers had a lion head on top of it, signifying her as a child of Rhea. "Do you remember the night I gave you this?"

"Kind of. The details are fuzzy. I remember thinking you were the most amazing man I'd ever met."

Ryse grinned, propping himself up on his elbow. His face fell, a deep scowl formed. "That night, you made me a promise. Tomorrow, I'll test it."

Avery dug through her memories, trying to look past the fog clouding some of the details. "Remind me?" She blushed.

"I promised you that I would never keep you in the dark. I promised always to be upfront about what I have to do. In return, you promised that you would never fear me."

The memory unraveled with every word he spoke. All she needed was the reminder. The emotions of that night came back and she vividly remembered making those vows. "I remember now."

"No matter what happens tomorrow, know that I love you with all my heart." He paused. "If I could keep you from this, I would."

"You promised not to hide the truth from me."

Ryse nodded. "I know. That doesn't make it easier to tell you."

Avery rolled over on her back and took a deep breath. She ran her hands over her face, wishing that all this crap would go away. Unfortunately, Ryse's phone rang and reminded them both that this was just the beginning.

"They're ready to take Dante to the portal." He stood and gave her a wonderful view of his backside. Wide shoulders, rounded with muscles, tapered off to a trim waist. His sword tattoo stretched from the base of his neck down his spine. It ended just before the curves of his bottom. Her heart ached with longing and, for a moment, she didn't want him to leave her.

"Ryse?" Avery whispered.

He turned, his eyes meeting hers. "What is it?" He fiddled with his shirt, trying to get the sleeves untangled. They hadn't exactly been careful with their clothing earlier.

"I love you."

He paused, his shirt halfway over his arms. The edge of his mouth tugged back and he sat down on the bed again. "I love you too, baby."

Avery stretched out over the bed, her body laid out before him. "I'll wait here for you, just like this."

Ryse clenched his eyes closed and his jaw tightened. "Do you know how hard it will be to concentrate on my task, knowing you are naked and waiting on me?"

"Don't forget aroused. I'll be naked and aroused, waiting on you." She sent him the most mischievous smile she could.

"You're going to be the death of me yet, woman." He gave her a light slap on her thigh that made her giggle. When he stood to stretch his shirt over his head, a whole new wave of desire hit her. Yes, she was going to be painfully aroused while waiting on him.

CHAPTER TWENTY-EIGHT

RYSE RENDEZVOUSED WITH THE ELITES AS THEY CAME OUT OF THE SIDE door of the palace. They carried Dante between them on a stretcher. Hayden led the way. Lysandra, Dynasty, and Hanna followed, with Hammon bringing up the rear. With every movement across the terrain, Dante cringed and moaned. His body was still in great pain. But Apollo promised to heal him.

"Where's Avery?" Brenden asked from his position at the front corner near Dante's head.

"Avery?" Dante moaned. His dazed eyes found Ryse.

"She's awake, but had to remain hidden still," Ryse answered his soldiers. Sweat covered Dante's head and chest. His eyes were cloudy and bloodshot. The boy looked terrible.

Nonetheless, a faint smile kicked up the corners of his lips. "Good."

Brenden, Cutter, Philippe, and Yankee walked him to the entrance of the portal. The large oval of liquid still glowed and rippled, actively open to the other side. They gingerly laid his pallet on the ground. The soldier of Zeus looked down at Dante.

"Well done, thou servant of the gods. Apollo has arrived."

Sure enough, the sun god stepped out of the portal, his eyes searching each person in the group. He wore a white robe secured on one of his shoulders. Navy blue ribbons trimmed the edges and a laurel wreath adorned his head. His entire body glowed with power.

They all went to their knees. Hayden spoke. "Apollo, we are humbled by your presence."

"Thank you, young prince. I am happy to aid this fine warrior. He should not have suffered this evil." The god gathered his robes and came to the pallet that held Dante. Apollo placed his illuminated hand on Dante's forehead and closed his eyes. He mumbled a few words that Ryse didn't catch before he lifted his hand. "Open his garment and let me see his wound."

Lysandra quickly fell to task. She pulled off his bandages and allowed Apollo to see the gruesome mess of his stomach.

"Oracle?" Apollo looked inquisitively at her, his head tilted to the side, like he'd just realized the obvious.

Lysandra sat on her knees, her hands folded in her lap. "My Lord."

"Why do you abide here?"

"Rhea sent me."

"What business have you with this man?" Apollo pointed at Dante.

"He is my—" She glanced up at Ryse. "He is my chosen mate, my Lord. If he shall have me." Her body trembled.

"You defy the vow of the Pythia?" Apollo frowned.

Lysandra, frightened but brave, looked full into the face of the god. "My heart belongs to this incredible warrior as strongly as my faith belongs to the gods. If you view this as an act of betrayal, I cannot help that and I am deeply apologetic. But…I pray you do not." She touched Dante's shoulder and looked at him. "I love him."

Ryse arched his brow. *Wow.* It took amazing courage to be so bold to a god. His affections for her increased when he saw that she would stand beside Dante and fight for their blooming relationship.

"I support this union," Ryse said. Several of his men and his mother agreed. None spoke up as loudly as Yankee. *Interesting.*

Apollo looked around at the men. Even kneeling, he was still nearly as tall. "Never has an Oracle left my temple."

"With all due respect, my Lord," Yankee said. "There's never been a *Thracian* Deity, never a second-born Deity Prince, never an assassin princess, or a Divine Grace brought back from the grave either."

Yankee shrugged his shoulders, held up his hands with that *who gives a shit* smirk on his face. "Is this really so shocking?"

Ryse could have sworn that the god's lips twitched.

"Fair point." Apollo addressed Lysandra. "So be it, Oracle. May you live a long and prosperous life with your warrior." He touched Dante's stomach and his hand glowed bright.

Dante screamed as black oil rose into the air, streaming from his wound and his mouth. It reminded Ryse of how the evil had spewed from Nikki when Apollo had healed her. And he knew exactly who had put that demonic crap inside of her. Ryse was going to pay much more attention to Ashton after this.

When Apollo finished, Dante lay breathing heavily on the ground, Lysandra gripping his shoulders as he looked around with a wild expression in his eyes. Once they settled on her, he calmed.

"It's me. Don't worry, my love." She talked softly to him, kissing his cheek and forehead.

Ryse wasn't the only one who turned their eyes away from the intimate moment.

"He still has traces of the dark magic in his mind." Apollo rose to his full height. "Only time will tell what becomes of it. Hades alone can remove it, although it is best that he not be involved in this realm. He is one of the gods who wishes your race extinct. He will find any excuse. He surely will not care about the life of one soldier." The god looked down at the couple on the ground. "His physical form shall heal in the next few hours. Take care of him, Oracle."

Lysandra shifted to grip his robe. She kissed his hands and feet, thanking him over and over again in Greek.

A strange expression crossed his face before he concealed it. He looked surprised by her worship. Apollo smiled a warm and loving smile down at his follower. "You are welcome, my child. Your prayers unto me shall always be heard." He tipped his head to Ryse, then went back through the portal. The soldier of Zeus took up his position and paid them no more attention.

"Let's get him inside," Brenden said, helping Dante to his feet.

"I don't know who summoned a *god* for me," Dante said, his voice tight. "But thanks."

Hammon reached out and touched his shoulder. "It is the least we can do. What you did was very brave."

"Stupid," Yankee said, "but brave."

Dante locked eyes with Yankee. "You and I have some unfinished business."

"Look," Yankee put his hands in his pockets, appearing to be bored, "get to the point of supporting your own weight, and then you can threaten me all you want. Until then, shut it."

"Gentleman," Ryse said, his patience gone for one day, "enough of the bickering. Lysandra, accompany Dante to his suite. Stay with him and tend to his needs. The rest of you, get some sleep. We will all need to be at our best tomorrow."

He kissed his mother goodnight and made his way back to his room. Avery had just taken her hair down and was standing in front of the mirror naked, save a tiny triangle of cloth over her plump ass. His footsteps faltered and he watched her bend to open a few drawers in the dresser, mumbling as she searched for something.

"Damn selective amnesia. I can light a friggin' candle with my mind, but I can't find my clothes." She saw him in the mirror. "Oh, hey."

He moved until he was right behind her and wrapped his arms around her waist.

"Ryse?"

"Shh. You're supposed to be naked." He met her eyes in the mirror as his hand slid upward to cup the weight of one breast. She shuddered, fire sparking in her green eyes. Ryse slipped his other hand between her legs. "I think I should worship you now."

Avery's eyes closed and her body relaxed against him. "Perfectly fine with me, darlin'."

Throughout the night, Ryse reacquainted himself with every inch of her body. He memorized every fleck of green in her eyes and every curve of her lips. Once he learned what made her moan and gasp in pleasure, he repeated it often. They drowned each other in desire. When she thought she couldn't take any more, he pushed her even further until they flew to the edges of the universe and back.

Somewhere in the middle of their exploration, he found a ticklish spot. Ryse took full advantage and had his sexy Princess laughing and giggling in between her sighs. Even with all the turmoil facing him tomorrow, he'd never been happier in his life than while laughing and making love with her. She collapsed on top of him, huffing and puffing after their last orgasm.

"Holy cow." She chuckled against this chest. "You really are the product of gods."

Ryse grinned, his body finally sated and lax. "You are welcome." They both laughed and tried to catch their breath.

When they finally fell asleep, it was soundly in each other's arms.

CHAPTER TWENTY-NINE

HAYDEN SIGHED WITH RELIEF WHEN HIS DREAM TOOK SHAPE. HE WAS once again in the gardens of the palace. White roses, with blooms so pure they could only exist in dreams scented the air. A fountain trickled behind him as he sat and waited. Please, please let her come.

Minutes ticked by and there was no sign of her. His heart sank. Had she given up? Was two months without him so long that this mysterious night angel couldn't believe in him any longer?

He leaned over and put his elbows on his knees. *Please, Zeus. If you're listening, please bring her back.*

A feminine gasp brought up his head. There she was. His angel, with her long, flowing black hair and deep black eyes, stood in a white gown that flowed around her body. A tear rolled down her cheek as a shaking hand covered her mouth.

"You're here." Hayden stood, but she never moved, never came to him. "What's wrong?"

"I didn't think you would come back," she whispered, her voice full of despair.

Hayden took one step forward. "I promised I would."

"I know. But I—" She closed her eyes and more tears fell. "I was so afraid. I feared you were gone forever. That you were some figment of my imagination."

Hayden held out his hand. "Will you not come to me?"

"You have to find me." She didn't move from her position.

Hayden's heart filled with dread and he took another step forward. "What's wrong?" he demanded, his voice rougher than he intended.

His angel wrapped her arms around her stomach. "You're not real. I'm going crazy. They all think I'm crazy."

"Sweetheart, *please*, let me hold you." Hayden took one more step. "Take my hand."

She looked up at him and he could see a pure but tormented soul in the depths of her eyes. "I can't do this anymore. If you're real, find me. But I can't keep living in a dream."

Unable to control himself any longer, Hayden closed the distance between them and brought her body into the shelter of his arms. "I will find you. I swear my life on it. I will use every means necessary. I won't give up." He tilted her chin up so she could see his eyes. "Don't lose faith. I'll find you and, when I do, nothing will keep us apart."

His angel gripped the collar of his shirt and pulled his lips slowly to hers. Heat and longing flooded his bloodstream as he felt the silk of her kiss. Dearest gods, if this was what it felt like to kiss her in a dream, what bliss would the reality be?

"I need you," she whispered.

"I promise, my love. Soon. I have a tracker, the best in the world. Can you tell me anything about where you are?"

"We've moved in with—Damn it." She let out a heavy breath. "My sister is dating this man. We moved in with him. I didn't want to leave that awful place in case it was somehow linked to you."

"Do you know him?" Hayden worried about his angel being in danger.

"He's one of us. Powerful."

Hayden felt his face bunch up. His voice came out rough. "Is he good to you?"

"Oh, yes." She touched his face, nodding. "Yes, don't misunderstand me. He's a good man. Honorable. My sister is crazy about him, and that makes me very happy. I'm only worried about being some-where you can't find me."

"Don't. I'll find you. If you're with a powerful Olympian, I have something to go on. Can you tell me what his power is?"

She said the word, but no sound came from her lips. She sighed in frustration; her head fell to his chest. "Why can't the gods ignore us for one minute?"

Determination filled him. Hayden took his angel by the shoulders. He knew she was in the human realm. She'd implied as much. He had to find out more. "Does he live in a major city?"

"Yes. He has guards."

"Thracians?" Hayden asked, excited that he got at least a breadcrumb.

"Yes. They are massive and well trained."

Hayden sighed. That alone was enough to give him a direction. It didn't narrow it down, by any stretch of the imagination. Powerful Olympians with Thracian guards lived throughout the world.

"Is it near an ocean?"

"No. Lakes." Those two words took great effort for her to speak. Wide, fear-filled eyes met his. "I'm leaving. I'm waking up."

"I'll find you." Hayden kissed her with passion, promising over and over to search.

His angel faded, her last words ringing in his head when the sun woke him up the next morning.

I need you.

⊸•· ⟞ ·•⊸

Lysandra helped Dante into the bed in his room. She couldn't take her eyes off him. Blessed be the gods, he was alive. Pale, but alive. He sat up against the headboard and she stood beside him, fussing with his blankets.

"Can I get you anything?"

He leaned his head back and closed his eyes. "No, sit with me for a moment, please."

She wasn't accustomed to this closeness with a man. Yes, this was

Dante, whom she loved. It still made her nervous to be alone with him. "Can you remember anything about that night?"

He scrubbed a hand over his face and took a deep breath, causing his barrel chest to expand. "I remember making you go for help. I remember seeing a demon and knowing I had to stop it. Everything else is blurred in my mind."

She took his hand in both of hers and he smiled up at her. "Do you remember the man who was with the demon?" He frowned. "You said you knew who he was, but you never said his name. Can you recall it?"

Dante's forehead wrinkled up as he thought back. "No. All I remember is the demon."

That was not a good thing. She nodded and gave him a reassuring smile. If Dante didn't remember, then how were they ever going to catch the person who summoned the beast?

"Can you do something for me?" he said, his throat scratchy.

Lysandra reached for a glass of water and handed it to him. "Anything."

Dante's eyes captured hers. "Will you kiss me? I need to feel your life and passion again."

Air left her lungs in a rush. She took off her overcoat and sat on the edge of his bed. Her long, black braid landed near his hands. He slid off the band and unraveled it. When she finished the job for him and shook out her hair, his eyes widened.

"Do you have any idea how beautiful you are?"

"I am if you think I am." Her stomach twisted and every nerve ending sizzled at his compliment.

Dante cupped her cheeks with his hands. "Inside and out, you are lovelier than all the roses in all the gardens in the world." He pressed his lips to hers and sparks flew. She loved the way his kiss started out soft and gentle, the most intimate brushing of satin lips.

This wasn't close enough for her. Dante must have felt the same because he pulled her up into his lap. Two strong arms encased her and his hands rested on her back. Her pulse raced and her head spun by the time she pulled away.

An adorable smile spread over his face. "Did I hear you tell Apollo that I'm your chosen mate? Or was it merely a pain-induced fantasy?"

Heat rose up her neck and into her cheeks. "You heard correctly. If you'll have me. I have nothing to offer you. I have no home, no family, no dowry of any kind." She didn't know if women these days still came with a dowry, not that it mattered. It was no secret she had not a penny to her name.

"Oh, Lysa." He ran his hands up her neck and into her hair. "I'll have you every way I can get you. Your love is all I require."

This time when he kissed her, it held desire and passion, lust and love, and hints of desperation. Her body came alive with sparks of fireworks and electricity. Suddenly, kissing him wasn't enough, touching his clothed body didn't suffice.

Then the truth of the situation became very clear. She might want Dante, but she didn't have the first clue about seduction or the art of sex. What if she didn't make him happy? What if she couldn't please him in bed? Would he still want her? Perhaps she needed to slow things down.

"I had a vision of you," she whispered against his kiss. "Of us, to be more specific. It was the reason I came to you that night."

"Tell me about it." He made his way to her neck and lavished his attentions there.

She could barely concentrate under his touch. "I had a vision of us together...*intimately*."

Dante's head jerked back, his eyebrows went up. "Having sex?"

"Yes." The temperature in the room skyrocketed.

"Oh. Were you okay with that?"

Lysandra smirked. "I was on my way to your room to make it a reality."

"Oh." Dante exhaled heavily. The pink that colored his face warmed her heart.

"Looking back, I think it was a good thing that you weren't alone."

Dante shook his head, refueling his aggravation. "I'm still kicking Yankee's ass."

"It saved us—me—from rushing into a situation I couldn't handle, Dante. I love you. But I'm not like other women. It's not in my nature to rush into a physical relationship, especially since you will be my first, well, everything. I don't want you to feel chained to someone who will weigh you down with my inexperience."

"Lysa," he said and smiled, melting her insides. "I'm going to let you in on a little secret. When I was nearly thirty years old, my father paid a woman to seduce me. I lost my virginity to a prostitute and I didn't even know it." Lysa gasped, appalled. "He justified it by saying that if he didn't pay someone to have sex with me, I'd be a virgin forever because no self-respecting Olympian woman would want to risk being with me."

"How dare he say such a thing? You're a much more honorable warrior than he will ever be. I'd like to give him a large piece of my mind." How could a man do that to his son? Xavier was less than scum. Gods forbid he ever say anything to Dante in her presence. She might forget her training and curse at him.

Dante chuckled. "I love your fierce heart." He kissed her and, for a moment, they got lost. "Such a distraction, those lips of yours." He sighed happily and returned to his story. "I only told you because that prostitute is the only woman I've ever been with. So while I'm not a virgin, I'm just as inexperienced in the sexual aspect as you are."

Lysa put her hands on his chest. "I want to do this right, Dante. I want to have a future with you that is blessed by the gods. You are a warrior, an Elite. I know your devotion is to Lady Avery and I respect that. Do you think you can make room for me in there?"

"Yes, my beautiful fantasy, I can."

"One day, when we are prepared, I will willingly give myself to you, completely, in every way."

"Until then, will you rest with me? Your presence eases me like no other."

She saw the weariness on his face. "Yes, mighty warrior. Rest and conserve your strength."

When she moved off the bed, Dante took her hands. "I love you so much."

"As I do you. Now get comfortable and I will sleep beside you. I fear tomorrow is going to be a rough day."

CHAPTER THIRTY

People filled the arena. Thracian students stood shoulder to shoulder around the perimeter as Olympians filed in. The crowd was fairly quiet. They looked expectantly to the stage that had been constructed on the north side.

Dynasty saw them from her place behind the wall. The royals would not take their seats until the arena was full. She'd not seen Ryse nor Avery this morning. Hayden had joined her at the palace and had ridden with her to the training center. He was quiet; none of his usual chipper attitude came through. Her son's eyes looked haunted, but when she asked about it, he shook his head and told her not to worry.

Of course she was going to worry. A mother always worried over her children. Since Troy's death, they were the only reason her heart kept beating. Ryse had Avery, and after today, they wouldn't have to hide her any longer. The couple could take on the world together. Hayden, well, Hayden was used to being a loner. Charm and charisma dripped from him, but not many people knew how he studied and wrote. He would stay in solitude for hours at a time. He had no mate, no friends that he could relax with. Hayden had even turned down having a Thracian guardian. Her guardians, Titus and Gabrele often looked after him as well. But Hayden preferred his privacy.

"Are you okay, milady?" Hammon stood next to her, his ebony

skin nearly disappearing in the shadows where they waited. All the Elites, Lysandra, the Avondales, their security, and the temple priests were waiting to be introduced.

Dynasty took a deep breath and turned her eyes to the tall man beside her. "I wish this day would be over." There was no reason to pretend otherwise.

"I concur, my queen. If I could save you from it, I would."

Dynasty smiled. "I know you would, Hammon. I am grateful for the sentiment."

He turned his lean body to face her full on. "If I can be so bold, I would like you to know that the Elites look to you as our counselor. You are held in the highest respects. We will not abandon you."

For some reason, his words brought tears to her eyes. She blinked rapidly. "Thank you, Master Hammon. I feel as though I am mother to you all. You make me very proud."

A hush fell over the crowd and General Falcon took center stage. "Olympians! Thracians! We welcome first the hosts of our temple." The four temple workers, two men and two women wearing white robes that covered their heads, came forward and sat in the front row.

"We welcome honored guest sent by the gods, the Oracle Lysandra, from the Holy City of Delphi." The crowd murmured. Dante escorted Lysandra to her seat. The people in the Haven were surprised by her appearance. Guessing by the way Charles gasped and Filene clutched her chest, they were surprised as well.

Lysandra was ravishing in her off-white gown. She'd picked the gown because of how it mimicked the one-shouldered drapes of the ancient Greeks, but still held the allure of modern-day fashion. Her long, black hair spilled out of an intricate bun on the top of her head. Gold jewelry adorned her ears and neck, a gold cuff on her upper arm. With Dante at her side in his Elite uniform, she radiated elegance and power, a goddess of old.

"They're sickeningly sweet together." Hayden grinned at his mother. "I think they might be worse than Ryse and Avery."

"It's good to see that something beautiful has come from this. They both deserve to be loved."

"Yeah, even if the rest of us want to gag." Hayden's smile didn't touch his eyes, but at least he was attempting humor.

Falcon continued on with his introductions. "I present to you our beloved Deities, Prince Hayden Castille and our Divine Grace, Queen Dynasty."

Hayden held out his arm to escort her onto the stage, looking every bit the Deity Prince. He wore black dress pants and a black formal shirt. Draped over his shoulders and falling about his modern clothing was a *chlamys* of deep green to pay homage to their Greek ancestors. A large, gold brooch depicting an eagle with a snake in his talons held the fabric on his shoulder. The symbols of Zeus were also on the ring on his finger and the crown on his head.

Dynasty paused before they were on the stage. "Son." Hayden looked at her. "I am so proud of you. Your father would be overjoyed to see you today, as regal and honorable as he was."

Hayden took a deep breath and held up his chin. "He can see me, Mother. And I know he's proud. I'm glad you are too."

Hayden kissed her cheek and they stepped out into the morning sunlight in front of thousands of their Olympian followers.

The crowd was on their feet, clapping, cheering, and waving. Dyna blew kisses to the crowd, waved at her people. Shouts of love and support overwhelmed her. A chorus of "bless our queen, bless our queen" began and soon the entire arena was chanting and pumping their fists in the air. Even the Thracians held up their right fists in a show of support. She looked at her son and he too was moved by their people. They both raised their right fists in the air. The crowd went wild, cheering even louder than before. To keep them from seeing how overwhelmed with emotion she was, she turned to be seated.

Her throne sat alone on the top of a pyramid of steps with three levels, split down the middle with a staircase. Titus and Gabrele took up their posts on either side.

Dynasty picked up the gown she wore as she was seated on the throne. Since she was still in the traditional mourning period of their people, her gown was black with a thin, gold belt winding around her from her breasts to her navel. Her hair was covered in a dark green and gold shawl. Her crown sat atop the silky fabric. It was the first time she'd been so formal in front of her people in decades. Perhaps it was past time.

On the tier below her were four smaller thrones, two on either side of the staircase. Hayden and Lysandra sat on her right. The two thrones on her left had to be for Ryse and Avery. Dyna searched the crowd and found Hanna on the front row, only feet from the edge of the platform. She nodded and gave Dynasty a tight smile. It was enough to let her know she was nearby if needed.

She took a moment to survey the area around her. Her family sat to the far right of the wide stage. In the middle were the portal and the soldier of Zeus. To the far left were three more thrones all in a line together. General Falcon introduced the Avondales and they came to sit on stage. Charles sat on the right, then Filene and Ashton closest to the edge of the stage.

Dynasty's stomach clenched when the cheers from the crowd quieted. The crowd gawked at the European Deities. The people had gone far too long without seeing other royals and the gods. This was quite the show to them. The other Deities wore their colors as well: blue, white, and silver. Filene's and Ashton's attire was very modern. Only Charles wore a brilliant royal blue *chlamys* over his suit like Hayden. He stopped and bowed to her. She inclined her head and smiled as best she could, given the sickness in her gut. Filene and Ashton followed, but their bows were forced and ire shone in their eyes.

Once the royals were seated, Thracians came to stand around them. Xavier and a couple others she didn't know stood behind the Avondales.

Falcon made another announcement. "I present to you the Elite Thracian warriors and the honorable Deity Prince and Master Thracian, Ryse Castille." His voice boomed the name proudly.

She heard a collective gasp from the people as the Elites came to sit in the six seats at the base of their pyramid. Hammon, Philippe, and Cutter on the right side; Yankee, Brenden and Dante on the left. All the men were dressed in a uniform of black, gold, and green. Their crest was different. On their right biceps was the emblem of Ryse: golden sword with the symbols of Ares and Zeus carved into the blade. Only Brenden's and Dante's differed. Theirs had a lion's head over the sword, exactly like Avery's tattoo. Each man also had a decorative golden sword hanging from his belt. While they might have been beautiful embellishments, there was no doubt that the swords could be used as weapons.

Hammon wore a beaded sash across his chest and a round, flat-top hat that came from his home country of South Africa along with a tall walking stick he often claimed had magical properties. He was the last one to take his seat, naturally, because he stayed right beside Ryse until the final moment.

Ryse stepped out onto the stage and the crowd went quiet. Dyna sucked in a deep breath. He was a glorious Thracian warrior of old from the black sandals on his feet to the golden helmet on his head. A black tunic hung to mid-thigh. His arms were bare and his chest was covered by a silver and gold breastplate. The symbols of Zeus and Ares decorated the front. A green and gold cape attached at his shoulders and hung down his back to his knees. The spectacle was both impressive and intimidating. Ryse was larger than life. Even the soldier of Zeus paled in comparison to his magnificence.

While others saw the executioner of their race, Dynasty saw a black-haired, brown-eyed little boy who loved to ride horses. She saw the teenager who didn't like to be touched, except by her. She saw a man so deeply in love with his wife that he'd challenged the gods to save her life.

When she looked at her son, Dynasty's heart filled with pride and a tinge of sorrow. The precious little boy she'd raised was now a warrior. The blood of their people was on his hands and it stained his soul. She couldn't fathom the weight he carried. Scanning the crowd, she could see the fear on the faces of the people. Ryse was a living legend. Ryse was death incarnated. Today, he was going to solidify the image as the most dangerous man in their universe.

He bowed at the waist to the Avondales. He went to his knee in front of Dynasty, removed his helmet, and spoke in Greek.

"My Queen, please forgive what I must do in the service of the gods. May the gods bless you all your days and fill you with their light."

Dynasty stood and stepped down to stand in front of him. Placing a hand on his head, she recited a prayer of forgiveness and blessings, also in Greek. Although their family didn't come from Greece, all ceremonies and rituals were done in the language of the gods. Olympian children were taught the language along with that of their home country.

Ryse rose and bent to kiss her cheek. "I love you," he whispered.

"I love you too, son."

Ryse stood straight, replaced his helmet, and clasped his hands in front of him. He spoke to General Falcon. "Bring the sacrifice."

The General brought a lamb to the stage. Dynasty hated this part. As archaic as it was, she asked Ryse to skip the sacrifice. But the gods had given him strict instructions. This same ritual would be performed at every Haven around the globe in order to call the gods down.

As man of the house, the task of blooding the lamb would have fallen to Ryse. However, since he was acting as executioner, the sacrifice fell to Hayden. The night before, Dyna had asked her son if he wanted Charles to carry this out. Hayden squared his shoulders, clenched his jaws, and told her that this was *his* home and he would do it. Whether Hayden was acting out of selfish pride, not wanting Charles to one-up him, or pride in his duty, she didn't know. Either way, Hayden stepped up and pulled a dagger from his belt. The handle of the blade was adorned in gold and featured jewels thousands of years old. The knife had belonged to Troy. Seeing it in Hayden's hands brought a bittersweet ache in her heart.

Dynasty backed away as Hayden knelt and expertly thrust the knife in to the neck of the lamb. The strike was so fast and so smooth. The lamb slowly eased down to the ground and died, its blood pooling on the wood. One of the temple workers gave him a cloth to wipe the blood from his hands, but there was none. He cleaned the blade of his dagger and put it away.

With her sons on either side of her, Dynasty raised her hands and face to the sky. "Holy gods of Olympia," she prayed in Greek. "We bring to you a sacrifice of purest blood. Come unto us. Walk among us and show yourselves, that we might be connected to you once more."

The portal began to roll like the ocean waves. Lightning flashed and thunder roared. Dynasty, Ryse, and Hayden turned to face the oval and went to their knees. Everyone in the arena followed suit.

Ares was the first to enter this realm. He was exactly as she expected him to be. Fierce in his glory, terrifying to behold, and cold as steel. Athena was next, a warrior princess clad in leather and weapons, as beautiful as she was deadly. Poseidon was less human than the other two. As hard as she tried, she couldn't see him as a man of flesh and bones. His form seemed to shift between liquid and solid. Only his face remained perceivable. When he looked into her eyes, she felt as though she might drown in their depths. She could see the abyss, felt the chill of waters so dark the light could not touch them. She shivered.

Zeus was the final god to step out of the portal. She couldn't take her eyes off of him. He was golden and magnificent, just as she remembered from when Ryse called him forth. He was resplendent in stature and elegance while still having a fine edge of danger about him. His white and golden robes cascaded down his large body. All the gods stood over nine feet tall, possibly ten. But Zeus seemed bigger than them all. His white hair and beard were the only indication of age. His body was as muscular and fit as Ryse's, his eyes were sharp and missed nothing.

"Rise and take your places," he commanded, holding out a hand to Dynasty. She slipped her hand into his, feeling infinitesimal compared to him. He guided her to her throne and then turned back to the portal.

"Bring forth the prisoners."

A guardian exited the portal with Nikki. She was subdued, complying without the guardian having to touch her. When directed, she knelt at the front center of the stage, close to the sacrifice, and didn't move.

Another exited with Salina—*Oh dearest gods of Olympia!* Was that Salina? This withered old hag who fought and screamed like a mad woman? No, there must be a mistake.

"What happened to my daughter?" Filene rose from her seat, but Charles stopped her from approaching. Her body shook and her face went pale.

"The former Princess," Zeus answered, "Salina Avondale, has been stripped of her gifts from the goddess Aphrodite. She stated her beauty was a curse, and the goddess rid her of the problem. Now all can see the true face of this monster."

"If you want to see a monster, look at your own reflection," Salina said with a voice that sounded dry and ready to crack.

The crowd was in shock. They had collectively moved away from the stage, not wanting to get too close to the rabid beast.

"Even now you refuse to repent? Knowing your head is about to be severed from your body?" Ares spoke up.

"I'd rather rot in the underworld than give my devotion to you."

Salina's words caused reactions from everyone. Filene could barely contain herself. She cried and kept shaking her head. The people gasped and booed, calling out names like murderer, traitor, and witch.

"Then you will have it your way," Athena said with a sneer.

Dynasty held her breath. She couldn't believe what she was about to witness. Already, tears fell down her cheek and before she even had the thought, Hanna was behind her throne, handing her a handkerchief. Titus lifted her up so she could sit at Dynasty's feet. The two women clasped hands.

Painful as it would be, Nikki would live through this. It was Salina who weighed on her heart. Again, her mind went to days gone by. Salina had been such a lovely child. Her big blue eyes, long, blonde hair, and dazzling smile had wrapped everyone around her finger. Dyna and Troy, not having a daughter of their own, had loved her dearly. When she was only a decade old, Salina had come to stay with them many times for weeks on end. They would ride horses, wander through the mountains on adventures, and read stories of the gods in front of the fire.

Where did that sweet, innocent child go? How did it come to this?

The more she reflected, the more she understood. Salina had been put on a pedestal. She was adored and spoiled. The people lavished her with anything her heart desired. Especially her parents. Charles and Filene had unknowingly bred a spirit of selfishness inside of their daughter. They catered to her every whim, never disciplining her when she acted out or when she began to demand more and more. As she grew older, more self-obsessed, Dynasty could see the greed taking root in her soul. Then, when her body developed, she found a new tool of manipulation. The sad truth was, Salina had been on this path of destruction for many, many decades, possibly even the last century of her life.

There is such a difference in knowing that each person has to suffer the consequences of their actions and seeing those consequences come to fruition. It's hard to watch people reap the punishment of the devastation they sowed. Because just like a farmer sowing his crops, the one seed he puts in the ground will bear multiple fruits. What a person puts into the world, positive or negative, comes back multiplied and amplified.

Now Salina would have to deal with her consequences. Unfortunately, her actions affected so many other people.

CHAPTER
THIRTY-ONE

RYSE GREW IMPATIENT AS HE STOOD ON DISPLAY WHILE THE GODS DID their tricks. He was ready to have Avery officially back and have this day over with. He was quite ready to get out of this costume.

Zeus waved his hands in the air and the portal shimmered and rippled. It rose and sailed through the air until it was positioned over the audience, like another set of watching eyes. Through its watery screen, the entire Olympian population could see the events unfold in their Haven.

"Before we carry out this sentencing," Zeus raised his arms to the crowd, "we would like to right a wrong committed against the house of Castille."

Ryse's heart leapt. Here it was. Avery. The only thing that made this day bearable. He stood motionless, even though he wanted to shake the god until he hurried up.

"During her capture, Salina Avondale took the life of the newly bonded Divine Grace, Avery McClain. Avery's soul has rested in the hands of the gods. However, we know that a Deity will need his Grace to rule by his side. In a measure to show our faith in the Thracian soldiers and the Olympian race, the gods deliver Avery back into the world of the living."

A blinding white lightning bolt formed in Zeus' hand. It hurt to look at it and many in the crowd shielded their eyes. He pointed the bolt to the sky. Clouds darkened and swirled, then turned into a red cylinder of flames. It was awe-inspiring, to say the least. The crowd looked panicked and yet they watched with rapt attention.

Ryse was spellbound right along with them. The flaming tornado touched down onto the stage, the wind blowing about like a storm. No doubt, every Olympian on Earth who watched the spectacle held their breath as the fires touched the stage with an explosive clash of lightning and thunder. As quickly as Zeus called the clouds forth, he sent them away. Left on the stage was a woman on fire, spinning in a circle until she crouched low. The flames receded.

Avery stood slowly as the fire left her body. She was dressed in what could barely be classified as clothing. The green sheath was more like a scarf that had been draped around her neck, crisscrossed over her breasts, and tucked into a belt. The skirt was little more than two sheets of fabric, one in the front, one in the back. A sliver of her thigh could be seen on each side. Except for the gold belt at her waist, and another right under her chest, her entire back was bare, hidden only by a thick curtain of deep red curls hanging to her bottom. Golden sandals adorned her feet and the straps wound up to her knee. A thin crown sat atop her head. The symbol of Rhea, two lions, was encrusted in jewels.

She was a true goddess come to Earth. Her ethereal beauty had everyone stunned. Even the Avondales gasped.

Ryse, humbled by the privilege of making love to this woman for the rest of his life, stepped to her side and offered his hand. The crowd broke their silence and roared as the couple lifted their hands.

"Hell of an entrance, huh darlin'?" she said without moving her mouth. Avery smiled and waved to the crowd.

"A little dramatic for my taste. But, damn, you're sexy." Ryse could barely contain the small smile that crossed his lips. Thankfully, his helmet hid his mouth. In the middle of his personal hell, Avery was heaven. He removed the helmet and lifted her hand to his mouth. When they locked eyes, the atmosphere crackled with electricity. "Milady."

As if she hadn't caused enough of a scene, Avery bowed to him, kneeling at his feet. "My Lord."

Those two words nearly caused him to come undone. Before he made a fool of himself, he ushered Avery over to the side of the stage.

As she passed Nikki, she paused, nearly tripping. She reached out and touched Nikki's cheek. Her whole body went stiff. Avery didn't move for a long minute.

Nikki flickered her eyes from her mistress to him and back. "What's wrong with her?"

Avery's eyes widened as recognition lit in her mind. "I remember," she whispered, her voice breathy. "Oh god, Ryse. I remember." She turned to Nikki and shivered. "Nikki, I—I'm so sorry."

"Have faith," Nikki whispered back, the women locked in each other's gaze. "Go."

Thankfully, Dyna was right there to take Avery's hand and lead her to her throne. She covered well, but Ryse's lover was about to fall apart.

Ryse stood once again in front of Nikki. Guardians tied her hands to the shackles of the whipping post. *Damn.* He was really about to do this. Acid rolled in his gut.

Athena addressed them both. "Shadow Lady, do you deny your role in the death of Grand Deity Troy Castille?"

"No." Nikki's body shook, her eyes closed, and she tried not to cry.

"Master Thracian, do you find fault with this woman?"

"No." Ryse pushed as much of his power into that one word as he could. If only it were enough.

"Are you willing to punish her based on the judgment of the gods?"

He swallowed and wished like hell he didn't have to answer. "Yes."

Athena handed him a whip. "Prove your loyalty to the gods, Thracian."

Every muscle in his body protested as he gripped the whip and took position behind Nikki. She was openly crying and had hunched down around the post, preparing for the worst. Athena used her knife to slit her shirt right up the middle, baring the pale flesh of Nikki's back.

He made the mistake of looking over at the three tiers of seats where his family sat. His mother's face was glistening with tears, but she kept her dignity about her. Avery's jaw was clenched so tightly it caused her neck to strain, a scowl on her face. Brenden looked downright mutinous. He was rigid in his chair, and his face showed the minute signs of his stress. He gripped the arms of his seat until his knuckles were white. None of them wanted to watch this. None of them thought Nikki deserved it. Yet all of them were going to honor the will of the gods. Ryse turned back to Nikki.

Why must I do this? Ryse thought as he cast a glance to Ares. The god watched with no emotion, no expression in his glowing features. He did not answer.

Although his face was partially covered, Ryse kept his expression neutral. The crowd could not see his indecision, not even in his eyes. They couldn't know what he was about to do would break his heart. All they were supposed to see were his devotion to the gods and his willingness to carry out their wishes, no matter what they were.

The crowd hushed as Ryse reared back his arm. This was not the first time he'd handled a whip. He knew exactly how to move his arm and flick his wrist to send the nine tails swooshing through the air to bite into flesh. As his arm came forward and the leather flew, he prayed that Nikki would forgive him.

The tails cracked, the sound of contact with flesh made him sick. Nikki screamed in agony. Ryse thought he might vomit when he saw the red stripes form on her skin and begin to drip.

Once. Twice. Three times he struck until his entire body shook, refusing to continue.

"Enough." Zeus held up his hand.

Thank the fucking gods. He wanted to sag in relief, but didn't. He faced Zeus. "My Lord?"

"Her punishment was to be whipped. You whipped her. That is enough." He waved her off. "She is not the real criminal here. Now that her blood has spilled, I absolve her from all wrong."

Blinding rage filled him. Ryse bent as if bowing and growled under his breath to the god. "Then why the hell did you even bother? She could have been spared."

Zeus glared down at him. "Part of this was your test, Master Thracian, as well as your mate's, your Elites', and your brother's. You have done well, so has your family, so has the woman. You all had something to prove." He addressed the crowd. "Tend to her wounds."

"Brenden," Ryse commanded, and the soldier quickly rushed to Nikki's side. Two of the Paeans aided him in gathering her up and rushing her out of the arena where she could be tended.

"Now for the murderer," Ares bellowed. "Executioner, come forth."

The weight of his next task settled heavily on his shoulders, the relief short-lived. As he approached Salina, her eyes widened, but she stayed silent. He opened his hand to his side and called upon the power of the gods who created him. The sword of Ares formed in his hand, perfectly crafted for him. The blade bore the symbols of his people and was sharp beyond measure.

Ryse stopped by Salina's head and put the tip of the sword on the stage. He crossed his hands on the handle and awaited orders.

"Salina Avondale," Zeus said, "you have been found guilty of murder and numerous crimes against our people. You are sentenced to beheading and an eternity in the depths of Hades. Your soul shall not see the Heavens. Do you have anything to say for yourself?"

The withered old woman with haunted blue eyes turned that gaze on Ryse. Tears rolled down her cheeks. "I only wanted you to love me," she whispered to him.

Ryse knelt down to be eye level. "You never knew the meaning of love, Salina."

"Will you even mourn me?" Her voice cracked, her lips quivered.

Ryse dropped his head and said the only thing he could. "No." He then looked her in the eyes. Even in her aged state, he remembered the happy child who played with the horses and twirled her dresses to see them fan out. Things could have been so different for her if only she had chosen wisely. "I shall, however, mourn the woman you could have been."

Salina sobbed as he stood and took up his sword.

"Let this be a lesson to all who dare to defy the gods." Zeus' voice reverberated throughout the arena. "We created you for a purpose. We have bestowed our gifts upon you. We shall rule with both love and justice." The god looked at Ryse and gave a barely discernible nod.

Ryse raised his sword, his heart ready to explode in his chest. He gritted his teeth. *Ares, give me strength,* he prayed. Power filled him, wrapped around his soul, and aided him in his task. In his moment of weakness, Ares was there with him physically and mentally, as he had promised. Ryse cried out as the blade sliced through the air and made contact.

The only thing he heard was Filene's screams.

CHAPTER
THIRTY-TWO

ASHTON SAT MOTIONLESS. HIS EYES TRACKED THE SHINING METAL OF Ryse's blade as it rose into the air. In that moment, Salina sent him a final telepathic message. In the heartbeat before the blade sliced through her blonde hair and her neck, her eyes flickered to him.

You're next.

Her head fell to the stage floor, her blood mixing with the lamb's and clinging to her hair. When it finally quit rolling, it stared at him. A withered face, relaxed in death, eyes open.

Filene screamed beside him. She turned her face into his father's shoulder. The whole world paused. His sister was dead.

You're next.

A princess had been executed. A Castille swung the blade that ended her life. For some reason, up until that moment, until he was staring at the bodiless head of his baby sister, he hadn't thought Ryse would actually do it. It was quite a shock to his system.

Ryse truly was the killer of legend.

You're next.

The earth trembled and the skies turned dark. Clouds rolled in and the wind whipped about them. Above the crowd, the portal churned with blackness.

Hades erupted from the oval, a cloud of oil and acid and brimstone.

He flew to the stage and formed an inky cloud above Salina's decapitated body. If he listened hard enough, Ashton could hear the screams of the souls suffering in the underworld. Chills ran over his skin and the temperature dropped until he could see his panting breath.

"This one belongs to me," Hades roared as he absorbed every last drop of her blood and flesh. The god of the underworld formed a mutated version of a body and stood before Ryse, staring him down.

The bastard deserved credit; he never shrank from Hades. He stood his ground. Thunder boomed overhead as the god spoke to Ryse. No one else heard. Ryse nodded, held up his sword at his chest, and bowed. Whatever passed between the two was a mystery.

As quickly as he came, Hades rushed back into the oval. The skies settled and the wind ceased. Sunshine bathed them once more. The stage area was clean of all evidence of Salina's execution. Given how his mother was acting, he was thankful.

"Before we leave this place," Zeus said, commanding attention once more, "I shall appoint a new Grand Deity to take the place of our fallen brother Troy and appoint his heir as the North American Deity."

Bloody fantastic. Ashton wanted to roll his eyes. Ryse had just killed his sister and now he was about to be worshipped as the new King of North America. All this political bullshit drove him insane.

On the up side, there was a possibility that his father might be crowned the new Grand Deity. Who else could it be? Charles was second only to Troy in age and experience. He was the only obvious choice. This had to be part of the reason their family had been asked to stay in this Haven instead of returning home. No other Deity came close to being prepared for such an undertaking. The Grand Deity was in charge of the entire population of Olympians worldwide. It would take a man like Charles to handle the pressures of the task.

"I ask Master Ryse, Prince Hayden, quondam Deity Hammon, Deity Charles, and Prince Ashton to join me." Zeus lined up the men and asked them to all take a knee, facing the crowd. "All the Deities around the world, kneel before the gods."

What the hell did they need Hammon for? That fool gave up his throne because of a broken heart. He was barely fit to be a warrior, much less be among the rightful royals. And Hayden, well, now there was a joke if he'd ever saw one. Ashton quickly dismissed him.

"Divine Graces, please come to stand behind your men."

Dynasty, Avery—who was damned fuckable—and his mother stood behind the men. He couldn't help glancing over his shoulder at Avery. Why the hell couldn't he have met her first? Damned Castilles, always having the upper hand. If Jerry had done his job better, Ashton would have obtained her. He wouldn't make that mistake again. What a prize he'd missed out on.

She met his gaze. His body hardened upon seeing the fire burning behind her emerald eyes. It was a shame this woman was now his enemy. She would have made him a good mate.

Zeus's voice called them back to attention and Ashton turned to face the crowd. "As the eldest son of Troy Castille, the crown should pass to Ryse."

Should?

"However, seeing as how Ryse is also acting as Master Thracian, I will give him the option of taking the crown or passing it to his brother, and second legitimate heir, Prince Hayden."

What the fuck?

The brothers exchanged a glance and a head nod. This was not the first they had heard of this plan. Ryse confirmed as much.

"I wish to pass the crown to my brother Hayden. He is more than worthy and competent to reign."

"Prince Hayden, do you voluntarily take the crown, understanding and accepting the duties of Deity of North America?"

"I do, my Lord."

"Are you sure?" Zeus asked, a hint of hesitation in his voice.

"I am ready to serve my people and my gods in whatever capacity they designate."

"So shall it be. A formal coronation shall be held after the appropriate time of mourning for our fallen."

Now for the most important part. If his father was anointed as Grand Deity, Ashton could consider his path much easier. Having constant access to the head of the snake makes it easier to chop it off.

"After much deliberation between the gods, we have decided who shall rule the Olympian people as Grand Deity. All the Deities and princes of the world were considered. We find this man to be honorable, devoted to the gods, and knowledgeable in the old traditions and customs that we long to revive, yet also able to relate to this time period and the people outside out of the Havens. Not only is he a strong leader, but his house reflects this same level of devotion."

Oh shit. That would not *be the Avondale clan, thank you, Salina.* Charles seemed to understand what this meant as well. His shoulders fell slightly. Of course the gods would consider the family of the man who would rule the world. *Fuck.* That meant even Hammon was in the running. He might have given up his throne, but his son, Eekon, was as devoted a king as his father.

"After seeing him stand up for the people while in the Heavens, the gods have all agreed unanimously. Your leader will be a strong advocate of the people and will rule justly according to the laws of the gods. Charles Avondale…"

Yes!

"…when you were in the Heavens, you stated you would stand behind Ryse Castille."

No!

"Would you also stand behind his brother, Hayden?"

You must be joking?

A collective gasp came from the crowd and those on stage. Even Ryse Almighty snapped his head around. Hayden looked pale, nearly green. If he blew chunks all over the stage, perhaps the gods would reconsider letting a pussy like him lead their race. Hayden being crowned Grand Deity was ludicrous. He was young, inexperienced, and a complete push over.

Then again, maybe he was exactly what Ashton needed as Grand Deity. The Olympian population was practically falling into the hands of the demons with every move Zeus made.

Charles lifted his chin and made eye contact with Hayden for what felt like ten damn minutes. The guy was an Elementalist, not a telepath. What the hell was he doing?

"I support him, my Lords. I believe, especially after seeing his passion when we were in the Heavens, that Prince Hayden Castille will make a fitting and honorable Grand Deity."

"Hayden Castille, Deity de jure, do you accept this position as offered to you by the gods?"

"I do, my Lords. On one condition."

"Speak." Zeus squinted his glowing eyes at the boy.

"Out of respect for my brother, and the birthright he deserves, I want the offices of Grand Deity and Thracian Master to be of equal power, accountable to each other, for as long as we serve together."

"Fair enough." Zeus gave in with no hesitation.

Ryse held out his hand to his brother and Hayden clasped his arm. Lady Dynasty took Avery's hand. It was all so moving and sentimental and chock full of hearts and rainbows it made him gag. He had to swallow the bile in his throat as the crowd cheered.

This was total bullshit. The entire Olympian and Thracian populations were going to be ruled by the Castille brothers as equals. Now, more than ever, Ashton knew he had to push on with his quest. The Castilles had to be stopped.

"Arise, my royal servants."

Ashton stood along with the others.

"Under the next full moon, we shall hold a coronation. Until then, I ask all my children to be in meditation and prayer for your new Grand Deity. Pray for the families of those whose lives have been changed by the events of today. When next we meet, we celebrate and feast."

Zeus put his massive hand on Hayden's shoulder in a show of support. Then he leaned down and whispered in his ear. Hayden's eyes went wide and he nodded quickly before smiling for the crowd.

More secrets. These gods were full of them and the Castilles were keeping them.

Using the portal as their gateway, Zeus, Ares, Athena, and the *might as well not exist* Poseidon went back to the Heavens, taking the guardian and the portal with them.

"I want to leave this place," Filene said to him and his father. "I want to go home and mourn my daughter."

Charles took her by the shoulders and hugged her. "Yes, darling. It's time to go home."

They couldn't get away fast enough. His fucking father had to make it a point to speak to Hayden and Ryse. Bloody hell, could he kiss their asses anymore? The man was going to get chapped lips.

Ashton stayed by Filene. He could deal much easier with her anger than his father's misplaced devotions.

"Filene?" Lady Dynasty came over to them. "Charles says you are leaving today. I pray you have a safe trip home."

Filene faced her and stared at Dynasty. "Your son killed my daughter."

Dynasty let out a sigh. "Your daughter murdered my husband. Which of the two was the real sin? Ryse acted as the hand of the gods. Salina acted as the hand of selfishness."

"You think you're so justified," Filene sneered. "Wait until you have to watch one of your children die."

"I have," Dynasty said firmly. The bitch had spine, he'd give her that. "Salina also murdered Avery and she might as well have killed Nikki for all the emotional damage this has caused her."

"Time will heal her wounds." Filene waved off the maid. "It doesn't bring my daughter back."

Dynasty clasped her hands in front of her and squared her shoulders. "Time heals some wounds; it festers others. I suggest you tend to your own so they do not become a disease in your soul. I'm sorry our time as friends must end this way." Her strength gave way to her sadness. "I loved you so dearly, Filene. I still do. Love is honest and does not hide behind pretenses. If you cannot accept this from me, then I understand. I pray, one day, you will accept my love again." Dynasty bowed her head and turned away.

"I will never forgive her family," Filene said under her breath. "She has changed. Her holier than thou ways make me sick. She hides behind the gods."

"Don't worry, Mother." Ashton touched her face, playing up the caring son card. "Everyone gets what's coming to them in the end. The Castilles will pay for their power-hungry ways."

He sent her to their rooms to pack their things. He had to check on something.

Ashton, confident that Dante wouldn't remember anything about their meeting in the woods, sauntered up to where the warrior stood with the Oracle. It didn't take a genius to figure out there was something between them. His body stayed turned into hers, and her dove gray eyes shone up at him. They were both talking to the temple workers who fawned over the lovely lady from Delphi.

Dante and the lot of them had lied their asses off about Dante being with Hanna. They were hiding the Oracle all this time.

"Dante." Ashton smiled and held out his hand. "Pleased to see you up and moving again. To face a demon on your own…" He shook his head, feigning shock. "Whew, you're a brave one."

Dante shrugged his shoulders and grinned. "My fellow Elites told me there was a fine line between bravery and stupidity." He rubbed his stomach where his wound was. "I haven't figured out which classifies me."

"Brave," said the Oracle. "Very brave."

Dante remembered his manners at that moment and presented her for introduction. "Prince Ashton, I would like you to meet an Oracle from Delphi. This is Lysandra. Lysa, this is Prince Ashton Avondale."

"It is a great pleasure to meet you." Ashton took her hand and kissed it, gazing into her unique eyes. "Welcome." He purred his words, sure to put a telepathic hint of sensuality with them. He thought he saw a hint of blush on her cheeks, but then her face went slack and her eyes clouded over. He looked back and forth between the two of them. She couldn't possibly have a vision involving him. That morning, he'd used demon blood and black magic to mask his aura and guard his mind. Not even a lady from Delphi could be so powerful.

"So, Ashton, will you be leaving today?" Dante's distraction was noted, but he kept looking at the Oracle as she recovered and smiled tightly at him.

"Yes. My mother is ready to return home and I'm just as anxious. Being in a Haven is nice, but we are accustomed to the human realm."

"If you will excuse me, gentleman," Lysa said cordially. "It was nice to meet you, Prince Ashton." She gave a quick bow and walked away.

"That is one beautiful woman. Well done, Dante."

The warrior blushed and cleared his throat. "She is far above my station."

Ashton chuckled. "You clearly have things keeping you here, but my offer still stands. You're welcome to come work for me."

"While I appreciate the offer, my answer is still no. Avery is back and she will need her guardians."

"And so will a certain Oracle." Ashton played up the camaraderie for a couple more minutes before making his exit. "I have to ask, before I go. How did you survive coming face to face with a demon?"

"I wish I knew. Perhaps I wouldn't have if not for Apollo."

"Perhaps." Ashton gave a quick salute and left.

The boy didn't remember shit. His secret was safe. Even if he did in the future, Ashton had his sister as a bargaining chip. Thanks to the Oracle, he had two.

CHAPTER THIRTY-THREE

AVERY SEARCHED THE CASTLE FOR RYSE. AFTER THE EXECUTION, HE'D vanished. She had taken a moment to change into jeans and a pullover, and now her man was nowhere to be found. He wasn't in their room or his mother's suite. A couple of the Thracian students thought they had seen him heading away from the training center arena. Finally, she found Hayden in the library with a tumbler of alcohol in his hand. He stared blankly into the fire, his chin propped up on one hand.

Avery sat on the edge of his chair and sighed. "You didn't expect that, didja?"

"No. I knew Ryse was going to turn down the North American throne, but Grand Deity. Whew." He scrubbed his hand over his face and pushed back his long hair. "Kind of makes me wish I would have kept my damn mouth shut in the Heavens." Half his mouth pulled back into a weak smile.

"You've never been able to keep your mouth shut, darlin'," Avery joked. "At least, this time, it was for a just cause." She reached over and ran her hand over his head, cupping his cheek. "Hayden, you're one of the smartest men I've ever met."

"Says the girl raised by cowboys in the backwoods of Texas. Thanks."

She tugged his hair. "Shut it and listen. If anyone can lead these people, it's you." He scoffed. "Look at me." Avery grabbed his chin. "I'm serious. Rhea and I talked about you. You're one of a kind, Hayden. You're the right blend of traditionalist and modern practice. You'll be able to help our race revive the ways of old and still usher forward a new era, a stronger one."

His brows dipped and he smirked. "Damn, Avery, Heaven changed you."

She leaned back and slid off the arm of the chair and into his lap. He chuckled when she slapped a big kiss on his cheek. "You betcha, darlin'. I think it changed you too."

"You truly think I can do this?" he said, showing the vulnerable heart beneath the mouthy exterior.

"I know you can. That's why I suggested you."

"You?" His mouth dropped open and Avery laughed. Hayden unceremoniously pushed her to the floor. "I knew having a sister was going to be a pain in my ass."

Still smiling, Avery got up and dusted off her butt. "Having a brother ain't all it's cracked up to be either." They exchanged grins. "Speaking of, where's yours?"

"When Ryse is upset, he usually goes to the top level of the tower. It's his place to be alone and think. I don't know if he really wants me telling you that, though. It's kind of our secret."

"I'm his mate, Hayden. We don't have secrets."

"Then you should know that the only way to get up there is through the secret door behind the tapestry. Only family knows about it."

"Thanks, love."

"Hey, Avery?" Hayden called as she walked away. "I know Salina, uh, *killed* you and everything…but keep in mind that we all grew up together and Ryse doesn't like to hurt women, much less execute them."

"I know. That's why I'm not going to let him be alone right now. He shouldn't have to bear this burden on his own." Ryse was over two and a half centuries old. By now, he was used to dealing with things in his own way in his own time. What he didn't realize was that having a spouse meant he didn't have to battle his demons—literal and figurative—without someone standing by his side ready rage war with him.

Avery went to the very top story of the tower where Dynasty had helped free her aura. It seemed like another lifetime. Technically, it kind of was. Behind the tapestry was a stone that seemed oddly broken away from the others. She pushed and pulled until a section of the wall clicked open. The door was barely big enough for a small woman. How did a huge guy like Ryse fit? She crouched down and stepped inside to find a ladder leading upward.

Avery's breath caught when she reached the top level of the tower. The open-air terrace was littered with broken furniture. Pieces of what used to be a couple of lawn chairs and a metal table were tossed about. A glass tabletop was shattered. Ryse was sitting on the floor to the far side, his knees arched and his head bowed. He still wore the toga, but his breastplate was on the floor among the junk. Blood dripped from his battered and bruised knuckles. She glanced around and saw the places where he'd used the stone walls as a punching bag.

"Man, I'm glad you beat the hell out of that rock. It was startin' to really piss me off."

"I'm not in the mood for jokes," he growled, his voice feral and dark.

"Good. Me either."

"I'm serious, damn it. Leave."

She turned over one of the chairs and, upon inspection, realized she would have to sit on the floor too. "I can't really do that, baby." She sat next to him, their shoulders brushing. A tingle of power rippled off of him. "I'll never forget the first time I met you. Even with a messed up memory, I remember you walkin' into my café, lookin like fresh-spun sin on a stick. I thought Izzy was going to have a heart attack. Between you and Bren, she lost her mind." Avery huffed. "All I could think about was your eyes. How even though you were there with someone, you looked lonely. Then I saw you and Hammon and Cutter sparrin' at the safe house and I realized that because of your power, you were very much alone."

Avery slowly, cautiously, reached her hand over and lifted his chin so he would look at her. His irises glowed white and she could tell he'd shed a tear or two. Mostly, he appeared broken. "You don't have to face anything on your own anymore, Ryse. You don't have to hide your emotions from me. I don't see weakness in your tears. I see compassion, *strength*. You have every right to be upset about today. That doesn't make you less of a Thracian. It makes you more of a man."

He stared at her with those deep brown eyes for the longest time. She stroked his jaw and face.

"I don't deserve you." His voice was hoarse and low, like he'd been screaming.

"I beg to differ."

Ryse slowly pulled out of his rage and the white glow faded from his eyes. "Why do you love me?"

"Well, you're hot." She grinned and Ryse's shoulders relaxed. "And because you were created for me; you make me whole the way no other man ever can. I love your honor, your stubbornness, your heart. I love your sense of duty and faith. You're amazing, Ryse."

"And I'm hot," he said with a sniff.

"Hell, yeah."

"You're pretty hot too, baby. That sexy goddess scarf on steroids thing you had on today was distracting."

"How about I put it on again for you tonight, and you can take it off…with your teeth?" It was the crazy way she wiggled her eyebrows that finally made him grin.

He leaned his forehead over to hers and sighed. "Thank you, for not being afraid of me."

"The only thing I fear is a life without you. As long as we're together, nothing in this world can stop us." She kissed him, strong and firm, relaying all the conviction she felt. "I have to go check on Nikki. I promised Brenden I would give them some time, but I want to see her. Will you come down?"

"In a bit."

Understanding that after a day like today, he might need more time to process his emotions, Avery nodded and kissed his forehead and left him to his thoughts.

After her whipping, Brenden took Nikki back to her room. Avery lightly tapped on the door, in case she was resting. Brenden sat in a chair next to her bed and waved her in. Nikki was belly down on the bed, her long, red hair fanned out on the pillow next to her. Across her bare back lay white bandages. A blanket covered her lower back and legs. She didn't move when Avery entered.

Brenden met her halfway across the room.

"How is she?" Avery whispered.

He heaved a sigh and rubbed the back of his neck. "The cuts aren't too bad; a few stitches, nothing major. The Paeans tried to heal her, but apparently, the gods want her to suffer a bit more. Their powers didn't work." He pursed his lips and shook his head.

"Has she spoken?"

Brenden nodded and glanced back at her over his shoulder. "She keeps ordering me to leave. Stubborn as a mule, that one." He grinned affectionately. "I told her I was in this for the long haul, but she seems to think I need to move on or some shit."

"Is she awake?"

"Yeah, but she stares straight ahead at me, at the wall, at nothing. It took her forever to quit crying. Maybe you can talk to her." He stepped close to her and whispered in her ear. "I'm not giving up on her. I love her. So you need to tell her to get that through her head." He pulled back and Avery nodded.

"Don't worry, Bren. We aren't going to lose her. I won't let that happen."

His eyes misted and before he could let his emotions show, he quietly slipped out the door.

Avery walked around the bed. Sure enough, Nikki was staring at the window with a blank expression on her face. It killed Avery to see the dullness of her eyes.

Avery curled up on the bed, facing her. She reached up and took Nikki's hand and held it to her chest. When their eyes met, tears fell freely.

"It's going to be okay. I won't leave you," Avery promised.

Nikki clenched her eyes shut, but the tears came anyway. They poured down her face, her sobs shaking the bed. Avery cried right along with her. They didn't speak. They simply cried together.

Avery opened up her aura and let it pour over Nikki, healing her body and emotional trauma as best she could. Shadows moved across the wall as the afternoon went on, but the two women never did. They cried and held hands; the rest of the world could wait.

Late that evening, Brenden came into the room, Lysandra and Dante on his heels. Lysa carried a tray full of food and drinks. "I've come with nourishment." She set the tray down.

Avery didn't take her eyes away from Nikki's. "You need to eat." She reached up and pushed a stray red hair from her face. "Please? For me?"

Nikki nodded and allowed Avery to help her sit up. Brenden had retrieved one of his button-up shirts and she wore it backwards so her chest was covered.

"I heard that you love chocolate cake." Lysa smiled warmly at Nikki, her voice kind and soft. "Mine might not be as good as Lady Avery's, but you might enjoy it still."

"Who are you?" Nikki asked.

"I'm Lysa. I was sent here to take care of Avery while you were both in the Heavens."

Nikki's eyes went wide and she looked at Avery in horror. "You… you *replaced* me?" Her lips trembled and she covered her mouth to contain her cries.

"No, I was dead. I didn't do squat." Avery sat on the bed and forced Nikki to meet her eyes. "Listen to me, now. No one could replace you. When my spirit was in the Heavens, the gods sent Lysa to help Dyna watch over my body. She's not my Shadow Lady, Nikki. She's an Oracle. Do you understand?"

The hurt in her eyes cut to the quick. Poor Nikki, she had such a long road of healing ahead.

Lysa knelt down in front of her and took Nikki's hands in her own. "Your mistress loves you very much. Fear not, sweet girl. You could never be replaced. Please, let me feed you. You will need all your strength for healing so you may stand at Avery's side once more."

That gave Nikki the incentive to eat. Lysa fed her like a child. Her kindness warmed Avery's heart. Brenden and Dante stayed in the far corner of the room, watching, guarding. When Nikki was full, they called a Paean to take a final look at her bandages for the night.

"Can I talk to you alone for a minute?" Nikki asked Avery.

Their friends left the room and Nikki let out the breath she'd been holding. "You have to tell Brenden to leave me alone. I'm not good for him and he can't waste his time on me. The gods have stripped my title, Avery. I can't be your Shadow Lady."

"Ya know, I can do a lot of cool things. But I can't make that boy stop lovin' you."

"He doesn't love me," she said through gritted teeth. "I'm not the same person I was before. I can't be. Too much has changed." She closed her eyes tight. "Please, Avery. I'm asking you to please make him back off. I…" She got a grip on her emotions. "I don't know who I am anymore. My whole life was devoted to being the best Shadow Lady I could be. Now I've brought shame to those who taught me. I've shamed my family." She wiped her tears and sniffed. "How can anyone love me, when I don't know myself, much less love myself?"

"Have you even considered that Brenden might be the person who helps you figure it out?"

Nikki shook her head and her red hair fell around her shoulders. Avery realized she'd never seen her hair down. Nikki always kept it up or in a braid. It was lovely.

"I can't deal with him, Avery. I need to figure out what I'm going to do with my life. Please," she pleaded, looking up with desperation in her eyes. "I need time to heal all the scars no one can see."

Reluctantly, Avery nodded and went into the hall to explain to Brenden. He listened, staying motionless until she was done. Then he barged into the room and shut the door.

"Now you listen up, damn it," Brenden said loud enough for everyone outside to hear. "You're not getting out of this. You may not know who you are, but I damn sure do. You want to find yourself? Fine. We'll do it together. But love doesn't quit, it doesn't give up, and damn sure doesn't abandon in the time of need."

"Why are you doing this?" Nikki demanded, just as loud.

Avery, Dante, and Lysandra all leaned closer to the door to listen.

"You're my heart," Brenden replied. "Period. The End. No take backs. My heart is broken right now, but we can fix it. Together."

The room was quiet for a long time and Avery slowly turned the knob and peeked inside. Brenden was kneeling in front of Nikki, their mouths fused together, his hands buried in her hair.

Avery closed the door and turned to Lysa and Dante. "I think we should let them be."

Lysa grinned with a deep blush across her cheeks. She leaned against Dante's chest.

"How's Nikki?" Ryse's voice carried down the hallway. Her heart leapt in her chest at seeing him. She prayed she never got used to the sight of his powerful stride, the set of his shoulders, and the aura of confidence that surrounded him.

"I think Brenden is going to take care of her tonight."

"Good." He faced Lysa. "Tomorrow morning, we will gather to discuss your vision. I think everyone should hear it. Hades spoke to me and Zeus passed Hayden a message. We all need to share information."

"Yes, sire. As you wish." Lysa bowed.

"Go rest."

"Yes, Master." Dante took Lysa's hand and they disappeared down the hall.

Once they were gone, Ryse turned his stormy gaze on her. "Didn't you mention something about pulling off clothing with my teeth?"

Avery laughed and threw her arms around his neck. "I did. And I love you, baby."

"I love you too." Ryse picked her up and carried her to their room next door.

CHAPTER
THIRTY-FOUR

RYSE STOOD IN FRONT OF THE GROUP AND TOOK A DEEP BREATH. HIS Elites, his brother, his General, and his handful of trusted soldiers filled the conference room. Everyone was quiet. Especially when Dynasty and Avery walked in with Hanna, Lysandra, and Nikki behind them. Lysa and Hanna surveyed the room, but Nikki kept her head down.

"Gentlemen," Ryse said. "I have asked these ladies to join our council this morning. We have a few things to discuss and I believe all of them should be included. Ladies." Ryse motioned to the five empty chairs around the table.

Once everyone was seated, he continued. "In the last twenty-four hours, the gods have been actively speaking to us. I've received calls this morning from the Deities all over the world that they have heard direction and prophecy like never before. I, personally, take this as a good sign. However, not all of it has been positive. We face a new threat. All this time, we've been so focused on rogue Olympians, that we have missed the real enemy. And he is at our door. Demons have found a way out of the underworld. They cannot stay in this realm for long, but their tolerance increases all the time.

"After conversing with Dante about his interaction, I believe the rogues have learned ancient black magic spells that conjure the demons. Right now, they harness the power of demon blood."

"Do we know anything about its power?" Hammon leaned forward and put his elbows on the table.

"Not as much as we would like," Hayden answered. "Since Dante's attack, I've been trying to find anything in the histories about demons and there's not much. Until recently, Hades has kept them on lockdown and no one had bothered trying to set them free."

"So why now? What did he tell you?" Yankee asked.

Ryse clenched his jaw. "He told me that this was our battle. Our people started this, and we'll have to finish it."

He didn't have to expound. This was one battle they would not have divine back up for.

"Hades has always hated us," his mother said. "Since our beginning, Hades has been jealous. He thought that by creating demons as his spawn, they would give him the same devotion that Olympians give to Zeus. But because he is cruel and hateful, they turned against him. Now he wants nothing more than for the Olympians to be destroyed out of jealousy."

"Not that I'm advocating our extinction," Yankee said with a scowl, "but why wouldn't he just wipe us out?"

"Rhea," Avery answered him. "She's the only reason he hasn't set demons free in this world. Zeus can't stop him; only Rhea can control him. She also has a responsibility to the humans. They might not pray to the same gods we do, but they are under her protection."

"What's our next move, then?" asked General Falcon, always looking ahead.

"We must focus on battling demons right alongside the rogues. This is going to take training for all of us. It won't be a quick battle. From intel we've gathered, the rogues are searching hard for another teleporter. They are still targeting any woman who might be a Divine Grace as well. Which brings us to our next concern. Hayden?"

Ryse sat down and Hayden took the floor. "For the last few months, I've been visited in my dreams by a woman who I believe is my Grace. We can communicate, but until night before last, our voices were silenced every time we might have spoken words that would lead us to one another. I know what she looks like, but I don't know much else about her except that she lives in a large city in the United

States and her sister recently started dating a high-level Olympian with Thracian guards."

"That should narrow our search somewhat," Hammon said.

"I think so too. Yesterday, Zeus told me that I had until my coronation to find her."

"Of course." Dynasty nodded. "A Grand Deity must have a Grace by his side."

"No," Lysandra whispered. She shook her head, her eyes misting over. "It's not simply that. I had a vision yesterday when I shook Prince Ashton's hands." Lysandra shivered and Dante touched her knee.

"It's okay, you can say it," he said, giving her a kind smile.

Lysandra lifted her gaze to Hayden. "If you don't find her in the next month, she'll be dead. Ashton will find her and eventually kill her."

Ryse felt the tension in the room amp up. He looked across the table at his beloved Grace. The terror of watching her die in his arms would not happen to his brother. Hayden deserved better.

Dynasty stood up and put her fists on the table, the expression on her usually serene face turned hard and cold. "Over my dead body," she growled. The room chilled a few degrees and Ryse saw his men exchange cautious looks.

Ryse and Hayden exchanged a quick glance. This was a new side of their mother and frankly it was frightening.

A white glow surrounded Dynasty, as if the gods were giving her power and strength. "I've had *enough* of those cursed Avondales bringing pain to my family. First my husband, now my sons and their wives. No." She stood straight and lifted her chin. Her lavender eyes glowed white and it sent a chill down Ryse's spine. "No more. I will not sit on the sidelines one more minute. I will fight with my last breath to bring this girl home."

"So shall I." Hanna stood beside her mistress. Gods forbid the poor fool who felt Hanna's wrath. Whatever Hanna spoke came to pass. If she uttered the word death...

Ryse swallowed. That demon had shaken the hornet's nest.

"I'm not much of a fighter, but I believe my skills of precognition could be useful in battle situation. I will do anything you ask of me," Lysandra offered.

Avery joined them. "Y'all know I'm not afraid to rush into the middle of trouble. At least, this time, I'm a bit more prepared." She held up her hand and twirled a small ball of fire around her fingers. Ryse's men chuckled. "I think it's high time Olympians join their Thracian brothers and learn how to kick some ass."

"I want to fight." Nikki stood. "But I—I will have to be taught."

Brenden went to her side. "You don't have to do this. You have nothing to prove here."

Her eyes burned when she faced him. "I have *everything* to prove. This has nothing to do with you. I serve Avery and if my mistress steps up to fight, I will be at her side. Just as you will be." Brenden hung his head. But Nikki stood taller and kept her chin high.

Ryse narrowed his gaze at the five ladies standing at the end of the table.

"Lucky for you, ladies," he said and spread his arms to encompass the warriors in the room, "you have the Elites to teach you." He met the shocked stare of each man. It was Hammon who stood first. One by one, the men rose to their feet. If these women wanted to become warriors, the Elites would make it happen.

"Change outta your gowns, girls," Avery said in her Texas twang, her aura flaring with power. She held out her hand and fire sprang from her palm, controlled completely by its master. "Trainin' starts now."

There was a gleam in her eyes, a spark of inner fire that engulfed Ryse. If the enemy wanted blood and fire, then blood and fire they shall have.

To be continued...

Continue your journey and meet twins with unique powers in *Divine Encounter.*

ABOUT THE AUTHOR

JoAnna Grace lives in a world of alpha males and strong females where true love conquers all—at least in her books! From the time she started holding a crayon she began to create magical worlds. Living in the real world was never an option. A proud indie, she has published over a dozen novels including The Divine Chronicles series, The Blake Pride series, Riverview Romances, and more. This writer loves to read contemporary, paranormal, and urban fantasy romance novels.

JoAnna's tales are spun at her home in East Texas where she lives with her Prince Charming, three kids, and a few dogs and cats. When not hiding behind the computer screen chugging coffee, you can find her having fun with family and friends, singing, camping, or managing multiple businesses.

Connect on social media!

Like, Follow, Tag Jo, and share this book with your friends.

Instagram @authorjoannagrace
Facebook @joannagraceauthor
Goodreads: goodreads.com/author/show/7173373.JoAnna_Grace
Bookbub: www.bookbub.com/profile/joanna-grace

Make sure you're in the know. Sign up for the newsletter today!
http://eepurl.com/B_DM5

Do you want to help an author? Leave a review
Your opinion matters.
Every review can help.

JoAnna Grace
Giving Wings to Words

Bonus images by Meg Murray Designs

Meg Murrey's
Designs
Book covers & more
www.cactusrosepress.com